BIOGRAPHY

A long time ago, Michelle Shine arranged travel for Peter Gabriel, Spandau Ballet, Boy George, Phillip Green and other famous names. Then in 1989 after the miraculous cure of her eldest son's epilepsy and allergic colitis by homeopathy, she was compelled to find out more about the medicine that the German pharmacist Samuel Hahnemann discovered in the very late 18th century.

In 1993 she graduated from the College of Homeopathy in Regent's Park, London and embarked on a career, spanning twenty years, as a homeopath in North West London. When her husband died suddenly and tragically at fifty-eight she gave up her practice to write full time. The result is *Mesmerised,* her first full-length novel.

Michelle Shine is the author of *What About the Potency?* A homeopathic textbook now in its third edition and *The Subtle Art of Healing,* a novella which was long listed for the Cinnamon Press Novella Award in 2007. Her short stories have appeared in *Grey Sparrow, Liar's League, Epiphany, Lover's Lies* and *The Book of Euclid.* She has an MA in Creative Writing from Birkbeck University, and is the mother of three grown-up children.

MESMERISED

MICHELLE SHINE

Indigo Dreams Publishing

First Edition: Mesmerised

First published in Great Britain in 2013 by:
Indigo Dreams Publishing Ltd
24 Forest Houses
Cookworthy Moor
Halwill
Beaworthy
EX21 5UU
www.indigodreams.co.uk

ISBN 978-1-909357-29-7

Mesmerised is a work of fiction.

Designed and typeset in Minion Pro by Indigo Dreams.

Cover design by Ronnie Goodyer at Indigo Dreams
Le Déjeuner sur l'herbe by Édouard Manet

Printed and bound in Great Britain by Imprint Academic, Exeter
Papers used by Indigo Dreams are recyclable products made from
wood grown in sustainable forests following the guidance of the
Forest Stewardship Council

AUTHOR'S NOTE

This story is a work of fiction where real events and people are intertwined with characters and happenings that are born solely of my imagination.

All the artists mentioned, their families, the Academie Suisse, Père Tanguy, Doctor Charcot, Georges de Bellio, and Blanche Castets really existed.

Victorine's letter resides in the Adolphe Tabarant archive at The Pierpont Morgan Library, New York. MA 3950.

Many of the homes, workplaces, and cafés have authentic addresses. Le Salon des Refusés really happened and the revelations of Edouard Manet's life and death are well documented.

Doctor Gachet did save Alfred Pissaro's life with homeopathy, and was called in to try and help Edouard Manet on his deathbed.

The London cholera statistics have been taken from the NHS, UCLH website.

Any mistakes that might be contained in this book are my own.

DEDICATION

To the man of my dreams
Jon Shine
1950-2009

and my beautiful children,
Matthew, Rebecca and Daniel

ACKNOWLEDGEMENTS

My gratitude goes to the lovely Nomads, my writing group who were instrumental in encouraging me to start the novel and continue it – Sarah Peak, Charlie Fish, Beth Cordingly, Helen Bain,Felix Harrison, Anna Baggaley, Deirdre Shannon, Skye Sherwin and Laura Allsop. And my early readers: Sue Young, Liz Shine, Elaine Ratner and Stacey Bernie. I'm indebted to the lovely people who worked in Paul Gachet's house in Auvers sur Oise, and spoke to me at length about his life, but whose names were sadly swallowed by a house fire. Also, Anna Cassale, Howard Robin, Lisa Goll and Louisa Dreisin for their good advice and having faith in me as a writer. David Ratner for being a great dad. Clive Goldman for helping me to retrieve *Mesmerised* from a burnt-out computer after the fire in my home. Ronnie Goodyer and Dawn Bauling for picking up this manuscript and wanting to run with it. John Griffiths, my editor. Caroline True for the flattering photograph. Sophie Lewis and Ruth Kaye for ideas for the front cover. Malcolm Sevren, Keith Woolf, Raymond Stoltzman, Gary Rose and Gary Bobbe, for much need help, advice and friendship at a very difficult time. Renee Rose for picking up the baton. Kate Bush, a huge source of inspiration, always. And Teodora Bergland and Elizabeth Adalian, for their passion, creativity and promotion.

Thank you.

MESMERISED

January 1863

I buy pure phosphorus from an old alchemist who lives in a slanted house on the hill that leads to Montmartre. His wife, Madame Armand, has a small plot of land where she grows vegetables and flowers to sell at the market. Many of the brown bottles in my collection contain fluids that were distilled from her produce.

In Monsieur Armand's laboratory, in the middle of the afternoon, all shutters remain closed. Thin streams of light trespass and fall in diagonal lines across glass vessels. Tubes lead from one to the other in a world of liquids that bubble and fizz.

'This is a very combustible material.' Leaning on his stick, he licks his lips, wrinkles deepening in concentration under strands of white hair.

'Monsieur Armand, I really appreciate this. I know that you originally acquired the substance for yourself.'

'Shh, say no more,' he says, his free hand at my back.

A baby cries.

'That's Madeleine, my grandchild,' he says, eyes lit. 'What are you going to do with the phosphorus?'

'I'm going to make a homeopathic remedy.'

'What's that?' He pulls down a book from a splintery shelf behind him. Dust puffs into the air like face powder in a thespian's dressing room.

'No,' he says, opening the leather-bound and gilt-edged tome. 'It's not mentioned here. And therefore …' He claps the pages shut using the outer cover, '… it does not exist.'

Moving Home
March 20th

'It is not enough to know your craft – you have to have feeling.'
Edouard Manet

It is 7 o'clock in the evening and deceitfully dark. I sit on a crate in the centre of the main room in my new apartment in rue Faubourg Saint Denis. I face two large windows which look out upon a full moon that throws a white smudge at my feet. Inside, there is no light. The fireplace is silent in its unlit state. My greatcoat hangs on a hook behind the door wearing a lunar streak. I don't feel cold inside although my feet are numb and when I touch my cheek with my fingers they are shockingly cold. The warmth in my chest brings me comfort. This room is embracing me.

There's the clip-clop of horses' hooves, neighing, the closing of carriage doors and the voices of easily affronted Parisians three stories below. My heart lurches with my good fortune, for this is a great room. The walls are high, luminous, practically begging for art to adorn them. My desk, which seemed so large and cumbersome at my last address in rue Montholon, proudly occupies less than one third of the space, and is tucked away at one end. I imagine receiving patients here, putting chairs out in the hallway where they can wait. I will make the alcove into a kitchen/dispensary for my medicine. But not only that, this room is conducive to artistry. The light is good. It is where I shall paint.

I will store my easel and my canvases in the cupboard in the small lobby leading to the bedroom, through the door to the right of the fireplace.

I shall be happy here.

A knock on the door jolts me from my thoughts. Without thinking to light a gas lamp or candle, I jump up.

'Who is it?' I call through the door.

'Victorine Meurent.'

Releasing the shiny new brass chain, I let her in.

'Bonjour *Monsieur Docteur,* my dear friend Paul,' she greets me. 'It's very dark. I wouldn't have thought you were a man who was into séance,' she says, bounding in and stopping short only a few steps beyond the threshold. She looks back at me.

'Victorine,' I tell her, 'your vivid imagination influences you. I've just moved in. I've been sitting on that crate contemplating my new direction and inwardly celebrating. Let me bring some light to the situation.' I rub my cold hands on my trouser legs and hunt blindly through packing boxes for matches, which I eventually find. I strike one and the phosphorus glows bright like the sun, dying as I spark up the gas lamps by their brass cords.

'I've come to ask you when it would be a convenient time to call. I knew that it wouldn't be now, but Camille gave me your new address and I'm desperate to see you professionally, so I thought I would stop by in passing just to ask you this question,' she says, her body as composed as Savoldo's Mary Magdalene, silver caped and waiting on a hillside wall above the port in Old Jerusalem.

'Forgive me if I don't ask you what the matter is right away,' I say, indicating with my arms the bareness of the space around me.

'It's the usual.'

'Ah!'

Victorine is a city girl who like so many others, lives on her wits, but she has a talent for life and there is very little that she cannot do.

'I'm not unpacked yet. You'll have to come back tomorrow at around eleven. I will have what you want to hand.'

'Paul, you're wonderful,' she tells me with her palms at my

shoulders and her red lipstick making imprints on my cheeks, as usual.

She leaves me alone again. Immediately, I extinguish the light and look around, re-focusing. Perhaps Victorine is on the street looking up, finding me odd to desire darkness in this way. I pick up the matches left on the mantel and strike a bulbous head against the grainy stone fireplace. Immediately it flares white gold and blinding. Phosphorescent. What is to be learned? I do this three more times then retire to bed.

March 21st

Dawn. There's a lacy, iridescent frost at the windows. I am up early, blowing heat through my fingers, unpacking logs, kindling, old newspapers, and lighting the fire. It is Saturday, like Sunday, a day of rest for me, although not always. Sometimes there is work to do at the hospital and very often there are callers with acute ailments. Today Victorine is arriving at eleven. Georges de Bellio, a medical colleague of mine, will come to help with the building of shelves in my kitchen/dispensary, which shall also serve as a pharmacy. There is even running water there thanks to Haussmann, Napoleon III's lackey, who rebuilt our city to a modern specification.

With the fire crackling, I hunt through six boxes for the medicine required by Victorine. My desk shall separate us. She will sit opposite me and say she wishes for some more Mercury, just in case. I will talk to her again about condoms and how they are to be used. I will lecture her on hygiene as prevention against disease. She will purse her lips, rest one elbow on my desk and sit with her chin neatly framed by her hand. She will stare directly at me, and say, 'Like I said, just in case'.

No doubt I will sigh and dispense a small two-gram vial that will contain around fifteen pillules. She will take one every time she beds a man unprotected.

She comes for this prescription once or twice a year, ever since I told her at the Café Guerbois, 'Mercury is the medicine for syphilis but it is also a poison.'

'Yes, but can you prevent syphilis, that's what I want to know?' she asked, blowing Turkish cigarette smoke up at the ceiling.

'The disease is endemic.'

Her attention wavered. She was looking at a man in the corner whose body was wrapped around someone smaller. He must have sensed Victorine's stare as he let go of his companion and looked directly at us. His left cheek had what appeared from a distance to be a botched scar. His eyes were steely and challenging. His companion was not much older than a child. She swayed as if drunk. Victorine shuddered and pulled her shawl closer around her.

'I met a man the other day. He sits on the board of the Faculty of Medicine. I can't remember his name. He knows of you. He said that the medicine you prescribe outside the hospital is rubbish.'

'Why don't you try it for yourself? Mercury prophylactically, in minute doses.'

'Fine. When can I come and see you?' she said, smiling broadly as she turned back towards me.

Georges arrives whilst I am still in consultation with Victorine. I make him a prisoner in my bedroom until she leaves.

Coming out of hiding, 'I propose breakfast,' he says good-naturedly.

I haven't eaten since yesterday lunchtime and run wildly fast down the winding staircase. My hand brushes the cast iron balustrade, burning my palm, and I almost trip on the stone steps.

'Take care, Paul, you're far too young to die,' Georges shouts down from under his bobbing handlebar mustachios, a robust figure in frockcoat, black and white spotted tie, opal pin and bowler hat. His voice is an echo all around him.

'Come and join me. Don't be pompous,' I shout back up.

Georges hails a hansom to take us to his favourite café in the Boulevard des Italiens, where green plants grow in pewter coalscuttles snaking around columns amid a passing scent of pancakes aux citron; sponged walls like marble in caramel and toffee; gilt-framed mirrors reflect black-tailed waiters carrying silver salvers. Women, with lavender and jasmine oozing from perfumed hair, are adorned in organza and lace. We order omelette aux pommes and drink bitter, Arabic coffee.

'How's the painting?' my Romanian colleague asks, tapping his cigar in an ashtray with his podgy forefinger.

'I've joined the Académie of Pére Suisse. I go twice a week.'

'I envy you your talent.'

'As a painter? Surely not.'

'As a physician – consultant in nervous disorders at La Salpêtrière – it's impressive.'

'No, what's impressive is that all your patients are artists and literati, and your consulting room is the Café Riche.'

Georges sits back and smirks.

'Clever me,' he says.

It's still morning and yet the candle flames wag like tongues on every table.

'Tell me, when did you last see Edouard?' Georges asks.

Needing to be back at my practice by noon, I had been in a hurry. I had spent the whole morning at the hospital, detained by a woman named Manon, a patient, who had just been informed that her father had died. Her pupils were dilated. I waved my hand in front of her face but there was no reaction, she just carried on staring without blinking. Months earlier, when she had lost her sister, she had cut off all her hair and run naked through the streets of Faubourg Saint-Honoré.

I wanted to sit with her, hold her hand and be of some comfort, but needed to get across town to Rue Montholon. I stayed for a short while then caught a crowded omnibus, giving up my seat to a young girl who was pregnant and swayed with the vehicle till it came to a standstill. I grew agitated at the prolonged stop and craned my neck see through the window. There was a rumpus outside the courthouse. The police were arresting a man. Crowds gathered and no one could get through. Edouard stood on the steps of the Palais de Justice. No doubt he had just visited his father, who was a judge, perhaps for lunch. He seemed very self-assured: his hands thrust into his trouser pockets, his top hat connecting him to the gods. He was in conversation with Victorine. She was wearing a black coat, open at the throat. She cocked her head at something he said. I imagined Edouard with his forefinger slipping downwards from the velvet ribbon at her neck.

I say nothing. That wasn't the last time I saw him anyway.

'He is not going to Académie Suisse?' Georges persists.

'Not of late, why do you ask?'

'I haven't seen him for a while that's all. He used to come by here at least once a week. I've had his prescription in my pocket for the last month.'

'When I saw him a couple of weeks ago, I noticed he had a slight limp.'

George winces, calls over the waiter and asks for the bill, which he insists on paying.

Academie Suisse
March 25th

'Blessed are they who see beautiful things in humble places.'

Camille Pissarro

Charcoal sketches on greying paper in simple black frames are knocked sideways on the wall as I climb. They boast the signatures of Courbet, Delacroix and Corot. It's impossible *not* to shoulder them and cause mini avalanches in the cracking wall paint. The stairs demand trudging, each one placed too high above the one before. About half-way up there is one that has almost collapsed into a chasm. I have to manoeuvre my way around it and take a chance where I'm stepping. It's an expedition. Only the brave come to Père Suisse.

He is hovering at the door as usual, making sure no one enters who hasn't paid a monthly fee. His suspicious eyes lift above his spittoon. He was an artist's model once, lucky to have inherited this perfect studio to paint in. And he is sufficiently pleased with himself. You can see it in the way he wipes his mouth with the back of his hand after expectorating tobacco-phlegm into a real silver bowl. Père Suisse is the proprietor of a school that has the arrogance to exist without any formal tuition. But there is always an atmosphere of camaraderie in this grimy studio.

'Ah,' I breathe out, arriving with aching legs at the summit.

Camille, Victorine, and Henri look around.

'I've arrived,' I say. Everyone's eyes are dreamy. They are lost in design. A young boy in a Grecian toga stands on a plinth, his hair cornfield yellow from some sort of dye. His lips scarlet, and

19

the manner in which he purses them, is distinctly feminine. He holds a bunch of purple grapes.

'Hello,' he says, waving.

I find an empty chair; take out my notebook and a pencil from my bag.

'You know, I'd rather you came in your own clothes,' Henri says to the model. He perches on a desk and pulls at the material the boy has wrapped around him. A pin comes loose and the costume tumbles from his shoulders folding itself over a belt at his waist. 'Far more interesting,' says Henri.

The boy's face looks rouged. 'I'm going,' he says, stepping down, holding his skirts like a sixteenth century maiden. He storms across the room and hurriedly puts on his street clothes. Père Suisse watches silently.

Camille, next to me, has already flipped a page and begun working from memory: an impression of The Boulevard des Italiens – a drawn reproduction of his painting *en plein air,* the road alive with a blue-white tinged surface, showing sunshine after a rainfall, blinding as snow, and countered by the starkness of a red and white awning outside a shop.

I admit to myself sadly, once again, that I must be satisfied with my lesser talent or live in depression forever. And whilst I strive for some lowly satisfaction, greatness seems to come so easily to him; his eye is so much keener. I long to fill up the walls of my home with his inspiration and decide to follow his lead, recreating the painting in graphite of Manon, lying on a low hospital bed in a cellar, her body slightly levitating.

Camille taps me on my shoulder with his pencil. He leans forwards. We are nearly cheek-to-cheek.

'The world is not black, my friend. Look up at the sky.' I lift my chin to the glass panes in the ceiling.

'What colour do you see?'

'Grey.'

'That's it? Can't you taste plum-purple? Cerise?' I cross my arms and marvel at his insight. He encourages me to imagine the use of colour to create a less heavy mood. I've seen him give similar advice to the other Paul, Paul Cézanne, my namesake.

The air is filled with anxiety. It crackles in heated silence. An alkaline scent taunts the dry air. We are still a long way off but spring is here and once again we will put forward our canvases to be considered by the committee at the Académie des Beaux-Arts. They will judge and decide whether our work is worthy to hang on the walls of Le Salon. It is our only hope of exhibiting before the public. We are, all of us, trying our best to be focused and pointed.

'What of Edouard, Henri?' Camille asks.

I look from Camille to Henri, to Henri's drawing, a bunch of white orchids tossed into a vase on a shaded background.

'He is not coming anymore. He feels that he has learnt enough from here,' Henri answers, broad shouldered.

'Do we come here only to learn?' Camille strokes his beard.

'You can visit Edouard in his studio. He likes people around him whilst he paints,' Victorine says, lengthening her spine.

'I can't, I will also be painting,' Camille answers.

'You visit Courbet,' she goes on.

'We all visit Courbet,' says Henri. 'Even Manet.'

'Papa Courbet,' says Victorine, shading the face of a spider-veined woman in ragged clothes. 'Why is everyone so interested in Edouard, all of a sudden?' she asks.

Henri shrugs. Camille carries on as if he has not heard the question. It is a while before anyone speaks. Henri puts his charcoal on the floor and appraises his own work. He combs the fingers of both hands through his mane. His work is sharp, his images exact.

'We're not all the same,' Camille says, eventually. 'Each of us has different aims and aspirations'.

'Have you seen his Salon entry this year?' Victorine asks.

No one answers.

She smiles. 'I wonder if you will be shocked.'

Protest Day
April 16th

*'When you do a thing with your whole soul and everything that is
noble within you, you always find your counterpart.'*
Camille Pissarro

A streetwalker stands, hands on hips, underneath a window on
the Boulevard de Clichy. She spits on the ground and treads
saliva into stone with the sole of her dirty pink shoe. She is small
and slight and too young. Shadows of horses and their carriages
run her over again and again.

'You bastard! I hope your mother dies of syphilis. I hope
your house burns down and your children fry. I hope you don't
eat because thieves take everything you own and when you're
working your wife is fucking another man!' she calls out.

I stop in my tracks on an island in the centre of Boulevard de
Clichy. Two street urchins run into me, one after the other.
'Excuse me,' I say, but they are already disappearing into the light
that shimmers through the trees.

I look up. A man bellows from an upstairs window. His
whole head is framed by the azure sky, and his round shirt collar
has swallowed his neck.

'Why *would* I pay you?' he calls down.

I hear the slight tat-tat of footsteps behind me – Victorine.
Fixed on the streetwalker, she doesn't notice me. A bourgeois
family descends from a hansom. They walk past as if we are all
ghosts. Victorine's gaze shifts to them, the expression on her face
questioning.

Until the streetwalker's outburst I was in my own world,

discovering how the clouds, sun and sky merge to make colours like peach and fuchsia. I was observing the light, the buildings that cut geometric dark shapes into the world when the sun is just so in the sky; the way darkness dampens mood and hardens contour and the leaves on the trees in the centre of the road – when they are caught in sudden brightness, even the earth beneath them is lightened.

'The devil will have his way with you; what about the first time?' yells the girl.

'A mere figment of your imagination … *Monsieur! Monsieur! Gendarme!*'

'Sir, do you know this woman?'

'Would I know such a cow?'

In the theatre, the crowds would be laughing. Hussies in satin dresses, escorted by lecherous men who seek out the smell of sex on a woman's clothes, would guffaw in the face of this everyday tragedy. Prostitutes cannot afford to be revolutionaries. Meanwhile, it is the playwrights who sit in the cafés that line the streets, drinking vin blanc and witnessing girls being treated unfairly, who, for money, tell these tales so accurately, so eloquently, catering to the amusement of the average male. Perhaps if I hadn't taken up a medical profession and not spent time talking to the likes of such women at the Salpêtrière, I wouldn't understand the injustice and would be laughing myself.

A crowd has gathered. Ladies wearing pastel hues of silk and satin mingle with those less fortunate whose clothes are dull and stiff. Two gendarmes restrain the streetwalker. Handcuffed, she tries to shrug off their grasp but their fingernails bite deeper into her arms forcing her to start walking.

'Come on love, it's not fair to dirty the street any longer than you have to,' one gendarme says to the amusement of the other.

'Get off me, you animals,' she screams.

'I saw everything,' Victorine calls out. The streetwalker cranes her neck to look over her shoulder. 'I'm Victorine Meurent. I live on rue Maître-Albert, number 17.'

Two men wearing black top hats turn to stare accusingly at Victorine. One of the gendarmes pulls roughly on the woman's arm. She starts to trot in order to keep on her feet. Victorine watches until the party of three turns the corner. Then, realising she is late, perhaps, lifts her skirts and runs. I follow her, feeling as if I impose on her footsteps. She stops running and I'm very close on her heels. She turns around.

'Doctor Gachet, Paul. I *thought* there was someone behind me.'

'I'm on my way to the Café de Bade,' I say.

'Of course you are. So am I. Shall we walk together?' she says, hooking her arm around my elbow.

'I saw what happened back there. It was very generous of you to give that girl your name and address.'

'Generous? No. It was very stupid,' she says, glancing at me and smiling warmly. 'I'll probably have that woman turning up at my door and demanding her rights to all my possessions.'

'And what will you do?'

'That depends if I like her.' She elbows my rib cage, teasingly.

There is silence.

'I'm not sure about Napoleon, but isn't Haussmann wonderful?' she says eventually.

'Yes, quite wonderful,' I answer. We are in a narrow street with tall white buildings carved to perfection. They too are art. Their front doors gleam proudly. Not so long ago, Paris was a series of alleyways with dilapidated housing stinking of shit and piss. There is no question that Haussmann, with his rebuilding of the city, is keen on hygiene, and it has given the populace the gift of greater health.

'His buildings are solid, interestingly-shaped and quite beautiful to paint.'

'Yes,' I say, and think, that too.

Outside the café, a multitude has gathered underneath the awning, spilling out into the street. Tables are pushed aside and the inside teems with people. I recognise fellow artists, musicians, actors and newspapermen amongst the throng. Tears prick at the realisation that so many have come out to protest against the decision made by the jury of the Académie. The only new artist's work they have chosen to exhibit this year is August Renoir's *La Esmeralda*. How *can* artists survive if they can't show their work?

Victorine pushes her way through to the front. At the entrance, Edouard's eccentric writer friend, Charles, acknowledges me with a wink. I touch the peak of my cap in reply. I can just about see through to the centre of the room and to the left where Camille stands on a table and speaks.

'It is amazing, what can be achieved by word of mouth,' he says. 'I think you have all come here today because you know that this meeting is not only about painting. Painting is just the beginning. The whole of our culture is at risk.

'Three hundred fewer artists were chosen this year for the Salon, and only one is not from the old school. All the others comply with certain precepts and conventions. None of them paint *en plein-air*. Colours are defined and used as designated: blue for sky; grass is green. Nakedness is fine, but only for nymphs and angels.' Camille hesitates whilst his audience chuckles. 'The government is an organisation that loves convention and only wants to help its own. I seriously believe this is more about convenience for the powers that be than excellence. This is censorship and many artists are starving in consequence.'

'We must fight for justice!' a gentleman calls out, thrusting his fist into the air whilst others whistle and clap.

Paul Cézanne and Henri help Camille down. A thoughtful-looking man with a jacket, waistcoat and wing collar climbs onto a chair and then onto the table. The room goes very quiet. The man coughs into his fist.

'I am Paul Durand-Ruel. My business is buying and selling paintings. I have come here today to say that I have seen some of the artwork that has been refused by the Salon this year. Of course, there were submissions that were never going to make it to *any* position on those hallowed walls, but there were others of such excellent quality, so innovative and emotive. Far superior to any of the works favoured by the judges, and yet they were refused.'

The crowd rumbles.

'If those talented painters continue to be shut out of the Salon and suffer prejudice for extending their creative ability beyond all foresight of their critics, then today marks the beginning of the end for any serious painter and for the soul of the art world. But I am of the opinion … .'

'Napoleon's lackeys reign, but what are we going to do about it?' A voice calls from behind me. Everyone starts to speak at once and the babble rises in an ascending scale. Durand-Ruel raises his arms and waits for the crowd to quieten.

'I am of the opinion that we can't allow this to happen. If I have to take the matter into my own hands, I will.'

Someone whistles.

'I think I've fallen in love with you,' a joker catcalls.

'I give my pledge here and now. I will risk my reputation to possess some of the worthy artwork made by these terribly modern painters.'

'Will you pay the artists? Some of us don't have enough money to eat.'

'I will buy the paintings. I will stand them on easels for the whole world to see and if necessary, I will take them out of Paris and exhibit them in London and New York.'

Someone has caught my attention – the only other female in the café apart from Victorine. She stands close enough for me to smell the patchouli in her perfume. I check my watch. It is nearing my next consultation time.

I arrive home a quarter of an hour late. Far too many people are waiting and there are only four chairs on the landing outside my apartment. Patients and prospective patients are leaning on the balustrade, sitting on the window ledge, above and below on the stairs. I am careful not to tread on clothing or skin with my footsteps as I ascend. At about every ten paces I stop. 'Good afternoon,' I say, to no one in particular.

One man, who does not sit or lean but stands upright, has a red bush of a beard and hazel irises that look alternately sparky and sad. Hands in his pockets, he catches my eye.

'You have nowhere to sit,' I remark as I pass him on the staircase. 'You'd better follow me.'

I feel the morale of my other patients sag and try to ignore it.

'How can I help you, Edouard?' I ask, closing the front door and motioning him over to the seat in front of my desk.

'I have a problem.' He interlinks his fingers in his lap and stares at his palms while he speaks. 'Georges is away, visiting family in Rumania, and Leon has a cough. I've come to ask if you would do a house call?'

'After surgery hours, although it could be quite late judging by the amount of people out there,' I say, pushing a leaf of paper and a pen towards him. 'I'll need your address.'

Georges has already confided that Edouard sometimes lives with Suzanne Leenhoff (his childhood piano teacher), and the boy Leon, in the rue de l'Hôtel de Ville. Painting is his only occupation but unlike my friend Camille, whose parents have all but disowned him for marrying the housemaid, Edouard has never been treated like a black sheep by his parents. His clothing is of the finest tailoring and fabrics, and his purse always generously open when he frequents the cafés.

'Doctor Gachet, how good of you to come. I'm Suzanne Leenhoff, she says, limply extending her hand out towards mine. 'Edouard apologises for not being here, although he's asked me to convey his gratitude to you for coming.'

'Leon is not well?'

'Yes. Please. I'm sorry,' she says, leading the way through the apartment to Leon's room, past a grand piano, cut glass lampshades and stepping on polished wood floors.

'Hello Leon,' I say. Leon lies in bed, propped up with pillows. He is a drowsy, dark haired, slim faced boy of around eleven.

'I'm Doctor Gachet.'

Leon smiles meekly. He has a rash like sunburn on his neck. Despite the sunshine and the mildness of the day, the window is closed. Glass percussions in my leather case as I place it on the floor.

'The window is closed,' I say, looking over my shoulder at Suzanne.

'Do you think he needs air?' she asks, her large chest straining against her plain linen dress.

'What do you think, Leon, do you need the air?'

'No, I'm cold,' he says, 'I asked Moedge to shut it.'

'Who?'

'Moedge, it is his pet name for me,' says Suzanne.

Moedge. I have never heard of this word. It's similar to the Belgian for mother, but not quite. I place my palm on his forehead. Heat radiates from his skin.

'Excuse me,' I say, pulling the sheets off him. It is as I thought; like opening an oven door.

Leon hugs his body and shivers. There's no sign of dampness from perspiration. Opening the buttons on his nightshirt, I can see that the rash continues all over his torso. I sit down beside him, and feel swollen glands just above his throat. 'Can I rinse this?' I ask, taking a spatula out of my bag. She shows me to a tap in the kitchen. Cloudy water sputters forth. I wait until it runs clear, then on returning to the bedroom I tip Leon's chin towards the light. 'Can you open your mouth wide?'

His throat is inflamed and pussy. I replace the covers on top of him, pull down his lower eyelids and look into his glassy eyes; his pupils are dilated. He begins to cough, a dry, barking sound.

'Is he eating?'

'He asked for raw vegetables, but he didn't eat them. His throat hurt.'

'Is this what he normally eats?'

'No, no,' Suzanne laughs as if the premise is amusing.

'Is he drinking?'

'Only a few sips, if I insist.'

'He has a high fever.'

'Yes, this is what made Edouard worry and stay at home today instead of going to the Café de Bade.'

I take my case on my lap and hunt through the bottles for some Belladonna and ask Suzanne to fetch me a spoon. I tip one pillule onto it then tip it straight into Leon's mouth. From a sheaf of small square papers I take one and sprinkle some sediment of Belladonna onto it, then wrap it into an envelope.

'If he has a bad night pour this powder into his mouth,' I say, handing the paper to Suzanne. 'I'll come by sometime tomorrow.'

'I have another envelope just like this from Doctor De Bellio for Edouard. How can I tell them apart?'

I take my pen from my jacket pocket and ask for Leon's surname.

Suzanne hesitates.

'His surname is Kalle. 'K-A-L-L-E,' she says.

I write it on the corner of the waxed paper. Suzanne does not ask and I don't wish to alarm her but my diagnosis for Leon is Scarlet Fever.

Bathing is not easy. It is no wonder that so many of the population avoid the performance. My bath is tin rather than cast iron, so that I can manoeuvre it into the main room.

I carry the great vessel with some difficulty, and place it on the rug between my living and work area. I light the fire so I won't catch cold, then begin the long and laborious process of heating large pans of water on the stove.

As I do this I think of Edouard. It is well known that he spends at least three nights a week at his mother's house, and uses her address for all his correspondence. The logical assumption is that Leon is his son, and Suzanne is the mother. So, Edouard is living with Suzanne to do the right thing by her, whilst at the same time pursuing his career and his freedom. Perhaps his parents have tolerated this behaviour as long as the relationship is not alluded to and the boy is not known to be his own or Suzanne's. I understand that it is all about saving face, and yet, this situation is bothering me. Something is not quite right with my assumption.

An abrasive bar of pearlash soap waits for me on the arm of an adjacent chair. It's getting dark and I am very tired, pleased to strip off and soak. Steam rises. The fire mesmerises with its leaping flames and the ghost of an acrid scent clings to my nostrils. I lay my head on the side of the bath and grow sleepy but I am troubled.

It's an old memory. I was a twelve-year-old boy. It was a Sunday afternoon. A trail of black threads crossed the sky. Thick soot entered my parent's house through cracks in the window frames. My mother and father held handkerchiefs over their mouths trying to stifle their coughs and I rushed outside to investigate. Wafting heat made the air hazy. The whole village had come out to see what was happening, blocking my way, so I ducked and dived through the throng.

'Everybody's out so don't go any nearer,' an old hunchback said, grabbing hold of my arm.

The inn was on fire. I heard the sound of horses in distress and wrenched my arm away. I ran like a river that spilled over its dam. As I neared the inferno my skin pricked and reddened but I was determined to get to the barn. Only seconds before the roof collapsed I kicked down the large doors and ran backwards, five stallions rushing past me like a glorious wind.

I lie there, for some time, watching black shadows dance upon the wall, then move over to the sofa wrapped in a towel, letting the fire penetrate with its warmth. I think about this morning at the Café de Bade: the speeches, the camaraderie, the calling out, the solemn backslapping and shaking of hands. The cartoonist who works for the newspaper, *L'Avenir Nationale*, as he sat on a stool by the bar and drew the scene – an image that will be presented to the populace by breakfast tomorrow morning.

And something wonderful. She wore a white lace dress that was both demure and shapely. Her eyes quietly demanded my attention. I looked away but found myself magnetically pulled towards her. She lifted the back of her hand to her lips and laughed. Her amusement created boldness inside me and without thinking I approached her.

'Hello.'

'Hello.'

'I'm Doctor Paul Gachet, from Lille.'

'Blanche Elisabeth Castets. I am a musician,' she said.

We agreed that I would call at her house on Saturday at eleven. We'd go for a walk.

'And will this suit your parents?' I asked.

'Doctor Gachet, if I had parents, I doubt I would be here now. Both my parents died in the cholera epidemic. I live in their house, alone.'

'And you play an instrument.'

'I play the violin – self-taught, for a living.'

'I have patients who will be waiting for me,' I said, glancing at my watch.

'Until the weekend then,' she replied, embracing me with a smile that captured and accompanied me for the best part of an hour whilst I made my way home.

La Salpêtrière
April 17th

'The physician's high and only mission is to restore the sick to health, to cure, as it is termed.'

Samuel Hahnemann, *The Organon of Medicine.*

The room is arranged like an auditorium. Twenty doctors and students sit on low chairs. These men are expectant, hoping to witness mastery over the human mind. Magic has been medically adopted here, and the place vibrates with the frisson of conversation.

We have been kept waiting for over fifteen minutes but no one seems to care. The sun peers through the clouds and throws a devilish heat into the room through a large picture window. I pull my collar away from my neck just as he appears with his entourage. His audience is silenced.

'Good morning gentlemen.'

He receives a rumble in reply.

'For those of you who don't know me I am Doctor Jean-Martin Charcot, Head of Neurology here at La Salpêtrière. This is a beautiful morning, don't you think?' He pulls his jacket sleeves towards the heels of his hands. 'I intend to give you a powerful demonstration that will change the way you think about the human brain. I have with me my helpers and a patient named Manon.' Charcot stands with his right hand on his heart, a handsome man, slightly hunched, with white swept-back hair and a serious demeanour. 'Come here Manon.'

My poor Manon has not been looking forward to this charade. She wouldn't let anyone come near her this morning.

Now she stands with her head bowed, still in her nightgown, and with the heaviest of frowns upon her face. Her hair is oily from fear and sweat and the way it hangs limply mirrors her mood.

'Madame Bottard, can you bring Manon over here?'

Marguerite Bottard is short and squat with grey, wiry wisps escaping her bonnet.

'Certainly Doctor.'

She places her hands on Manon's shoulders and guides the patient towards Charcot.

'No, let her stand back a little so there is space between us and stay behind her, only slightly to the left, so these gentlemen can see. Thank you nurse, I don't know what I'd do without you.' Charcot smiles with some difficulty and Marguerite blooms. Charcot pulls a gold watch on a long chain from his top jacket pocket, testing its weight in his hands.

'Hypnotism, gentleman, is not just entertainment for the café-concert. It is supreme power over the neurological functions of the human brain. Please watch carefully. Look up Manon!'

Marguerite shoves the patient from behind. She falls forward a step and looks up at Charcot. He starts to swing his pocket watch before her eyes.

'Do not blink. Just watch, Manon.'

Her head flops towards her chest.

'Look up!' Charcot cries.

Manon lifts her head again and Charcot clicks his fingers suddenly in her line of vision.

'Your grief will come out!'

Marguerite Bottard licks her lips and smooths her pinafore with her hands.

Manon lifts herself up and yells heartily for several moments. Then her eyes focus on something in the middle distance. For several seconds she is quiet. She starts to cry. 'Don't leave me. Please, don't leave me. I can't go through this again. No, no, no, don't make me go through this again.' And she collapses in a sobbing heap.

33

'Aha!' Charcot turns towards us medics, a slight smile appearing on his thin lips as if he has just won the war. He bends down and clicks his fingers once again in front of Manon's face. She doesn't move. The sound of her weeping is unnerving. I'm not the only one to squirm in my seat.

The nurse and a student haul Manon off the floor. They make a support with their arms behind her back and walk her out through the door. We hear their footsteps slapping marble into the distance.

'So you see gentlemen, we have power at our liberty to overwhelm our patients. We can transfix them. We can ignite their emotions. We can induce hysteria. And this morning you have witnessed just an iota of our capabilities as scientists and physicians. Gentlemen, we are on the threshold of great discovery.'

At Home
April 17th, eve

'Besides the stomach, the tongue and the mouth are the parts most susceptible to the medicinal influences; but the interior of the nose is more especially so ... .'

Samuel Hahnemann, *Organon of Medicine.*

My kitchen/dispensary is almost finished. There are now half a dozen shelves along the wall facing the window. They support my brown bottles of mother tinctures: *Chamomilla*, Calendula, Arnica – all plants from the *compositae* family. Pulsatilla, *Staphisagria*, Aconite from the *ranunculaceae*, and so on and so forth.

I have twenty-one of these bottles all in all, and one very large, transparent, glass decanter, which is full of pure alcohol. I keep it on the floor. My high-potency liquid remedies are in a big cupboard at the top, in medium-sized blue bottles. Crude minerals that I have collected over the years are at the bottom. Next to the cupboard is an Admiral's chest with over a hundred small drawers filled with little vials of pillules: different remedies, in different potencies, in alphabetical order. Opposite are the sink, the gas stove and the surface where I make and dispense.

My pharmacy has a semi-circular window with frosted glass that shields me from the sight of the well. There is no gaslight, so I have quite a few candles burning on plates. Moonshine stubs the window. I sit on a stool in front of the worktop grinding down phosphorus with a porcelain pestle and mortar. Voices rise up through the well and squeeze through the glass.

'My God, I'll hit you if you ever come home with another

woman's sweat on your clothes.' – Two shadows in the window like puppets. Both have an arm raised as if to strike. I try to concentrate on Phosphorus.

'You'll not hit me because I'll hit you first.'

'Then I will cut off your balls to make soup.'

'But you won't, my dear, because I will have murdered you first. But tell me, why are we fighting when nothing has happened, Mathilde? We're fighting and nothing's happened, don't you see?' he begins to laugh.

'I see. I see. Oh, Jean, it's funny, isn't it?' She laughs too.

The silhouettes merge.

I reach for the sterilised Egyptian kohl pot on the shelf. It brims with sugar powder. I fold small pieces of paper in a particular way, lay them out on the worktable and pour a small amount of powder onto each of them. Only one gets the phosphorus. Individually, I weigh them on a pair of brass scales. They must all weigh exactly the same.

Piano music seeps in from another apartment. I must make sure that I don't forget which paper contains the phosphorus as I wash the pestle and mortar thoroughly with soap and water, before putting them in the oven to dry. I pour the phosphorus into a clean mortar and add the contents of another envelope. Then I mill the mixture with a pestle for six minutes and, with a spatula, scrape the contents down into the bowl for four. I do this for an hour, with the addition of the contents of another envelope after each twenty minutes. It is a hypnotic affair. At first, I am conscious that my wrist is quite weak. Then that sensation dissipates as white powder circles around and around in the bowl like shifting clouds. A ring forms. I see an albino monk's head. There is the chinking of china. There is the grazing of a spatula in downward motions from the sides. An avalanche that ends in gentle snowfalls that bank against the sides of the container and pushed into the centre becomes a mountain range. Candlelight. Fire. White fire. Phosphorus. The substance becomes finer. My pestle starts to glide. I have no body. Just a mind expanding like a balloon. Thoughts vie for my attention. Of how deeply Manon grieves. I see Camille's kind face superimposed upon a portrait of his impoverished family. I feel as if it is me experiencing poverty and rejection. I push the mortar away from me. Drops of blood are falling from my nose onto my arm. I have, thankfully, saved the contents of my proving experiment. I escape into my consulting room, crying. Enormous sobs of vicarious sorrow. Feeling alone, older than my years, exhausted and thirsty, I sit on the chair in front of my desk, pinch my nose and start to pant.

I am experiencing the true nature of Phosphorus.

Wonderful Weekend
April 18th

'A multitude of small delights constitutes happiness.'

Charles Baudelaire

As agreed, I arrive at the home of Blanche Elisabeth Castets on Saturday at eleven. It has taken me over an hour to walk there under a clear sky in kind air. I find myself pleasantly expectant and whistle along the way.

She lives in a house set in a small courtyard close by Quai D'Orsay. After I ring the bell, I sit and wait for her on the bench outside, elbows on my knees, chin cupped in hands, staring at my highly polished brown shoes on the cobbles. The winter sun is uncharacteristically warm and induces a heady feeling of wellbeing similar to the experience of Cannabis intoxication. All my thoughts have wafted away.

'Doctor Gachet, I've kept you waiting all this time,' she says, without a hint of regret.

I look up, quite surprised to see her beside me. 'That's quite all right, I've enjoyed the anticipation.'

I stand and we begin to walk.

'Your eyes are quite mesmerising.' She shakes her head slightly. 'I know, that seems forward. I have always been outspoken when I'm nervous. As a child, I used to get reprimanded for it. Obviously, I am a slow learner and now it's too late.'

I raise my eyebrows. The word mesmerising reminds me of Charcot's experiments and I am especially interested in her positive use of the word.

'I think you are lovely just as you are.'

She gives me a sidelong glance.

'You do?' She interlocks her arm with mine.

'We can walk along the banks of the Seine, if you like. I often do that, in search of an inspiring place to paint and draw.'

'You're an artist *and* a medic? Of course you are, but how is it that you have so much talent, Doctor Gachet? Stupid question, no, please don't answer that.'

'Paul.'

'Pardon?'

'Paul. I'd like you to call me Paul.'

'Blanche.'

'Blanche, and you manage quite well without them, your parents, I mean?'

'I don't have a choice. I am here. I must carry on.'

'Not easy.'

'No, you are right, it's not, but no one said life would be.'

'I agree, things are easier without preconceived ideas, but not everyone can manage that. You are blessed if you do.'

'I suppose you've got to be blessed with something.'

We speak in this easy flowing manner until the saffron sun smudges the horizon. We watch the spectacle from the bridge of Alex III and are speechless before it.

Reluctantly, I leave her on her doorstep. She closes the door and I realise that I would gladly forego my place at Père Suisse in the morning for another few hours of being in her presence. I scratch my head wondering if I should knock to tell her this, when a window springs open above me.

'I don't have to practice my violin tomorrow.'

Her voice trails towards me like the scent of roses on a summer's afternoon.

I am in excellent spirits when I arrive at the rue de l'Hôtel de Ville to check on my patient. Once again, Suzanne Leenhoff greets me.

'I'm so pleased you called, Doctor,' she says, anxiously. 'Come in.'

'He is no better?' I ask, as she leads me through to Leon's bedroom.

'Doctor, I am very worried. He has a violent cough.'

My mood flattens instantly. I regret taking full responsibility for his health. I could have easily arranged admittance to the Hospital for Sick Children, but my experience in these matters led me to believe he was better off at home. However, when I enter the room I find several reasons to have faith in my instincts restored. The window is open. Leon is no longer drowsy with glassy eyes and dilated pupils but sitting up and reading. The rash has gone from his neck.

'Is he eating?' I ask, making my way over to his bedside in order to perform a more in depth examination.

'Yes, he had a breakfast of bread, cheese and sausage. He ate quite well.'

'And drinking?'

'Not so much,' she replies.

'The body needs water, Leon. How are you feeling today?'

I place my wind-chilled hands upon his neck, which sends him into a bout of coughing that severely grates the air, and his face reddens. I let him finish then unbutton his nightshirt. The rash on his chest and stomach has faded from crimson to pale pink. I rub my palms together for warmth and rest my fingers for some moments on his brow, which no longer exudes a steamy heat. Angling his head towards the window I ask him to open his mouth, although the fact that he had eaten a hearty breakfast is already indication enough that his fauces are on the mend.

'Now,' I say, turning round to face his mother. 'How was he yesterday, after I left?'

'At first, I thought it was a miracle. Within ten minutes of having that little pill he brightened and he has not been so hot ever since, but in the night he was coughing and coughing, so I gave him the powder like you said, and that's when his cough got very bad, frighteningly harsh as it is now and I thought at one point that he wasn't going to regain his breath,' she said, all in one go, as if she was coming out in sympathy with the boy's arrested inhalation.

'Miss Leenhoff, my prognosis is very good. He is so much better in himself and this is a major indication. His body will repair itself now. I'll pass by again tomorrow.'

'Aren't you going to give him anything for his cough?'

'His body will heal itself.'

'Oh,' she says. 'I'll have to go to the shop for linctus then.'

I pick up my bag. Inside it there are bottles neatly separated by a metal grid. I look for the one with *Sac Lac* – sugar powder – written on its label. I pour twenty pillules into a two-gram vial.

'Give him one every two hours, and you won't need the linctus.'

'Thank you, Doctor,' she says.

April 19th

Sunday. Blanche and I stroll along the river once more. Like a homing pigeon I walk her in the direction of rue Faubourg Saint Denis, all the while pointing out the merits and the drawbacks of a scene from a technical, artistic, point of view. I speak about the light, such an inspirational factor. The way in which my friends see colours inside colours, which they blend on canvas, bringing purple to the heavens, yellow to grey paving stones and blue to grass.

'Music has tones and hues too,' she tells me.

She stops walking and hums. When she's finished, she asks, 'What colour did you see?'

'The colour of light.' But I wanted to say, 'The colour of you'.

We eat lunch in the Café Guerbois. I introduce her to the writer, Charles Beaudelaire. His face is powdered white and eyelids kohled like a geisha. He sits amongst a small entourage of young men and women, each dressed in varying degrees of eccentricity and style. I look from one to the other: An angelic face. A blond curly wig. A swish of royal blue velvet. The rustle of organza. The glint of gold. An amused expression occupies them all. Charles makes a show of kissing Blanche's hand whilst gazing up into her eyes. His friends let out a collective and precipitating, 'Woah.'

'What a wonderful secret friend you have, Doctor Gachet,' Charles says. 'Will you join us?'

Blanche takes a deep lungful of air and says, 'This is only our second rendezvous. I think we should be alone.'

I am relieved and flattered. Once at our table, after a game of 'No, after you', she says 'Your accent is strange.'

'I grew up in Lille.'

I unwrap a piece of charcoal from a cloth and sketch an unnamed bird of prey on a napkin.

'It's for you,' I say, pushing the drawing towards her.

'I'll frame it, but you have to sign it. Put Paul van Ryssel,' she says, pushing the drawing back to me. I thought about it briefly then wrote under the date Paul van Ryssel – Paul of Lille. From now on it is how I will sign all my artwork.

We order a feast of onion soup followed by goose with bacon and peas. But a strange spell of enchantment has been cast over us; we can't eat and the food congeals on the plates.

On my way home, once again, I return to Edouard's second household, a strange family of sorts where every member proudly bears a different surname. This time a very hurried Suzanne Leenhoff greets me.

'Oh, I forgot you were coming,' she says, wearing a coat and quite clearly just on her way out.

'How is Leon?'

'He is quite well. He is in the studio with Edouard who wants to paint him. I am just on my way to collect him now.'

Monday Morning
April 20th

'Symptoms, in reality, are nothing more than the cry from suffering organs.'

Jean-Martin Charcot

I am late. Disorientated. Staring at the open wardrobe when I need socks from the drawer. Stirring salt into my coffee. Outside the arched entrance of Sâlpetrière my stomach groans as I anticipate the smell that overwhelms so many of my days: the stink of boiled cabbage mixed with ethanol.

Moving through the lobby, I bid Madame Lemont, the concierge, a good morning. As usual, her bonnet barely nods in reply. My footsteps echo on the stone floor. I've been told that prostitutes were once massacred here and if you listen carefully you can still hear their screams in the buzzing silence. I am barely past reception when the sight of Victorine Meurent accompanied by another female surprises me. They sit on a bench attached to the wall.

'Victorine, what are you doing here?'

'Doctor Gachet, Paul, we need to see you immediately!'

'I am already running late,' I say, but the look on Victorine's face is a determined stare.

'Come this way.' Looking over my shoulder, Madame Lemont's countenance shrivels in disgust. I wonder if it is only here, in this wintery hallway, that she finds human compassion so difficult to abide.

Victorine holds the arm of her companion with both hands and follows me through to the atrium and up some stairs. I can

44

hear the rustle of petticoats as we climb. We go into a ward that I know to be unoccupied. I perch on one of the beds. The women stand.

'What's going on?' I ask.

Victorine's friend has her head bowed. She has a skull full of thick, matted blonde curls. I look down at a pair of dirty pink shoes. When I raise my eyes Victorine meets my gaze and vigorously shakes her friend's arm.

'Tell him,' she says. 'Tell him what you told me.'

Her friend lifts her head. There is lightning in her glare. The girl tugs her arm away from Victorine's grasp and hurls herself towards me. Her nails are talons directed at my face. I catch her wrists. She thrashes and tries to bite me.

'You bloody men are all the same,' she screams. 'All you want to do is to cut off my head,' and in seconds she's a snake on the floor reaching for my ankles.

'Go on, tell him who you are,' Victorine calls loudly.

'He knows who I am. It's him. He betrayed me.'

'Tell him anyway,' Victorine goads.

'I am,' she says, on all fours now, wobbling her head like a coquette, 'Marie Antoinette.'

Silence.

I stand with my chin in my hand. Victorine's eyes are questioning mine. This maniac is hardly out of childhood.

'Wait here,' I tell Victorine.

In the corridor I bump straight into a young nurse who I have never seen before.

'We're in the midst of an emergency, come with me.'

There are often screams reverberating in these halls, hospital staff huddled together to contain a dangerous patient. But the girl is quiet now. It must appear to be a silent emergency, like a suicide.

Victorine paces as we enter the room. Her temporary ward rolls on the floor and moans.

'Nurse?'

'Yes Doctor.'

'Your name?'

'Morrisot. Catherine Morrisot.'

'Nurse Morrisot, this woman on the floor, her name is ... .'

'Bella,' Victorine interjects.

'This girl Bella, I have good reason to ask you to look after her for an hour or so. Please keep her here, in this room, and be kind. If anyone asks what you're doing, tell them you're acting on the orders of Doctor Paul Gachet. Do you understand?'

Nurse Morrisot nods. I gesture to Victorine, and to the sound of our footsteps we exit the building. When we reach the arched entrance to the courtyard, I thrust my hands in my trouser pockets, turn towards Victorine and ask her to explain.

'Yesterday, I was at home about to begin painting. I'd set up an easel by the open window. I quite liked the feel of the dim light making a grey background for Notre Dame. It was damp. There was a horrible smell of manure and a mean wind blew the candle out.

'I said "*Merde!*", then someone called through the door, "Mademoiselle Victorine Meurent, I have a note for you from Bella Laffaire." It was a very young male voice. "I'm sorry, I don't know Bella Laffaire," I said.'

Victorine paused and I pictured the scene. I had been to Victorine's garret once when she had a sore throat. It was just one room with a bed and a chair, some clothes, cooking utensils, and a guitar.

'He said, "You saw her a few days ago at La Pigalle. Mademoiselle Meurent, it was when Bella was arrested."

'You remember, Doctor Gachet ... Paul? You were there.'

I gave my assent.

'Well naturally, I was reluctant to let the boy in. I remember swaying a little, trying to think of an alternative, but I could not think of a satisfactory reason to refute him. So, I drew back the bolt and threw open the door. He could not have been any older than nine or ten, wearing a double-breasted coat with silver buttons. He had pale and sickly skin and a rivulet of mucus ran out of his nose. "You have a note?" I asked, without inviting him in. He was like a little soldier handing me a message.'

Victorine takes a crumpled piece of paper from behind the ruffle at the neck of her blue velvet dress. She hands me the note.

Mademoiselle Victorine Meurent I am dreaming of your kindness and that you will come and get me because the policemen are animals who think that when a woman needs to sell her body she should give it away for free and that it is a game to beat her and whilst this goes on there is no hope of making enough money to pay for the keep of an invalid mother some snotty-nosed kids and a father who drinks spirits till he beats her Bella Laffaire

"'I need to paint," I told the boy, but he just stood there silently until I waved my arms in the air from the sheer frustration of being disturbed and said, "Where is she?"

'He led me to the police station where they kept me waiting for half an hour. Then a gendarme with a fat stomach said that I could take her if I gave him twenty francs. Twenty francs! He thought I was her madam. I paid the money and believed that would be the end of it but she followed me home. She stood on the pavement for half an hour shouting up at me about the French court, many lovers and having her head cut off, and that's where I found her this morning, trying to sleep off her madness under a tree.'

Meeting with Charcot
April 22nd

'The highest ideal of cure is rapid, gentle and permanent restoration of the health, or removal and annihilation of the disease in its whole extent, in the shortest, most reliable, and most harmless way, on easily comprehensible principles.'

Samuel Hahnemann, *The Organon of Medicine.*

Charcot comes towards me. He has a doctor at either side and his commanding voice fills the air.

'Doctor Gachet, the other day a new staff nurse was confined to a room with a young madwoman who was not yet admitted to this hospital. Your orders, I believe. Perhaps you would like to enlighten me?'

'Well, yes, I've been wanting to talk to you ... .'

'Lots of paperwork and we still don't know who brought her here.'

'It was a friend of mine. I'd like to talk to you about her treatment.'

'I've booked her in for electroshock therapy.' Doctor Charcot takes his watch from his top pocket and studies it. 'If there's anything more, you'll have to keep up with me,' he says, walking away hurriedly. His accomplices and I follow like a snake on his tail as he continues to speak. 'I've read your thesis on melancholia. There is no doubt that you have been very thoughtful on the subject. You should study hypnotherapy amongst other practises. Embrace the future, Gachet. You know, I've started to wonder if memories live on long after we are conscious of them, and influence who we are to become. Doctor

Gachet, do you believe that to be true?'

'Yes, I do, and I also believe in another of your theories, that symptoms are the expression of a diseased organ. Doctor Charcot, why not the same theory for symptoms expressed by the mind?'

'"Why not?" indeed.'

Charcot pushes his way through a series of heavy wooden doors and lets them swing backwards. I must slip through quickly behind him or else be struck.

'I think that when a person is fragile and cannot face their own emotions, something shatters inside them – but supposing there is a medicine that mirrors a patient's disturbance exactly and, in doing so, strengthens their inner resolve?'

Charcot stops and looks at me.

'What type of medicine?'

'A dynamic medicine: homeopathy.'

Charcot's cronies laugh into their fists and turn around to try and hide their mocking amusement. The man himself remains serious but silent then after some time continues to march.

We have entered the hospital library and arrived at the staircase leading down to the reading room: oak-panelled walls, a huge drawing room fit for Napoleon himself; bow-legged walnut sideboards; portraits of Generals; tasselled sofas; a man smoking a clay pipe, tears continually falling down his cheeks, mumbling, turning round in circles, shouting an obscenity; a child with her back wedged into a chair, raised legs out in front, clutching a china doll and sucking her finger. Actually, she is not a girl but a woman with creases on her face, bleeding scarlet lipstick and thick black, uneven kohl lines along the margins of her eyes. Another man: he is wearing a monocle, pocket watch, round glasses, and a suit full of holes. He talks only of doom and haughtily introduces himself to everyone as Jesus Christ. There are others. Two nurses stand like soldiers observing the scene. One has her back to us, clanking metal against porcelain.

'We are the leading hospital in the world for diseases of the mind. You won't see another one in all five continents that allows mentally ill patients to wander in a room like this,' he says, chest puffed.

I am talking to an eminent man, a very brilliant man. A man who recognises disease syndromes and names them. They bob towards me with every nod of his head – Tourette's … Multiple Sclerosis … Parkinson's.

There are many polished medals pinned to his silk embroidered coat, and there are scuttling rats and damp cells in the basement that serve as patients' bedrooms.

I look him in the eye and say, 'What about cure?'

That Evening

'I am an artist ... I am here to live out loud.'

Emile Zola

On my way home I buy a copy of *Moniteur,* Napoleon's propaganda paper. I am intrigued by the headline, *The Emperor's Salon. An exhibition of all rejected works will open on May 17th, at The Palais de l'Industrie, a fortnight after Le Salon itself. Napoleon has said, 'Let the public be the judge of the nation's art!'*

'Ha!' I say, looking around.

A surly woman clutches her handbag close to her bosom. She watches me closely and widens the space between us as she walks past. Other pedestrians follow suit.

Blanche sits on the stairs outside my front door, a silhouette in the dim light. I look over my shoulder, key poised in the lock.

'If I'd known you'd been waiting ... .'

'I've only come to invite you to a café-concert. Tomorrow evening, I'm playing violin,' she says, standing up, brushing the dust off her coat. I look down and notice that she carries a wicker basket filled with bread, salad, cheese and ham.

'Do you have dinner?' she asks.

'Come in,' I say. 'Be at home.'

I sit on a stool in my pharmacy. Blanche stands at the sink. She washes leaves covered with salt, shakes out the water and absently eats some. There is a leather-bound notebook in front of me open at a blank page. I write 'Phosphorus' and the date in my best calligraphy. I haven't taken the remedy myself yet but such startling symptoms, experienced during its making, are embossed on my brain. I must record them for posterity.

'If you come tomorrow evening, I hope you won't judge my playing too harshly. I tend to get nervous if someone I know is in the audience. Anyway, enough of that. How was your day?'

I look up and Blanche is smiling. All thoughts of Phosphorus disappear from my mind.

'Go away!' – a female voice. A neighbour screams from somewhere outside the window. 'Just go away. Get out. Will you just get out?'

'Madame,' a male voice calls back. 'You have one more night then you must pay the rent. One more night, do you hear? Tomorrow I will bring an eviction order and the police.'

'You fucking swine, just get out of here. What right do you have turning a young mother with three children out onto the streets?' another male voice intervenes.

'You sir, have drunk your inheritance. It's not up to me to protect your family.'

'I have a knife inside. I suggest you run away while I get it.'

'That poor woman,' Blanche says, coughing into her hand.

'Are you all right?'

'It's a cough. I've had it on and off since childhood.'

'I could treat it.'

'No. Don't be silly. It's fine. Ssh now, I need to concentrate whilst I cut up the ham.'

The pages of my notebook have fallen open, fan-like, onto words copied some time ago from a Materia Medica:

Platinum: Platina,

Mentals: Ailments from, vexation, humiliation. Hauteur with contemptuousness for those around her. Conceit. Delusions of superiority; thinks she is a queen ... .

I read again, *thinks she is a queen.*

Blanche says something.

'Pardon?'

'Do you have olive oil?'

'I don't usually eat here.'

After supper, we sit in my apartment before the soporific warmth of the fire. I'm on the sofa. Blanche is on the floor leaning against my legs. I tell her of my childhood: my mother's kitchen with fine herbs that hung from oak beams and aromas that never failed to entice the gastric juices; my father's study, its roaring fire and comfortable high-backed leather chairs; the scent of linseed and turpentine when learning to paint. I hold a lock of her hair loosely in my palm and run a finger from the base of her skull to the top cervical bone in her spine, an area that's soft and special like an oyster. I like the fact that I am able to impress her with my story about saving the horses.

'Really?' she asks.

'Really,' I answer.

And I make her gasp at the tale of jumping off a rampart.

The clock on the mantel strikes midnight.

'I don't … '

So fearful of the negative thing she is going to say, I feel my heart begin to pound.

' … want to go,' she says.

'We still have hours until morning.'

'Then I'll stay just a little bit longer.'

'Tell me something about you,' I ask.

She takes the slippers from my feet.

My toes look waxy in the candlelight.

'I would like to travel to China, Africa, India and those little islands on the Caribbean Sea.'

'How would you get there?'

She laughs as I wriggle my toes.

'I always thought I'd get there on a boat with a handsome captain. You probably think I'm too old to dream about such things. Anyway, lately, I've thought about going there with you.'

I don't speak for a very long time but join her on the floor, take her hand in mine. It is cold and I hope to warm it.

She coughs.

'I'd like to treat your cough.'

'No, it's fine. I'm all right, really.'

Her face has lost its translucence. Her cheeks are red from the hacking spasm. Earlier, she stood by the mirror and slightly rouged her pale lips. When I looked at her she half-smiled and turned away, embarrassed.

'And I want to bed you,' I say, with immediate regret.

Blanche says nothing. She stares at the fire. We are silent. The fire crackles. Time passes too quickly. She leaves in a hansom in the early hours. I stand on a kerbstone in my slippers to wave her off. When I turn to go back home the perfect night evaporates. Left behind is concern. Her cough frightens me.

It's dusk and I am running through trees. Light flickers. I trip over roots and thick ropey weeds but manage to stay on my feet, just. A russet squirrel swishes through brittle autumn leaves, scuttles past me, and climbs up a pine. A bee hums at my side. I hear a screech and the flapping of wings. My breath and my heart create percussion in my ears. Colette in her calico dress and hobnail boots has already reached the clearing.

'Come on,' she calls. 'Run, run.'

Colette does something strange to my organs. She makes me desperate to catch up and touch her. There is so much I don't understand. I run as fast as I can. When I reach the edge of the forest I pant for a while and hold my chest. There is something unreal about the light here. The sun lies low on the horizon and the sky is muddy. It is neither night nor day. It is in between.

Colette dances round in circles in the clearing with her arms stretched out to the sides. The wet grass makes her boots shine. I laugh at her unashamedness.

'I'm coming,' I yell, determined to get ahead, pushing myself forward, flying beyond her with the might of a conqueror. Then scrabbling up the hill on all fours towards the castle, handfuls of

grass threaten to slide from my grasp and caked mud creates pressure under my fingernails.

Behind me Colette screams in playful competition, 'No, wait, wait, wait.'

I'm ahead. I'm the winner. Hero. And king. Thwack. Thwack. Thwack. I run across the slack drawbridge, which is conveniently down, shouting, 'Ho, ho, ho' with my arms in the air. I climb the nearest wall, my limbs in superb co-ordination, until at the top I look down. Twelve years old and full up with the notion that this is not a child's game, but neither is it the way that adults behave. It is in between, an unidentified space that hardly exists at all. Nothing feels real here and therefore I can do anything, anything at all.

Colette throws herself up the hill towards me. With every lungful of breath it feels as if she's jutting into me, merging with me, becoming my own flesh. My want is enormous and I must do something courageous to mark this moment, this omnipotence. But I don't know what to do and so I jump, expecting to land like a cat. The moat is dry and stony. I arrive with a lump of skin grazed from my buttocks and with my ankle twisted beneath me. My foot is limp and hanging. I moan like an animal in pain.

The Day after the Night Before
April 23rd

'Colour is a matter of taste and sensitivity.'

Edouard Manet

I awake. Panicked. Soaked in perspiration, kicking off the covers. Daylight and birdsong tumble into the whitewashed room that is too square and too small for all its furniture. The brass bedstead rattles behind me as I move. The cupboard opposite overwhelms like a schoolmaster. There's only space to get out of bed on one side, there's a too narrow gap between the window and sink on the far wall. I splash my face with water and wash the putrid sweat from all areas of my skin. I have to go to work. To the hospital where I am never as productive as I would like to be, held back as I am in my therapeutic capabilities.

My first thought is of Bella Laffaire, admitted to the hospital but not on my terms. She will be exposed to hypnotism, electrotherapy and genital manipulation. In my understanding, these therapies are contrary to the Hippocratic oath – *primum non nocere* – first do no harm.

I'm not sure that I have a valid alternative. I have no experience of treating such deep mental pathology with homeopathy, although my experience in general suggests that it is definitely worth a try, especially if I think the catalyst is well known to me. I intend to make a fuss.

My watch says it's early, which after such a late night surprises me. I have only slept until my usual waking time. Too few hours and yet I don't feel tired. Good. I will go to Père Tanguy and buy paint.

When I arrive he is busy, entangled with the artistic needs of Victorine. I stand in line anticipating my next art project: Blanche has agreed to model for me.

It is mostly dark in the long narrow shop that is situated in a back street just off Pigalle. Sunlight slips through a gap between two houses across the street and just about manages to permeate the bald mat by the door, but ignores the window where one of Camille's paintings, a blue-tinged impression of the Boulevard des Italiens, sits on an easel looking out onto the street. The place is cluttered. Madame Tanguy in her thinning black dress and greying apron sits at a small table at the back of the shop. In front of her are a cash box and a sales register where she scrupulously records every business transaction her husband makes. She has a clump of steely hair tied in a bun. Each parched strand denotes an element of stress caused by her husband's open heart and generosity.

Old Tanguy wears a blue work shirt and a pair of wide black trousers. He bends over and looks for something amongst a pile of equipment: half constructed easels, paint pots, rolls of canvas and brushes. On the walls hang numerous works of art, coy in the darkness.

I imagine the old merchant coming down at night carrying a lantern that he holds up close to an image he has framed, his heart swollen with pride as he illuminates the magic of Paris streets, country scenes, café culture, the railway station and models, by the young artists whose visual delights are as delicious as ice cream.

Old Tanguy hands Victorine a brown paper bag that is full to the brim. She holds it in front of her like a baby. She faces me but I don't think she can see me. I would guess that I am in silhouette with the low-lying sun falling in from behind me. So, I am not surprised when she does not say 'hello' nor realise that I am watching her: her winsome smile, head tilted slightly to one side, an affectation which is both childish and suggestive. Tanguy wipes his palms on his trousers and says, 'Mademoiselle

Victorine, pay me next time.'

'I will bring you in a painting, Monsieur Tanguy. You are so kind.' She places her gloved hand on his shoulder, leans over and kisses him delicately by his ear.

'I will bring you a painting next time,' she says again, in a whisper that is shockingly intimate, especially with the old man's wife looking on. I have moved forward and am standing next to the couple. Now, Victorine can see me well. In the background Madame Tanguy is half-standing in her chair, presumably to catch a better glimpse of what is going on.

'Doctor Gachet,' Victorine says, placing that same gloved hand fleetingly in one of mine. 'Nice to see you.'

Tanguy and I watch as she sways out of the shop, her satin bustle a polite invitation.

Madame Tanguy brings me coffee. When I leave it is nearly ten. I have just enough time to take my purchases home and then get to the hospital. On the street, I am caught unawares by the sight of Victorine.

'I've waited for you,' she says, toppling slightly as the heel of her shoe gets caught between two cobbles. There is a horse and cart behind her. I grab her elbow to pull her away from the middle of the road. 'And the things you've bought?' I ask, noticing her arms are empty.

'I've dropped them at my mother's,' she says motioning with her head across the street. 'She is the laundress.'

We walk and I give her time to continue.

'It's about Bella. I'd like to come to the hospital to paint her.'

'Do you have her permission?' I ask.

'Do I need it?'

'I can ask Doctor Charcot. I have to see him this afternoon.'

I realise that I am walking very fast. Victorine is almost running to keep up. I slow down to be courteous.

'How is she?' she asks.

'Nothing can change in such a short period of time.'

'Were you able to admit her in the way that suited you best?'

'No. No, I wasn't.'

'Doctor Gachet, can I ask you, what was the problem?'

'I'm not sure it is appropriate for me to tell you. It's hospital business. Internal affairs. Why do you ask?'

'I care about women.'

'Women in general?'

'Yes, women in general,' she says.

I nod and think about this.

'I want to treat her using homeopathy, which is perfectly legal, valuable and effective, but beyond the credibility of the medical establishment.'

'A bit like the situation for modern painters then.'

'Yes,' I say. 'Exactly like that.'

'And what will happen to her if you don't get to treat her with your remedies?'

'She'll be hypnotised by Doctor Charcot and everyone will applaud. I won't get the opportunity to speak to her. She will become institutionalized, confined – probably for life.'

'And homeopathy will cure her?'

'It's worth a try.'

Victorine stops. We have come to La Pigalle.

'Doctor Gachet, Paul, you're an honest man, I like you,' she says in parting. I watch her walk away and reach with my fingers for the peak of my cap. I am upset. It is unprofessional. I have said too much.

In his office and separated by his desk, 'What is it Gachet?' asks Charcot. 'I am busy. I trust you will be quick?'

'Doctor Charcot, I want you to seek permission from The Faculty to practice homeopathy on the new patient, Bella Laffaire.'

'I'm sorry Gachet, am I losing my mind? Haven't we had this conversation already?'

'Not conclusively and to my satisfaction.'

'I see.'

'Doctor Charcot, with all due respect, I have been working at this hospital for longer than you have and the only difference between our positions here is that you have been allowed to experiment with your brand of science and I have not.'

'For a reason.'

'Please, share the reason?' I ask, sitting down and pulling up my trousers by the creases at my thighs.

'I don't have the time for this,' he says.

'That is not a good enough reason.'

'You will have to come back.'

'Then give me a time,' I say, leaning forward and bringing my fist down on his desk.

Charcot stiffens and there's an involuntary twitch in his cheek. He marches to the door, looks sideways along the hall, closes the door softly and comes back and seats himself behind his desk.

'Maybe we should do it now. Homeopathy is frowned upon because of its absurdity.'

'And mesmerism … .'

'Hypnotism.'

'If you wish … then hypnotism is not absurd?'

'You can see it man,' he roars, raising his body from the seat with his hands on his desk, his face coming, phantom-like, towards me. 'The reaction of hypnotism, you can see it clearly.'

'And you can see the response when you give a homeopathic remedy.'

Charcot sits down again and stares at his clasped hands.

'Doctor Gachet, I have no words for you.'

'Then send a letter.'

'You will turn this establishment into a laughing stock.'

'I will prove something. Either that homeopathy is a valid form of medicine or that it is quackery. Tell the Faculty that it is an important experiment that you wish to conduct under the roof of Salpêtrière.'

Charcot sits back and turns his head to look out of the

window. When he faces me again I can just about discern the briefest of nods.

I do not believe in coincidence. I believe that forces of the universe dictate when certain fates collide. That is how Victorine and Blanche, two strangers with only my friendship in common, both happen to be performing at the Café de Bade on the same night, and how I find myself sitting next to Edouard Manet.

'Doctor Paul Gachet, you don't normally come here in the evening,' he says, pulling off his lemon suede gloves, and loosening a silk cravat held at his throat by a topaz clip. 'It's hot in here.' He looks around and back again as if he is a little lost and says, 'Do you mind if I sit with you?'

'Of course not, help yourself. I've come to see Blanche Castets play the violin.'

'Really? I thought you'd come to see Victorine.'

'That is a bonus.'

Fascinated by his captivating aura, I watch him flick away the tails of his frock coat, ease himself into a chair and rest a palm nonchalantly on the gold pommel of his cane. He says, clearly to his own amusement, 'Yes, Victorine is definitely a bonus.'

At which point she arrives, squeezing between tables and pushing past staff with a steady gaze and a flower in her hair.

'Two of my favourite men sitting together,' she says, offering us in turn a very confident hand. 'You're not drinking. I'll get the waitress.' The crowded room absorbs her.

Edouard looks at me out of the corner of his eye. I smile and his old grin widens. Then the light touch of a woman's fingers rests against my lids from behind and blinds me to everything but the colour red.

'Blanche?'

She takes the shutters away from my eyes. I stand, introduce her to Edouard who, like Charles, kisses her knuckles while looking up into her eyes. She turns towards me and raises her eyebrows. She wears the lace dress that she wore the day we met.

'Your friend Victorine will be playing before me,' she says, sitting down without waiting to be asked. I sit down too, noticing Victorine has found a waitress who she steers in our direction before the maitre d' entangles her.

'Would you like a drink?' Edouard asks.

'Just water,' Blanche says.

'Just water, are you sure?'

'Yes, I am. Yes.'

'Gachet?'

'A beer.'

'A glass of water, one beer and I'll have a cognac,' Edouard says, then turning towards Blanche. 'Mademoiselle Blanche, what is your act?'

'I am a musician. I play the violin.'

'And do you write your own music?'

'I do, but if you notice Monsieur Edouard, there is a prejudice against original material. The owners of all the café concerts seem only to be interested in popular melodies.'

Blanche reaches for my hand and holds it in my lap.

'Ah, here come our drinks,' Edouard says.

A waiter climbs on the bench next to me and twists the valve on a kerosene lamp. The light dims. Victorine sits on a stool in the centre of the café with lamps all around her on the floor. The flower has gone from her hair. She wears pantaloons, a white blouse and a wide brimmed hat. She looks like a matador and plays Spanish guitar with verve and great accomplishment. 'Mesdames et Monsieurs, I will play a song for you,' she says, strumming. 'That Bonaparte's military men sang when they were at war and away from their loved ones. Imagine. A young man lying in a bunk – all around him are more robust less sensitive souls – playing cards – drinking spirits from a hip flask – laughing – sweating in their underwear from the heat in the belly of the ship.' The notes on her guitar become more defined. She starts playing chords and humming. She sings.

I never wanted to leave you
But we knew I had to go
The pale light of morning came much too soon
I should have told you so.

Voices from the audience join her.

I should have told you so.

At the next table, a woman wearing a silver brocade dress, hair high in a chignon, croons with a far away expression. Her hands rest on the table in front of her. It is as if she is making a confession. The barman stands mesmerised with his arms behind his back. Edouard pats his own knee in time to the music and I squeeze Blanche's fingers gently in my own.

Then Victorine's performance is over and Blanche goes behind the bar to get her violin. She holds the instrument by its neck and walks through the applauding crowd. As she stands inside the ring of lamps with chin-rest at her neck and eyes closed, she raises the bow and waits. The whole room is encompassed in a rich, commanding sound as the bow slides over the strings. Then a breath-taking silence for several seconds before Blanche plays an old melody. Her soul is inside the music, to my mind, not exactly like a picture in sound but suggestive, so that at one point I feel the warmth of a summer sea at sunset lapping against the shore at Deauville and the next minute I am tasting something cold like a snow flake upon my tongue. When she finishes people are standing, handclapping, and shouting 'Bravo'. She walks towards me, laughing with her eyes. Edouard leans over and whispers in my ear, 'You must bring her to one of my mother's soirées.'

My Work
May 1st

'Paint the essential character of things.'

Camille Pissarro

As a medical student, I did my apprenticeship in the Hospital for Sick Children. Those vivid times taught me to become the doctor I am today. I can still see those hurrying nurses carrying vessels filled with body fluids amid the choir of maternal wailing that accompanied the moans of children. Patients lying still and dumb in the cacophony; overheated flesh and dull pleading eyes between sheets stained with blood and shit. Big rectangular rooms like barracks, spirited by disease; floor to ceiling windows bringing light and brightness for the too sick to shun; pockets of silence hanging around the few beds that were stripped back to their greying mattresses, and the families that once surrounded them disappeared into the ether.

Memories of Doctor Emile Trousseau, in his white coat and scorpion tail moustache entering the scene:

'Next!' he used to shout, clapping his hands.

A nurse pulls a baby away from its mother. 'He has diphtheria. He must have the operation.'

Then being told in the staff room how it all made sense really. That yes, the majority of the babies do die, but best to perform the tracheotomy anyway, and remove the laryngeal obstruction. Science will one day arrive at a place where the babies will live to tell the tale. But whilst we wait for that to happen, those who haven't the time queue on the stairs to my apartment. Once again, I am careful not to pinch skin or cloth with my footsteps. Every few yards I say hello to no one in particular. The door to 2C is slightly ajar. An old and wizened person with an androgynous face pops their head out into the hallway. 'Get away with you,' their world-weary voice calls in my wake. 'Get away with you and your fucking circus here every day.'

The door slams, the sound reverberates and the walls and floor send tremors as if from an earthquake. First in line are a mother and child. I open the door, usher them in, stooping to pick up my post.

It is a fine day. Through the window, the sun is so bright and warming that I have to close the shutters. I sit behind my desk and wave for my patients to sit down in front of it. The mother wears a brown serge shapeless dress. She has fair hair and ruddy cheeks as if she has been drinking. The boy sits beside her with no shoes, picking his nose.

'How can I help?' I ask.

'I am Madame Bonnet,' she says. 'And this is Gustave. It's not all the time, Doctor, but when Gustav shits there is no time for him to get out into the yard. He ruins his clothes with it and our house stinks.'

I watch the boy. He kicks his legs and stares at the wall. The mother smacks his arm. He turns around to face me. I make a guess that he is about six years old.

'What's it like?'

'What's what like?'

'The stool, his motions.'

The mother looks at me. Her brown irises are vacant.

'The shit,' I say.

'It's like water, green, with jelly bits and it keeps on coming and coming and coming,' she is making waves with her arms.

'All day? He seems all right *now*.'

'No, only in the morning but his stomach makes noises like those machines in the pub.'

'Gustav, will you come and stand next to me for a second, I

want to have a look at your belly.'

Gustav ignores me but swings his legs with greater gusto. His mother lashes out again and he stands abruptly then slowly saunters over to my desk.

I rub my hands together to make them warm, lift the boy's holey chemise to reveal a swollen abdomen beneath dusty, grey skin.

'How often does he have a bath?'

The mother guffaws.

'Do you have a standpipe close to your house?'

'Just outside. We don't live in the country, you know.'

'Make him wash his hands before he eats. Actually, it would be better if the whole family did this. Do you feed him vegetables, meat?'

The mother guffaws again.

'Do you get pain, Gustav?'

'Yeah.'

'Where do you get your pain?'

'Here,' he says, pointing to his navel.

'And what do you do when you get your pain?'

The boy comically walks around the room, holding his middle, bending over and crying, 'Aw, it hurts. It really hurts.'

His mother and I share a smile.

'Any vomiting?'

'Yeah, but not 'im,' she says.'

'You?'

Madame Bonnet rubs her belly. At least, hers is a healthy condition. I know the remedy that will alleviate Gustav's symptoms, but the problem is from eating rotten food and lack of hygiene and I doubt this will change. I leave them alone whilst I make up his medicine in my dispensary. *Podophyllyum*, common name, Mayapple. I pour about twenty tiny pillules of the 30th potency into a small vial. I tell the mother she must administer the prescription twice a day until he's better. She must not leave the medicine in direct sunlight. I show her how I have made an indent in the cork so she can pour the remedy into it and directly into Gustav's mouth and I tell her to come back next week. She takes four grimy sous out of her pocket and places them reluctantly on my desk. The money barely covers the cost of the medicine.

'Next week I won't charge but I want to see him, even if he's better.'

The mother nods. When they leave, I open my letters quickly before I invite the next patient in. One is from my friend Camille. His wife is in labour. The midwife has just arrived. Would I come along whenever I can? The second is from my father, which reminds me that he might be interested to learn I will be exhibiting a painting at the Salon des Refusés.

More memories.

A conversation with my father:

'You're a sympathetic young man, Paul. Can't you forget art, which is never going to earn you a decent living and, I don't know, be a doctor?'

'Be a doctor?'

'Yes. Go to Paris. Study at La Sorbonne.'

Those last few months at home were bittersweet. The weather had been fine. I'd taken my easel outside, to paint what was left of the inn in a series of canvases that caught the light at different times of the day. I did not want to leave Lille. I was already practising the only thing I ever wanted to do. But my father had paid for a place at the university.

'I've heard there are studios where you can receive art tuition in your spare time. I know how important the subject is to you. It can be your hobby. More than a hobby perhaps, but not a career.'

The days shortened and, as they did, I felt a tug of rebelliousness. I was curt with my father, offhand with my mother, slamming doors and hitting the wall with my fist. My father cornered me, slapped me verbally with good reason until I had to admit that helping people with their ailments could, possibly, be a satisfying profession.

I tear open the envelope. As usual, his writing is full of concern. He asks if I am being over generous with my time and if I have enough money to eat. I have told him I do well enough several times but still he sends me a cheque every so often for several hundred francs. I rub the cheque between thumb and forefinger, finding it something tangible to show he cares.

I take a hansom to La Varenne. On the ride into the countryside, I realise that I didn't have an opportunity to mention to Charcot that Victorine would like to make portraiture of Bella Laffaire. It is not within my nature to feel comfortable about letting someone down and I am upset by the realisation that this is exactly what I have done. Modern art is important and not just aesthetically, it is a visual historical document of our world.

To the clip-clop of horse's hooves, I travel down an avenue where the tall trees filter light as if through a lace curtain. The fields to either side are Camille's current inspiration. I recognise the vivid greens and pale yellows.

When I arrive, I walk through Julie's vegetable garden that is less than luscious at this time of year, and enter the equally spare house with its timber walls and copper pots. Camille meets me at the door. He is brimming with pride.

'It's a boy,' he tells me excitedly. 'We'll call him Lucien. Let me pour you a glass to celebrate.'

I missed the birth but they did not need me. Julie is wan. She has Lucien at her breast. Both mother and baby seem extremely content.

'Will you give the baby something, to keep him well?'

I sit down at the wooden table with its hand-embroidered tablecloth and Camille brings over a bottle of local red wine. He pours two glasses and pushes one towards me. I take a sip.

'You can't be more well than well, Camille.'

'It's a dangerous world.'

'In an epidemic we can give a remedy to ward off any symptoms. In the meantime, I will come here anytime you are worried. This is excellent wine,' I say, tipping my glass to the light to watch it glow.

'Would you like a glass Julie?' Camille calls to other side of the room.

'Do you want to get your baby drunk, Camille?'

'He'll get drunk if you drink wine? Through the milk?'

'How come men don't know anything?' Julie asks me.

'Anyway, I need to pay you for coming,' says Camille.

'We're friends, it's all right, I would have come anyway.'

'I am a friend but you still have to survive.'

I look around at the humble surroundings and so many canvases stacked up against the walls. 'And so do you,' I say.

'This is your work. You must take something. I'll be affronted if you don't.'

'A painting then.'

Camille's dry, fleshy hand reaches across the table. I grasp it. The deal is done.

It is late in the evening. I'm outside Blanche's home, leaning against a street lamp, blowing clouds of frozen air towards the starry sky. I wear my old coat and scarf but my nose is so cold it reminds me it's there. This time it is I who has brought her dinner. A friend of mine, a fellow artist, owns a restaurant where they make the best onion soup. His wife has sold me a pot, together with a chunk of pungent Gruyere and a freshly baked baguette, all packed with pink tissue paper in a straw bag. When Blanche arrives we don't speak, she simply takes the bag and opens the front door.

'I've run out of kerosene,' she says eventually.

By the light of the moon, we manage to spark a fire in the small square room at the front of the house. There is a velvet armchair but no other furniture. Blanche has brought in a stool and a music stand. I have a large piece of paper attached to a canvas on a frame, which I place on the music stand. I sit on the stool facing the armchair where Blanche has settled. Charcoal pinched between my fingers, I take it to the page. The music stand collapses. Blanche laughs and I fumble to set it straight again. Flames lap up the sides of the chimney and glow on her face. All around me are candles so I can see what I draw, but I don't think I can draw now. I stare at her face. Look away. If this is going to be a portrait I must ascertain her physiology. I must understand how her clothing falls over her person. I must contemplate the flesh beneath, her breasts and the muscle of her thighs. My lips and my mouth are dry. She coughs into a handkerchief and dark shadows appear on the cloth.

'Please humour me, let me find you a remedy,' I say.

Day of Leisure
May 3rd

'If you shut up truth, and bury it underground, it will but grow.'
Emile Zola

I'm once again at Père Suisse with my painter colleagues. Camille, of course, is nearly always there, and when he misses a session those that have turned up are temporarily in mourning. He is like a father figure to us all. Paul has turned up. He is the one that I believe Camille has a special eye on, although his paintings are to my perception bizarre, with every subject and object outlined in bitumen, quite childlike, quite admirable. Claude pays us a nostalgic visit, and Victorine, as usual, is here.

'We're going to amaze the public,' Camille says excitedly.

'I think we will shock them,' says Paul. 'Whistler's "White Girl", *Dejeuner sur l'Herbe* ... .'

All eyes turn to Victorine. She is the female model in Edouard's painting.

'I agree, they won't understand,' she says, shrugging her shoulders. 'But actually, we are naïve if we ever thought they would.'

I find myself nodding. 'You are prepared then, Victorine?'

'We will cause a furore, of course, and everyone will be talking about our revolution. But it takes time for new ideas to be accepted by the people; the general public are sheep.'

'Quite the philosopher, Victorine,' Paul says.

'It's our chance to exhibit. We must hope for the best,' says Camille.

Claude remains quiet, shifting his long black hair behind his

71

ears, twitching his drooping moustache and focusing his jet eyes intently on his painting. It is of the view through the window, another depiction of his beloved Seine.

'Maybe no one will turn up,' says Paul.

Victorine is finishing her watercolour of La Notre Dame. She noisily drops her paintbrush into the jar.

'Aren't you friends with Zola?' Camille asks. 'An article from him to whet the public appetite, why not?'

'Promising something novel packed with diversity and spice,' Paul laughs.

'Why don't you invite him to preview our art?'

'Perhaps I will.'

Silence. There's a sudden commotion in the building. It's coming from the landing just outside the studio. Père Suisse scratches his stomach and shuffles out to see what is going on. With the door open, the din tumbles in with greater volume. Two youths push past an aggravated Père Suisse. The concierge stands behind them.

'I will not have you louts in my building,' he says holding his stomach and waving his index finger above his head. 'I know your sort with your thieving, grubby hands.'

The two boys stand panting as if before a headmaster.

'Mum sent me,' one of the boys cries.

It's Gustav Bonnet.

'All right everyone,' I say, standing up. My chair scratches noisily backwards across the wooden floor. 'I know this boy. Gustav what are you doing here?'

'A man called de Bellio was knocking at your door and the concierge told everybody to get out.'

'He was screaming that all the other tenants had had just about enough of you,' said the other, elder boy, panting.

'I don't follow. Why was the concierge vexed?'

'They're queuing right around the block for you and right up to your door,' Gustav says.

'Who's queuing? I don't understand.'

'It was my mum. She told everybody that you cured me of the shits. Some man died in his sleep because of them. Another man said that it was in all the newspapers that the water had become poisoned and everyone's blaming Napoleon and his lackey Haussman for saying it's all been cleaned up.'

'And Georges, I mean Monsieur de Bellio? He's meant to be in Romania.'

Both boys shrug. 'Told us where you were,' Gustav's friend says.

I make my excuses and follow the boys back to rue Faubourg Saint Denis. They run ahead of me, looking behind every so often to see that I am still there. With every step, I become angrier. Not with the queue outside my front door or with the concierge who views the incident as a disturbance of the peace, but with the bloody mindedness of those who won't acknowledge the validity in treating epidemics with a medicine that works. Where's Zola now? I ask myself. Where's the writer who continually tells the knuckle bone truth about our society? Will he cover this? I seriously doubt it. The last time someone wrote a piece highlighting the success of Hahnemann's medicine, its detractors, our eminent professors, shot him down in print for favouring fakirs and witches with murdering ways. He was not gainfully employed again, so I am told.

I arrive at the tenement to find only a few stragglers hovering in the courtyard. The concierge and a policeman with a paunch and stony eyes are there to greet me. My guides have made themselves scarce.

'This is him,' Monsieur Breton says.

The policeman takes my arm. I shake it free and say, 'What's going on?'

'Let's go inside,' he says, with one hand on my back pushing me along.

I sit on a chair in Monsieur Breton's tiny kitchen. He leans on the portal wiping his hands on a cloth. The heat from the stove is stifling. I can smell stale hops and garlic on the policeman's breath. 'Your friends started a riot in the street whilst they were waiting for you,' he says, motioning with his head towards Monsieur Breton. 'He says you're a doctor, but I've listened to the evidence about your behaviour. You have followers amongst the common people and I just want to warn you that the government will not take kindly if you've started your own anti-establishment party.'

'I am not a politician.'

'We don't need another revolution.'

'I'm a doctor. I'm also an artist and I rushed back from a painting session with some of my peers because I was informed that those people who were queuing outside here were potential patients ... all of them not well.'

'They were overheard discussing that this was because of a defect in the new water supply.'

'Apparently an article in a newspaper made that suggestion.'

'And you found a crowd to prove it, isn't that so?'

'I had nothing to do with it.'

'Don't worry, I am not going to arrest you,' he says, moving away from me. 'I am sure that Monsieur Breton will do his job and keep an eye on you. I don't want you to be the cause of any more fighting on the street – in my area – do you understand?'

I remain silent with indignation. His open palm slaps my ear. I hear the crack then a ringing sound. The flesh of my lobe burns

'Monsieur Breton, you didn't see that, did you?'

Monsieur Breton slowly shakes his head.

I say that I understand.

When Blanche arrives at eight o' clock with wine and a cassoulet, there are not many left outside my door, I advise the remaining few to come back tomorrow. She is cold and I put the fire on whilst she warms up the food which she tells me took all afternoon to shop for and cook. Then we sit on the floor facing each other with our plates in our laps and I tell her how my day has been.

'I didn't realise that to be true to myself my life would be so controversial. Sometimes it's like fighting the whole world.'

'If you want,' she says. 'You can give me a remedy.'

'You have to answer some questions. Did I tell you already that this is delicious?'

Her smile is magnanimous. 'Yes,' she says 'And Paul, you can go ahead and ask.'

'Ask what?'

'You know. Ask.'

She is holding me steadily with her gaze. For one moment I think that she is giving herself to me.

'Ask the questions you have to ask, for the remedy.'

'Yes, of course, of course, when did the coughing start?' I say, rising up off the rug and almost dropping my plate. I run over to my desk to get paper and a pen. 'Hold on,' I tell her. 'I don't want to miss a thing.' I run back, pen in mouth, paper flapping underneath my plate. She laughs, tells me I look like a kid in an egg and spoon race and kisses me spontaneously on the cheek as I once again sit down. Her eyes glow warmly in the firelight.

'It started two months ago. I was teaching violin to a pupil in a school. It was nearly the end of the lesson and I was writing down instructions for the boy's homework practice.'

'You haven't had it on and off since childhood?'

'Yes I have, but this is different.'

'How is it different?'

'It's gone on longer and it's worse.'

'And this bout first began two months ago, you said.'

'Yes.'

'Is there any reason for your cough to have started then? Did anything happen that could have upset your system?'

'The boy upset me.'

'Forgive me for prying but it will help me find your remedy; in what way did the boy upset you?'

'He's a very sensitive child.'

'And?'

'I'm sorry Paul, but I would be breaching a confidence if I told you. I know that you know his father and I'm not going to say.'

The fire crackles and spits embers into the flue.

'Blanche, I only need to know your reaction.'

'I felt upset for the boy.'

I wait a moment to see if she'd say more.

'When is your cough worse?'

'At night, when I am outside in the cold.'

'Is there anything that makes it better?'

'Warmth. Hot drinks. When you rubbed my back the other night.'

'Any other symptoms?'

She does not answer and I can see from her face that it is a wilful silence. I place my hand on her shoulder.

'I need to know.'

'Sometimes there is blood when I cough into the handkerchief.'

I have been writing and listening and observing and taking notes. Some gravy from my fork falls onto the page. It appears to me like the blood on my arm that fell from my nose. I think of giving Phosphorus immediately. When the problem began she was feeling sympathetic to the plight of another, this is how I felt when I was making the remedy.

Sympathy equals Phosphorus.

'I have your remedy. I am in the middle of making it. I will do it tonight,' I say.

She places a hand on my thigh and mouths the word 'no'. She takes my plate into the kitchen and when she comes back she kneels before me. She reaches for my hand, pulls me down until I am kneeling too. I feel the heat from her fingers in my hair. There is an invisible cloud of patchouli perfume. I want to touch but I am afraid of hurting her. 'Oh Christ,' I mutter, but she has found my lips with a finger and then the warmth of her breath is upon me and I am aware of her lips, her tongue … .

With first light, I open my front door and two painted canvases lean against the wall. One is a gold, bejewelled jug on a tarnished background with a message attached to it. The note says, 'Thanks for all your help,' and like the painting is signed Victorine Meurent. The other artwork is of the countryside around Paris and boasts rich green foliage. It is signed Camille Pissaro.

I hang Camille's over the fireplace and Victorine's on the wall behind my desk. When I look upon these two works, I breathe a lighter air. The spirit of the artist is not confined to the canvas. It flies around the room and sits on my cheek like a kiss of hope.

My Mentor, Clemens
May 4th (A reflection)

*'When we see men of worth, we should think of equalling them;
when we see men of a contrary character, we should turn inward
and examine ourselves.'*

Gustav Courbet

Emotions hang out like shirttails and are not so easy to tuck in.
I've set up an easel, placed paints on top of a board, but when
feelings grab, they stun, and now I'm sitting on the windowsill
watching the view of the street two stories below.

There's a man down there I think I recognise, a grey haired
gentleman with a youngish face. He holds an ebony cane with an
elaborate gold pommel in one hand as he brushes the dust off his
clothes with the other. He looks up at this building and I jolt my
head backwards so as not to be seen. He looks down again,
checks his watch, then walks off towards La Chapelle. The man is
Alain Desmarais. As his carriage pulls away in the opposite
direction, huge red and yellow wheels catch me in their circular
motion. They turn back the years to 1848, a lecture hall:

'You drill holes here and here.' Doctor Jacques Canard pointed at
a drawing of a skull, with a stubby finger. 'It helps with malaise.'

'But has it ever cured anyone?' I called out.

'Monsieur Gachet, you always pose the most irksome of
questions, probably because you wish to be perceived as someone
a lot cleverer than you really are. I would like to remind you, and
everyone else at this point, that you are not learning to be gods
here, you are learning to become physicians. It will be your job to

help *manage* suffering, *not* to become a healer. Monsieur Gachet, if that is your ambition I suggest you enrol at The Institute of Psychic Studies. That is if you can ever find it from your lowly position down here on Earth.'

With laughter ringing in my ears, I walked out, resisting the temptation to slam the door.

'Well, Gachet?' Professor Bernard asked. He sat back, crossed his legs, placed an elbow on the arm of his chair and made a wave of his fingers. Late afternoon sunrays spilled in through the sash window creating a veil for his face and blond hair.

'I am struggling, Professor.'

'In what respect? Can you be more specific? I have not heard from any of your tutors that you are lagging behind.'

'I am morally challenged by the way the course is taught,'

'Ah,' Bernard said, rising from his seat to look out of the window at the courtyard.

'What is the most stupid thing you have ever done?' he asked. He sat down again, gesturing with his wrist for me to take a seat and smiling through teeth that matched his dark grey suit. I lowered myself into the chair on the other side of a large mahogany desk and leaned forward.

'When I was twelve, I jumped off a rampart into a moat.'

'Reckless lad,' Bernard said quietly, as if speaking to himself and then louder, 'Well, I suppose you could have answered, "To enroll on this course", but you didn't, so clearly you still have a mind for the profession. Exactly which part of your studies here do you find a challenge to your finer instincts, Monsieur Gachet?'

'Lobotomy is barbaric, I have a right to question it.'

'You are not questioning. You are making a statement about an accepted form of treatment. You are a first year student, Monsieur Gachet, what can you know?'

The Professor stood and walked around his desk. He looked at me with dull staring eyes. Rancid sweat mingled with sweet perfume surged through my nostrils and I tried not to breathe.

'Enough. Time for you to go.'

At the door, with my palm on the porcelain knob, he hissed, from so close behind me that his breath wavered the hairs on my neck, 'You're an idiot, Gachet! You'll end up dispensing herbs from Culpepper's quackery, and cheating the world with homeopathy.'

They had been waiting for me. Hands in pockets, backs against the wall. As soon as the door slammed they fell in line behind me. Ran down the stairs like an avalanche in my wake.

'Hey Gachet, slow down. Have you seen any ghosts lately? Woo, woo, woo,' called Alain Desmarais, the handsome son of a banker who had once informed me that I should be very careful about what I think, and what I say, because his father had direct access to the only god that mattered.

I pushed my way through big wooden doors into the courtyard, and was strangely comforted by a slap of cold air to my face. An aristocratic looking gentleman, with a silk scarf and greatcoat tails flapping, handed me a leaflet. I put the piece of paper in my pocket and walked away from the university as fast as I could.

I took a holiday. One day away from Bernard and Canard. I sketched the professor with rays of sunlight concealing most of the features on his face. It was a dark morning. Rain fell through cracks in the skylight onto the end of my nose, and soaked my moustache. It splashed onto my eyelashes, drowning out my vision, and I was suddenly hurrying to open the cupboard and pull out the bucket.

Some ghostly force took my breath away. I needed to get out. In the street I walked fast through the onslaught of a massive downpour. It was before the rebuilding of the city. There were no pavements and the roads were cobbled. Terraced houses and shops had holes in their roofs. Huddling in the doorway of a tavern, I searched my pockets for change that would buy me dinner and a beer. As I pulled out some coins from my trouser pocket, they slipped through my fingers, rolled and lodged themselves in the dirt between stones. I came forward, dodging a horse and cart, to retrieve them. I brushed mud away and dropped the money back into my pocket where I felt a piece of paper and pulled it out to investigate.

Baron Clemens Maria Franz von Boenninghausen will be giving a talk in the chapel of the hospital Pitié-Salpêtrière at half past the hour of seven tomorrow evening for all those interested in Samuel Hahnemann's Homeopathy by the means of which I have been cured myself of tuberculosis, some twenty years ago.

I nearly balled the leaflet in my fist and threw it away. *'You're an idiot, Gachet! You'll end up end up a quack, dispensing herbs from Culpepper's quackery, and cheating the world with homeopathy.'* I resolved to go to the meeting.

It was a small chapel, a place for the newly grieved to kneel and say their prayers. By ten minutes before seven it was already twilight. Candles burned all around the altar. It had stopped raining hours ago but a cold wind rattled the windows and seeped in through a multitude of fissures in the structure. I sat in a pew in the middle of three rows and breathed heat through my hands. I was alone, wondering if anyone else would come, and was starting to question whether even Baron Clemens Maria Franz von Boenninghausen had changed his mind on such a miserable evening. Just then, a group of young men burst through the door. They were dandyish in tight fitting trousers, long collared shirts and frock coats. They were the same three students who had pursued me before. They sat next to and behind me. The scent of fermented hops was heady in the air.

'It's "I'm going to save the world Gachet" come to listen to a talk on homeopathy,' slurred Alain Desmarais, an arm resting on the back of the pew and a leg along the seat, his foot almost but not quite touching my thigh. 'Yes, I bet you are interested in all this poxy stuff.'

'We've come specially to keep you company,' someone said from behind me. I could feel fingers digging into my shoulder through my jacket. The door squeaked on its hinges. I turned to see the man who handed me the leaflet, very tall, upright and elderly with a shock of white hair and bushy whiskers around his baldpate.

'Good evening gentlemen,' he said, walking down the aisle.

He sat on the dais at the front, very casually, pulling up his trouser legs.

'We are a very small gathering,' he called out in a foreign accent. 'I have prepared a speech but I would rather not read it out. Instead, I would like to speak to you honestly, man to man, off the cuff and from the heart. My subject tonight is homeopathy. And no, before you ask, I am not a medical doctor. Neither will I advertise myself as being one. What I am is a homeopathist, amongst other things. And you are all medical students?'

Alain Desmarais laughed, and choked on his saliva.

'I see, so first, let me tell you who I am and why I'm sitting before you tonight, for I am sure that you are all very sceptical indeed. I will start by telling you my story, so you can see that I have no need to set myself up as a charlatan.'

'Oh, but you are!' Alain Desmarais called out.

The Baron continued.

'I started my career, after graduating, as a Doctor of Civil and Criminal Law at the court of Louis Napoleon, King of Holland. I am also an agriculturalist. I formed the first agricultural society in the west of Germany, and have acted as President of the Provincial Court of Justice for the Westphalia district, evaluating land. But in 1827 I suffered from a serious derangement of health. I will not bore you with the symptoms, suffice to say that I had tuberculosis.

82

'The allopaths worked on me for a whole year. I was tossed into cold baths and had leeches thrown at me to swell and drop off my skin as they sated of my blood. I was administered mercury and heroin. For a long while those medicines put me into a state where I would not have cared whether I lived or died, quite frankly. My dear wife tells me I was a nightmare to live with and no doubt at times, prayed for the latter. I was far from cured.

'In the spring of 1829, I wrote to my good friend, Doctor Weihe, believing it to be my last correspondence. I had no idea he was a homeopath. I knew him as a botanist. He wrote back lecturing on hygiene and asked me of my symptoms. As he was interested, I drew him a lengthy account of my suffering. He sent me back a small vial of pillules that contained a highly dilute form of the windflower pulsatilla. I took my friend's medicine twice daily and by the end of the summer I proclaimed myself cured.'

Alain began to clap slowly. 'Quack, quack.'

'Tell me, Monsieur, why are you so angry that this anecdote happens to be the truth? Do you really think I would have come here to talk to four students instead of eating a hot dinner and drinking fine wine at my son's home, if it was not so? I am not peddling snake poison in the city square, for God's sake!'

Alain Desmarais stood, aimed his arm backwards and threw a tomato as if he was bowling a cricket ball. The orb splattered in the space between Baron von Boeninghausen's eyebrows. His friends laughed and catcalled. The Baron rose to an imposing figure. 'I think you'd better leave,' he said.

'Deluded old fool,' came a voice from behind me.

'Come on, let's go. This is boring,' said Alain Desmarais.

Pushing and shoving at each other, the gang departed.

I stayed in my seat. He shook a red satin handkerchief out of the top pocket of his greatcoat and wiped his forehead. I watched as the fruit juice seeped and darkened the fabric as if from blood.

'We are alone,' the Baron called.

'I think so.'

'And you are, Monsieur?'

'I am Paul Ferdinand Gachet of Lille.'

'I've seen you somewhere, recently. Where have I seen you?'

'I don't know.'

'Come, think man; I've just been attacked by hoodlums!'

'Maybe down by the water, on the banks of the Seine. If I have time, I go there to paint *en plein air.*'

'If you are an artist, why are you here tonight? The subject I intended to focus on is very much a science.'

'I am also a medical student, and with respect Monsieur, Leonardo Da Vinci was both an artist and a scientist.'

'Are you interested in homeopathy or have you also come to wear me down?'

'I am interested in a gentler medicine that works. I know nothing about homeopathy.'

'Its practise requires an endurance of flying tomatoes.'

'I would like to learn how to do it.'

'Homeopathy is not something you do. A homeopathist is something you become. Here ... ,' he said, waving a book with a brown suede cover in the air. ' ... *The Organon of Medicine* by Samuel Hahnemann, I suggest you read it. You will be doing me a favour if you take it. Please,' Clemens thrust the book forwards as he walked towards me.

I did not turn my head to watch him leave. But I heard the hollow sound of his leather heels on the stone floor, and the protest of an opening door. I lowered my gaze from a wooden cross bearing a suffering, roughly painted china Jesus, to the book. Slowly, I opened the front cover and stared at Clemens's elaborate calligraphy, noticing his home address in Prussia, and further down in print, that the volume was first published in 1810.

I stretched out my legs underneath the pew in front and read until the gas lamps on the floor had stopped whistling and the majority of candles on the altar had spluttered their last hint of light.

Phosphorus Three
May 5th

'The truth is in nature, and I shall prove it.'

Paul Cezanne

Monsieur Armand doesn't answer. I knock again on his door. Eventually, Madame Armand lets me in. She wears a grey serge dress and a white starched apron. She has a linen kerchief pinned in her hair. She waddles. But despite the simplicity in her looks there is wonder in her grey eyes.

'You're always so positive. How do you do it?' I once asked her over a cup of home-grown chamomile tea.

'Growing things,' she said. 'They have a passion for me.'

'And you for them.'

'And me for them,' she agreed, lifting her cup in a toast.

'Ah Madame Armand, I was just wondering … Monsieur Armand, is he in?'

'I'll go and get him for you,' she says, the wideness of her hips inhibiting the climb up the narrow stairs. 'Would you like a tisane?' she calls down.

'I would love a cup. Your tea always makes me feel better; there must be something of your spirit in it.'

I can't see her face. I hope she is smiling. I look around the hallway at lilac walls and a gilt-framed convex mirror, shaped like the sun. By the door is one of my sketches of the Seine.

Monsieur Armand takes me by surprise. His wiry old frame leans over the balustrade.

'Young Gachet, how can I help?'

'Last time I was here you had glass tubes in a wooden rack.'

'I have them still.'

'May I use them?'

'If you come up to my laboratory, yes you can.'

I reach into my pocket, pull out a homemade envelope, and wave it in the air.

'Come upstairs then, follow me. I've figured out a way to clean the blasted things so that there's no trace of a previous element polluting the glass.'

'With heat.'

'Yes, with heat.'

As I climb the stairs black motes swirl in a cone of light.

'It's the chimney flue, it's not drawing properly, and the sweep's gone missing. Smoke's billowing out into the house. The other evening I heard this scratching and flapping and the next day a roast pigeon fell into the grate: Dinner, a mistimed Christmas delivery, but too charred to eat. The old sod should get it right.' He chuckles. 'But anyway it's caused clouds in the house and my wife hasn't stopped complaining about the soot.'

The acrid scent hits my nostrils and I flinch. We arrive at the laboratory door. Monsieur Armand stands before it with his hand immobile on the handle as if waiting for permission to go in. Then he opens it. Inside, the room is quiet and still.

'It is as I left it last night,' he says.

Misty sunlight half obscures my sight, but the tray with glass tubes gleam on the worktable before me. I marvel and hesitate.

'Go on,' he says, waving me forward. 'Start. I'll sit over here.'

He sits down on a stool in the corner of the room, lifts a tome from a bookshelf onto his lap and heaves it open. I stand before the table and carefully open my envelope until it is a symmetrically creased piece of paper, then I make a funnel out of one of the sides. I take a tube and nearly topple the rack. Glass chinks, threatening to break. Armand and I lock eyes. I pour several granules of Phosphorus 3c into a tube: the result of several hours work. My heart pounds; I am afraid of my own clumsiness.

From my jacket pocket I pull out a bottle of neat alcohol and suck it up through a syringe. I squint and squirt 99 drops, each one a silken, transparent veil for the glass tube. There is a box full of corks on the table. I look towards Armand who is still staring straight at me.

'Go on,' he says, 'Take.'

I pick up a cork and stop the cylinder.

'I need a leather bound book,' I say, with a rasp in my throat. He raises his eyebrows and I gingerly lift a volume onto the desk. With the tube secure in my fist, I pound the side of my hand against animal skin several times, fiercely agitating the liquid.

'Phosphorus 4c,' I tell Armand.

He nods. 'Why 4c?'

'It's been diluted by one part in a hundred four times. Sometimes I go to 1M by diluting a thousand times. The more dilute, the higher the potency. Less is more.'

'Less is more,' he repeats and I can see that although he is intrigued he does not believe it.

From another pocket I take more syringes. Using a new one, and squinting to be accurate, I force one reluctant drop from the mixture I have just made and watch it skate down the glass. Once again I bang the solution against the book.

'5c,' I say to Armand, already starting to repeat the process again.

I use up all ten bottles in the rack but when I finish I have only raised the potency to 13c. To achieve 30c I will have to return a couple of times. I explain this to Armand.

'Seems like a lot of cleaning up to do for an experiment that is all about shaking up pure alcohol. But of course, my friend, you may come back,' he says, with one hand against my back leading me out into the tiny hallway. 'Before you go, some homemade wine? A little bit stronger than the wife's herbal,'

'I'll take both,' I reply.

'Both,' he says, chuckling. 'Such a diplomatic man.'

Arrival of Spies
May 6th

'People don't realise what it feels like to be constantly insulted.'
Edouard Manet

There is an outbreak of men from the Faculty at the hospital. There are clusters of them at Charcot's hypnotherapy demonstrations, walking up and down the main staircase, holding meetings in the corridors. If it weren't true, it would be comical, the way they divert their attention away from me each time I turn around. I catch Charcot in the corridor.

'Doctor Charcot,' I call, running towards him as he begins his descent of the big stone stairway. Whenever we cross paths in the common parts of the hospital, he purposefully accelerates his step. I slide across the marble floor towards him then pace down the steps behind him. 'You yourself have said that the therapeutic effects of my consultations with Manon are helping her. I'd like to have the opportunity to do the same thing with Bella Laffaire.'

Charcot stops midway on the stairs. He eyes me suspiciously and dismisses me with a wave of his hand.

'Catch me tomorrow Gachet. I have an important meeting that I have to attend. Can't be late.' He turns around and continues on his way.

I'm starting to think I should have left this post years ago. I should have seen the signs and taken my cue to walk away. I am clearly not appreciated for what I have to offer. I'm a firm believer that humans are like trees, in that if we allow our branches to be blown in the direction of the wind, we will be all right. If we fight the force and pull in the opposite direction then something eventually snaps. Melancholia keeps me rooted to this place and I'm starting to wonder if the condition might be catching.

Manon sits on the side of a bed, arms rigid, hands clutching bedclothes, legs swinging to and fro. I prop myself up on the bed opposite, and sketch her bowed head, then squint to look at my work.

When her sister died, Manon ran naked and screaming through the streets, a temporary insanity that soon turned into melancholia with taciturnity and glumness and little interest in eating, sleeping or anything else except for causing self-harm.

'Doctor Gachet, I need to talk to you,' she says now, looking up at me with shining eyes.

She is in one of her excited moods. My role is to administer medication but I find if I allow patients to relax in my company and converse at their free will, they feel less isolated and very often do not need a high dose of any drug to control their mood.

'Talk then, I have time.'

'My mother came to me in a dream. She was chasing me. There was meanness in her. She used to love me. Now that she is dead she hates me,' she says, balling her fist and biting down hard on her knuckles. 'I'm a horrible person, that's why. That's why I'm here.'

'Because you are a horrible person?' I ask.

'I am, aren't I?'

'Why do you think that?'

She laughs.

'Is that a picture of me?' she asks, feeling her face with her open palm as if exploring why she might be a good subject to draw.

'It is, but it's only the start of one, a vague outline. Would you like to see?'

'That doesn't look like me,' she says, screwing her face up like a prune.

'Try squinting.'

'Nah.'

'You were saying about horrible?'

'Have you ever seen the sea? I've seen a picture. My mother is a mermaid under the sea,' she says.

May 7th

'Ah, Doctor Gachet,' Charcot says, with a slight spring in his step as if he is pleased to see me. He smiles broadly. 'This is Doctor Ipsen.'

Doctor Ipsen clutches his hands behind his back. He has fawn coloured hair, round wire-framed glasses magnifying his small eyes, and lips pursed as if to hide a supercilious smile. I recognise him. He is one of the fanatics who have been following me around.

'We have good news for you. As you ingeniously suggested, I wrote to the Faculty of Medicine, you know, about your request. Most surprisingly, they replied asking for an invitation to make numerous site visits. I'm sure you've seen Doctor Ipsen walking around with his colleagues.' Charcot gestures towards the other man who nods again, this time smiling broadly. 'They think your suggestion is a very good idea.'

As much as I'd like to believe in the marvel of this offer, there is something not quite genuine about these two men. It is a feeling that I cannot quite prove but I do acknowledge to myself that to be out of synchronicity with the world in one's thoughts, is yet another symptom of melancholia. My legs tremble slightly.

'Doctor Ipsen will sit in with you when you consult. He'll note down your prescriptions and monitor the effects. I trust you are delighted with this arrangement.'

'We might as well start the first session now,' Doctor Ipsen says. 'Bella Laffaire, I believe, is waiting in the room you first brought her to. It is thought that it would be a good idea for you to pick up on her treatment exactly where you left off during her admission.'

'Fine, but right now, I have a busy schedule.'

'We've rearranged your schedule,' says Doctor Ipsen.

'I believe regularity of appointments to be an important part of my treatment here. Patients wait for and expect my visits. They shouldn't be disappointed.'

'We're here to treat patients not to please them, Doctor Gachet,' says Charcot.

Ipsen's chin is propped on his fingers. He wears the same detached expression that Charcot often directs at his patients. I hesitate for a few seconds.

'Perhaps Doctor Gachet has changed his mind.' Ipsen says.

'Well, all right,' I say.

'Then lead the way.'

As I walk down the corridor I hear the rustle of my perpetrators behind me. The odour of the usual cabbage wine brings on a sudden nausea. We arrive and I open the door. Bella Laffaire is already inside, slumped on the floor. There is a chair beside her. I am pleased to say it is Nurse Morrisot, not Marguerite Bottard, who bends over her.

'Bella,' I greet her, half-bowing. 'Nurse Morrisot.'

Nurse Morrisot turns towards me, smiles and lowers her head.

'Well gentlemen, are both of you staying, or just Doctor Ipsen?' I look around. There is a hospital bed against each wall, and apart from the chair, no other furniture.

'I notice there is only a chair for one,' I say.

The air is a little stifling. I turn to open a window and hear the door slam.

I turn back.

Charcot has left the room.

A blast of cool air seems to have blown away my negativity. I realise that if I can relax into things I might even have some fun. I have allowed Doctor Ipsen to claim the chair and he is moving it to a more innocuous position. Nurse Morrisot instinctively goes to help. With a hand on her arm I hold her back.

'It's a man's job,' I insist. 'Like putting out the rubbish. Wouldn't you agree Doctor Ipsen? ... Nurse Morrisot, would you grab some notepaper and a board to lean on. The bed over there will be your chair. I want you to jot down every word anybody says. Don't worry if you miss a few, it's bound to happen. If there's silence then I want you to write down any observations you might have. I don't want your opinion, just things that you can substantiate, things that you notice going on in the room. I need a piece of paper and a pencil too for my own observations. Paper, Doctor Ipsen?' I ask.

Ipsen's body goes into a voluntary spasm as if my words sicken him. He is wide-eyed with his chin in his hand as I sit on the floor with my legs crossed in front of my patient. Nurse Morrisot returns with the writing materials.

'Bella ... may I call you Bella?' I whisper, reaching out a hand to stir her. She lifts her head from the floor and I look into her hooded eyes. Her pupils are very small. She is obviously drowsy. Someone has dosed her with an opiate.

'I can't take Bella's case while she is in a stupor. The drug acts like a curtain, leaving us in the dark as it shuts out her symptoms.'

'But didn't you see her before she was admitted? There were your symptoms. According to reports they were very vivid I believe.'

'I need to monitor the progress. If you hand her to me like this at each consultation I will have nothing to go on. I will see her only in one drugged state after another. This experiment will be useless.'

'She is violent, Doctor Gachet. Do you suggest we put other patients and more importantly, staff, at risk?'

'She needs to be on a minimum dose. What is she on?'

'Laudanum,' Nurse Morrisot replies.

'Very well, you will be in charge of her medicine then that too can become part of the experiment,' Ipsen says. He narrows his eyes as if he has smoke in them. 'But you have to prescribe something homeopathic too.'

'I'd rather wait till I see her next and just reduce her laudanum for now.'

'I believe the first time she sat amongst these walls you saw her in all her vivid madness, did you not? What more do you expect the patient to tell you? Do you expect to have a polite conversation?'

'Doctor Ipsen, is this your diagnosis?' I ask.

He does not answer.

'Are you diagnosing mania?' I ask again.

Once more he does not reply.

'Perhaps lunacy, insanity, madness, as you have already stated.'

His lips remain glued together.

'I'll prescribe *Platina* 1M, one dose, based on my initial impression. But I'll have to bring it with me when I next come to the hospital on Thursday. Nurse Morrisot, what dosage of laudanum is she on at the moment?'

'One spoonful, hourly.'

'That dosage could kill an elephant, drop it by half, and send a messenger to come and get me if that causes any problems. Doctor Ipsen, I'd like to see Bella again on Thursday during my session here. I would appreciate it if someone tells Doctor Charcot that I wish to see Manon on that day as well. Doctor Ipsen, I thank you for this opportunity but I have patients waiting for me at home.'

Doctor Ipsen leaves the room hastily without responding. His abandoned chair falls over in his wake.

The scientist
May 8th

'If the physician clearly perceives what is to be cured in diseases,
that is to say, in every individual case of disease (knowledge of
disease, indication), if he clearly perceives what is curative in
medicine (knowledge of medicinal powers) ... then he understands
how to treat judiciously and rationally, and he is a true
practitioner of the healing art.'
Samuel Hahnemann, *The Organon of Medicine.*

In Café Riche, with its sponged walls that look like marble, and
luscious plants and candles on all tables, I read *l'Avenir*
Nationale. Waiting for Georges, I am overjoyed to see a small
piece about cholera. A Doctor Quin of London reports the
mortality rate in 1854 at the London Homeopathic hospital as
16%, compared with 59.2% in the nearby Middlesex hospital. He
asks why more doctors are not studying the healing art. Why
indeed?

I do not think such a small column in the back pages of a
newspaper will change anyone's thoughts; it only serves to
remind me of my own frustration. Nevertheless, it is heartening
to witness those figures in print. I flick through, but there are no
articles about our forthcoming exhibition and I close the paper.

'You don't appear too enamoured with today's rag.'

I look up. Bowler-hatted and carrying an ebony cane,
Georges has arrived.

'I was hoping for a mention about the Salon des Refusés,
even something derogatory. We can do with the publicity to
bring in the crowds. Anyway, I won't be disheartened, at least

Napoleon has sanctioned that our works have a right to be shown.' I fold the newspaper to expose the homeopathy article and place it in front of Georges.

'Good for homeopathy,' he says.

'How was Romania?' I ask. I clasp Georges' hand and rise to kiss him on both cheeks.

'It was a duty. I had to attend a family occasion. One of those members who you only vaguely know exists until they send you an invitation. Still, I suppose, one has to do something to be worthy of one's keep.'

'I came to visit,' he continues. 'They were queuing up for you like they do for Sarah Bernhardt, *and* it appears, you were wanted by the police.'

'It was a mild cholera-type epidemic. The allopaths were floundering and I administered *Podophyllum* to a small boy. It cured him. Word of mouth got about and brought the droves to my door. The concierge called the police. I was accused of causing a political uprising.'

'An adventure – that's why I am here. It's what motivates me to practise homeopathy and live in Paris.'

'I have something exciting,' I say, taking a vial of Phosphorus 30c out of my pocket and placing it on the table before us.

A waitress appears. Looking the other way, one hand on her hip, tray under her arm, she says, 'It's busy, what can I get you?'

'A coffee,' says Georges.

'No,' I intervene. 'He'll have water, the same as me.'

'We have it from a spring, it is slightly effervescent.'

'No … .' Georges starts to say.

'That's fine. That's fine,' I wave her away.

'What are you doing?' he asks.

'We're going to conduct a homeopathic proving.'

'I didn't consent to this.'

'Hahnemann says in the *Organon* that in order to understand the nature of substances, the earnest physician will test them upon himself.'

'I should sacrifice myself for mankind. Tell me, have you used yourself as a human instrument before?'

'Of course, many times. Take it three times a day for three days and keep a diary,' I say pushing the bottle towards him. 'No alcohol, caffeine, mint or garlic. Live simply. I propose we meet up again in five days, to compare notes. Same time, same place.'

'And I owe this noble gesture of yours to what?' he says, pouring a globule from the bottle into the cork's indent and then throwing it into his mouth. He pours another one for me, and watches intently as I take it. The waitress returns with a brown glazed pitcher. She pours water into two glasses.

'To the desire for advancement in our ourselves as physicians,' Georges says.

'A santé, to greater health and understanding,' I say, lifting my water. Georges chinks his glass against mine and takes a reverential sip as if tasting the world's finest cognac.

'Actually,' he says, 'it's very good.'

I look up. Camille, and his mother Rachel are coming through the doorway. They come over to our table. Camille stands before me in a huge brown great coat, making a cradle with his hands and rocking back and forth on his toes. His mother holds an embroidered handkerchief to her thin lips. Her eyes are narrow, red-rimmed and puffy.

'Paul, forgive me, I've been all over Paris asking where you are. It's Alfred, my brother. He is dying of no one-knows-what. I was at Courbet's studio and he reminded me about your genius. Doctor de Bellio,' he adds, turning to Georges with a slight bow.

'I'll come, of course. Georges, forgive me,' I say, rising and retrieving my hat and coat from a peg on an oak column. 'In five days, here, same time,' I remind him.

Alfred lies as still as a corpse in the small guest bedroom in Rachel Pissaro's apartment. Heavy oak furniture is set against claret walls. The curtains are drawn. I ask for light and Rachel brings me a small lamp. I place it on the bedside table and survey the room.

'No daylight or windows open, is this at the patient's request?' I ask.

No one answers. Eventually, Camille prompts his mother.

'Maman, you must reply.'

'Er yes,' she says.

'Did he say why?'

'The draught,' she says 'aggravates the pain and so does the light.'

'Alfred, I'm Paul Gachet, the doctor, and I need to ask some questions. Are you able to talk?'

Alfred opens his eyes. 'Hurts to talk,' he croaks, grabbing hold of his throat.

'Is there anything which helps the pain, makes it feel better?'

'Stay still.'

He closes his eyes. His skin is dry, very pale. His cough has a hollow sound and makes him bring his hand to his chest. Sitting on the edge of his bed, I place my case on my knees and open it. Bryonia cures pathological states where the symptoms are better for stillness and pressure and worse for any disturbance. Standing over Alfred, I ask him to open his mouth and place one pillule of Bryonia 200c between his gum and lower lip. I give the vial to Madame Pissaro and ask her to administer the remedy every four hours until my return. If there is a marked improvement she should reduce the dose radically.

'To what?' she asks. 'Reduce it to what?'

'To one every 6-8 hours,' I say. 'Excuse me, I have to get to the hospital for an afternoon session. I can see myself out.'

Camille catches me in the hall as I am leaving. His large frame is cumbersome.

'Paul, let me pay you, please. My mother can well afford it.'

'I'd rather a painting.'

'If Alfred gets better you can have both. In the meantime, take the money,' he says thrusting a one hundred franc note into my palm. To refuse would be an insult.

The Lover
May 14th

*'I can barely conceive of a type of beauty in which there is no
Melancholy.'*

Charles Baudelaire

It's that Thursday already, the date of Madame Manet's soirée. I
have been invited and Blanche has been requested to play the
violin. The days have passed by like pedestrians along the
Champs Elysees. The effect of this on my life is shocking. But
there is reprieve. I sit in a wickerwork chair in the corner of
Blanche's bedroom, wearing black trousers, a frock coat and very
soft slip-on shoes. The clothing feels unusual, uncomfortable and
unnatural. I make a spire with my fingers and peer over the top
to watch my love get dressed. Her movements are slow and
definite. At the moment, she is wearing ivory silk pantalettes and
a matching corset that I helped her to tie. Unselfconsciously, she
approaches her mirrored dressing table and lifts a velvet choker
to her throat. A silver locket dangles against her skin. She lowers
her chin to her breastbone, fastens the button at the back and
swiftly lifts her head as if she is enjoying her long flowing hair.
She sits down to pin her freedom up into a chignon. Her
petticoats and lace dress are like coverlets for the bed. I feel the
warmth of our intimate memories and see pictures of us naked
reeling through my mind.

'I won't be long,' she says.

'Don't worry,' I tell her. 'We're early. Take your time.'

There is a spray at the window behind me and I look around
to see splashes of rain sparkling against the glass like stars.

'But you'll get bored sitting there waiting.'

I take my hands apart in a submissive gesture.

'I owe you a good deed,' she says.

I cannot hide my smile.

'You're laughing at me.'

'Honestly I am not.'

'Well, what are you thinking, then?'

She faces me, hands on tilted hips, one leg thrust forward, knee bent accusingly.

'That I could not be more entertained.'

Madame Manet's Soiree

'The truth is on the march and nothing will stop it.'

Emile Zola

We are late. We walk quickly and our voices do a jig. When we arrive at the impressive four storey building in rue des Petits-Augustins and walk through the stone portal into a large courtyard, Blanche says, 'I thought all your artist friends were struggling to survive.'

'Most of us are lucky that our fathers were born before us. Edouard especially. His mother, Eugenie, hosts a dinner almost every Thursday evening and now that Edouard's father's passed away, most of the guests are Edouard's friends, at least so I hear.'

'You've never been to one before?'

'Never – and only invited this time because Edouard was quite taken with you.'

'Is that true?' she says with a sidelong glance.

'Quite true.' In spite of myself I smile.

'Really Paul,' she tells me. 'I can't trust anything you say these days.'

The apartment is large. Thick wool rugs lie on parquet floors. High floral walls frame gilt-edged painted doors whilst delicate furniture poses under cut-glass chandeliers. The rooms appear fragile.

'Does Madame Manet think she is Napoleon the third?' Blanche asks as we walk in the door. Her lips are feathers at my ear.

In the main room, guests stand in small groups whilst waiters hand out food and drinks on silver platters. Blanche carries her

101

violin case protectively in her arms. I catch sight of Edouard on the other side of the room. He is in conversation with a woman, but someone is standing in front of her and I can't see who she is. The person moves slightly to the left and I gain a better view. Edouard holds a glass by its base, poised as if someone is just about to paint it. He looks to the glass as he talks to Victorine.

Behind him is one of the doctors from the Faculty who followed me. Not Ipsen, someone else whose name starts with Q, I think Quenton, Quiggly, Quackenboss, something like that. Anyway, I shall call him Quackenboss. He is, in my opinion, noteworthy. At the hospital amongst his peers, he is humble and quiet, almost paling into insignificance. Here, he stands tall with his head high. He has toast with caviar in one hand, a glass of champagne in the other and he is looking my way with a sullen expression.

Eugenie Manet comes forward to greet us. She has a coil of dark hair at either side of her head and a black silk dress buttoned to her throat. Large white pearls rest heavy upon the fabric at her breastbone and sit like shields on her ear lobes. From a distance she could be mistaken for a young widow, but up close the lines around her mouth pinch inwards, whilst those on the outside of her orbital bones fan outwards, bringing attention to the lacklustre of her eyes.

'You must be Blanche,' she says offering a hand. 'And you must be Paul Gachet. I'm so pleased you have both arrived. Edouard's friend will be playing for us too. Come this way. Have you met Suzanne?'

Suzanne Leenhoff is standing by the piano, alone, as we approach.

'Oh Suzanne, this is Mademoiselle Blanche Castets, who I was telling you about. She plays the violin.'

Blanche thrusts her hand forward. Suzanne briefly shakes it, then briefly shakes mine.

'Suzanne, how is Leon?'

'Leon's fine but now *I* have a cough,' she says and she is

gripped by a spasm that makes it difficult for her to breathe. At which point Camille taps me from behind. I turn around. He clutches my upper arm and pumps my hand. His eyes are watery as he looks into mine.

'He's the man to cure your cough,' he says. 'Alfred is so much better.'

'Yes, didn't he cure Leon's?' says Madame Manet.

Suzanne nods, still coughing, unable to stop. She signals this with her hands.

'Well then, my dear, have him cure yours,' Madame Manet says, walking off.

'He cured mine,' Blanche tells Suzanne and I realise for the first time that Blanche hasn't coughed all day.

'I hope I'll be all right to play the piano,' Suzanne answers.

'I'm sure you'll be fine. Somehow I never coughed when playing the violin,' Blanche tells her.

I am a little embarrassed by the praise and not sure where to look. I sense a presence behind me. Doctor Quackenboss. He's standing next to me with his hands behind his back as if he is giving a lecture. He takes a step forward into our crowd.

'Don't let this man fool you,' he says. 'The Faculty does not recognise that homeopathy has any healing potential at all. The medicines have nothing in them. They are made from plain water. He merely gives you a placebo.'

'Then how can you explain that my brother Alfred was dying and no other doctor could heal him?'

'Your brother was lucky. He obviously went into some sort of spontaneous remission. But can you imagine if such a non-medicine was given to someone who needs proper intervention and doesn't get it? Your friend can easily become a murderer just for taking on the case. Excuse me,' he says, looking around. 'I think I'm wanted over there.' Heat rises to my face. Discomfort rankles. I want to get away. I grab hold of Blanche's wrist pulling her over to the side.

'We don't have to stay,' I say. 'You can tell them I've been called out on urgent business and I'm taking you home.'

'No, really,' she says. 'This is work for me. I want to stay. I have to stay. Anyway, what's wrong with you? That man's an idiot. Everyone knows it. You don't need to go.'

'Blanche, men like Quackenboss, or whatever he's called, are powerful and they're damning not just me but an honourable profession.'

'I have to play show tunes for money all the time but I'd rather play Vivaldi.'

Over Blanche's shoulder I see that Madame Manet has joined Victorine and Edouard. She whispers something in his ear. He nods emphatically and walks towards us. He arrives before I can answer Blanche.

'Paul,' he says. 'Congratulations on helping to achieve the Salon des Refusés and Mademoiselle Blanche, I am looking forward to hearing your hauntingly beautiful recital again tonight.'

'Monsieur Manet,' she responds politely.

'Edouard, please,' he says clearing his throat. 'This is very embarrassing. Georges is over there but my mother insists that I ask *you* to pay a visit in order to prescribe for Suzanne's cough. I am going to need your discretion.'

'Is Suzanne a patient of Georges?'

'No, not technically, although I most certainly am.'

'There is no conflict of interest then, Georges will understand.'

'I hope so.'

'You can tell Suzanne that I will call on her tomorrow morning at nine.'

Victorine joins our group. 'Edouard,' she says placing a gloved hand on his back. 'We were mid-conversation when you said you'd be back. I decided that I'd waited long enough and had to come to find you. Doctor Gachet, Paul,' she says, offering me her other gloved hand which I accept and lower my head.

'Mademoiselle Blanche,' Edouard says. 'Where did you learn

104

to play the violin?'

'Did you gain permission for me to do a portrait of Bella Laffaire?' Victorine whispers, moving closer towards me.

'No,' I say, in equally hushed tones. 'You'll probably have more luck if you write to the hospital directly.'

'Excuse us,' she says to Edouard and Blanche, then links her arm through mine and walks me to a corner. I glance over my shoulder at Blanche who is still carrying her violin case and watching us in the mirror above the fireplace.

'I hope you don't mind,' Victorine says. 'How is Bella?'

'I don't understand. Why have you brought me over here?'

'Her father keeps coming to my home. He is looking for her.'

'Haven't you told him where she is?'

'No.'

'Why not?'

'He looks mean.'

'That's not a reason …'

'Look, how do I know that he really is her father? I have his address – if you wish to go and see him,' she says, placing something in the pocket of my frock coat.

'Now I really think we should go back,' I say, but she is already making her way into the centre of the room.

'Is there something between you and Victorine?' Blanche asks when I return.

I open my mouth to answer her, but Paul appears at our side accompanied by a grey haired man.

'I want you to meet my father. He is very interested in homeopathy,' he says.

We drink champagne from fluted cut glass and eat canapés from silver trays. As the evening wears on I become more and more transfixed by the sorry figure of Suzanne. She is as out of place here as a chimpanzee would be in the Louvre. She stands alone by the piano as if looking out to sea. I wonder if she is still under the employ of Eugenie Manet, on call for Thursday evenings and ladies' afternoons. When the chairs are brought in and she finally gets to play, she shifts uncomfortably on the stool and I wonder throughout her recital if she's stifling a cough. She plays Chopin note perfect: competent, definitely competent. Her body is hunched as she turns to the audience and receives a light ripple of applause.

Blanche, on the other hand, stands tall before us, her instrument enslaved by her chin. She confidently plucks strings with her eyes closed, warming up. It is a while since Suzanne has finished her piece. The audience stand. They are restless, noisily conversing with each other. Behind me, Henri tells Charles that he is going to make his fortune in England.

'London is so much more receptive to new art,' he says.

Edouard climbs over chairs to the back of the room to greet his tardy friend Charles who has just recently arrived. He slaps him on the shoulder and kisses his cheeks.

'You made it. I thought the bordellos had claimed you, but you got here, I'm so glad you did.'

Blanche doesn't say a word. People sit. The room goes quiet. She sways as if to a secret rhythm, back and forth, back and forth. She raises the bow. Back and forth, back and forth, in double time back and forth, the bow is lowered to string and the music flows evoking the perfection of a summer's day. When she finishes, Charles stands on his chair, fingers to his lips, he whistles at a nerve-racking pitch. The clapping is hearty. Edouard, Henri and others call 'Bravo!'

The silence in the street is deafening by comparison.

'I'll walk you to your house,' I say, lightly squeezing Blanche's hand in mine, and purposefully kicking a stone. 'I'm not staying. I have to be up early.'

'You're not staying.'

'That's right.'

'No, you misunderstand me. You're not staying. It's also *my* choice.'

A bawdy song spills out through the open doors of an inn down the road and I hear the rustle of a lover's clothes in the shadows around the corner. Tears well up in my eyes. I sit down on a boulder and put my head in my hands. Blanche perches on another boulder, opposite, and waits.

'I don't know what came over me. I'm sorry,' I say eventually, looking up and mopping my face with a handkerchief. 'You must think I'm strange. Here, catch,' I say, tossing a bottle of Phosphorus 30c into her lap.

'What's this?' she asks. 'Isn't it the same remedy you gave me for my cough?'

I nod.

'My cough's better; why are you giving me more pills?'

'It's an explanation,' I say, and then blow my nose. 'It's to let you know that I'm in the middle of a homeopathic proving. The remedy is Phosphorus. I'm taking it three times a day until it brings out characteristic symptoms.'

'Meaning?'

'Pathological sympathy. I am crying for your sadness, Suzanne's loneliness and Victorine's frustration, all at once, and it is making me look a fool.'

'Do you think I am a fool, Paul? Is this why you gave it to me?'

'Absolutely not. No. No. I gave you the remedy because a sympathetic act was your cough's aetiology – its causation – and you also had a Phosphorus-type cough.'

'You know what?' she asks. 'Sometimes I feel like I really need to get away. Have you ever thought of India, Paul? I met a man who told me that Indian priests wear saffron robes and walk elephants across the beach in Goa on a pilgrimage for peace. In Africa, apparently, elephants trumpet at dawn. Whilst Paris can be stiflingly complicated, don't you think?'

'Why are you angry with me, Blanche?'

'I'm not sure I want this.'

'Me?'

She nods.

I look away as tears come again. When I'm ready, I get up.

'Come,' I say. 'Let me walk you home.'

It is a miserable night. I toss and turn and watch the shadows of carriages become grotesque upon the ceiling. The street lamp flickers and distorts the image. I haemorrhage again, this time, from my back passage. I am afraid of homeopathy's other worldliness and its power is humbling. It is loneliness that stifles me. Not complications. Not Paris. I know if Blanche were with me, I would not feel like this. Strange, amongst all of this melancholy uncertainty I feel the need to have her nakedness against my skin. I have the desire to make love.

When I awake I feel wretched but I have learned something. As I make my ablutions, I realise that I could recognise the need for Phosphorus in a patient without ever having to look in a textbook again, for I have lived the experience twice now – once before I'd even ingested a dose. You can't explain that to anyone. It is like when someone speaks of messages from the dead or strange objects in the sky.

I also know Blanche's remedy is not Phosphorus. It is close but it is not exactly right. Her wanderlust is too essential to her character for her most similar remedy not to mirror this. I have a nagging suspicion that my love's cough has abated for now but is nowhere near cured.

Suzanne's Consultation
May 15th

*'Even in a high potency, Ignatia is a main remedy in cases of
vexation in subjects who have no tendency to break out violently or
to revenge themselves, but who keep their annoyance to themselves;
in whom, in a word, the resemblance of the vexatious occurrence is
wont to dwell in the mind, and so also especially in morbid states
which are produced by occurrences that cause grief.'*

Samuel Hahenmann, *Materia Medica Pura.*

'Suzanne,' I say, pumping her hand over-zealously. She is still in
her nightdress, rubbing her eyes. It appears that the boy Leon has
gone to visit family in Holland. The soiree finished long after
midnight. She apologises, she has woken up late.

'That's fine,' I say. 'Don't worry about any of it. Where do
you want us to conduct the consultation?'

'In the drawing room?' she asks.

'Yes,' I say. 'That'll do fine.'

I sit down and start pulling out writing paper and a pen from
my bag. She sits opposite on the edge of her seat. My pen is
poised and ready to go to work, I look up into her face and say,
'Tell me about your cough. When did it start?'

Suzanne hesitates. 'Actually, it started a while ago but
recently it's got worse.'

'Was anything stressful happening immediately before the
cough came or around that time?'

'No, nothing stressful.'

'Then tell me about the cough itself. When does it come on?
Is there anything that initiates it?'

'Talking, but if I consciously suppress it, it's better.'

'How do you do that?'

'I swallow, you know,' she says, with fingers resting against her throat and conspicuously swallowing to demonstrate what she means.

'Tell me more about the cough.'

'Well, it is a lump in my throat as well. This is how it comes. It starts with a lump and I have to cough to dislodge … it's the phlegm, I suppose. Doctor, would you like a coffee? I am so rude I haven't thought to offer you … .'

'No, I'm fine, thank you.'

'Do you know what remedy I can take to get rid of my cough?'

'I have my suspicions as to what you might need, but I wouldn't be happy to prescribe for you straight away.'

Cough better for not coughing, worse for talking, and sensation of a lump in the throat are all symptoms of *Ignatia*. *Ignatia* is a grief remedy. Is this a case of grief? My training forbids me to assume that it is. 'Tell me a little bit about yourself first?'

'I don't know what to say.'

'Tell me anything. What do you find difficult, stressful?'

'I'm sorry,' she says, leaping out of her seat and hastily leaving the room. When she comes back she is dabbing a handkerchief to the corners of her eyes. I wait for her to settle in her chair.

'Are you all right to go on?' I ask.

She nods briefly.

'Please, I don't mean to pry, but in order to find your correct remedy I'm going to have to understand just a little bit more.'

At which point, the dam breaks and she cries hysterically, loudly, taking in huge gulps of air between sobs and I do something that I don't normally do. I rise to go and sit on the arm of her chair, take her hand in mine and wait for her to calm. Then I speak again.

'This is obviously very difficult for you and I understand if you prefer me to come back another day but in my opinion whatever is making you so upset is what is causing the stress in your body, which in turn, is what provokes the symptom of a cough. Do you follow?'

Once again she signals the affirmative with her head bowed. Simultaneously her hand pulls away from mine. She places it in her lap on top of the other one. I return to my chair. It isn't long before she speaks and I try to write down every word without looking away from her face.

'This cough began some time ago. It's hard to say exactly when. But you are right Doctor Gachet, I have stress in my life.'

'Go on.'

'No, I cannot say. It's too difficult. If you cannot give me a remedy now then I sincerely understand. But I cannot speak of what you ask me to and I think I would rather live with my cough.'

I sit in my chair for some time staring out ahead of me. Hysterical weeping is another symptom of *Ignatia*. But is this grief? I have to complete the symptom picture. Right now, I am just assuming that it is. I can hear Clemens's words to me:

'Don't assume anything Paul. You are not the patient. Only the patient knows what he thinks and feels. You may think at some point, because you are making all of these beautiful cures, that you are a god and know better than your patients about themselves. Forget it. Do you understand? You're a man. We are both men. Ordinary men with an extraordinary job, maybe. But if you ever take the path of bringing conjecture into your prescribing, I hope that one day you will be wise enough to realise, through experience as I have done, where you have gone wrong.

And don't be fooled. Whatever they say … whatever they say … it is about themselves. If they say, 'she is a very jealous woman' they mean 'I am sensitive to jealousy; jealousy is in my nature'. If they deny something – 'I'm not a jealous person' – again you know they are sensitive to jealousy and it is a characteristic that is in their nature.'

'Suzanne, would you be willing to talk more about your cough? In that way we might be able to avoid talking about your stress. For instance, when it happens, how would you describe it?'

'I think I have told you everything.'

'Please tell me again. Humour me. What is the effect that this cough has on you?'

'Doctor Gachet, it tears me to pieces, if you must know.'

'And how would you describe being torn to pieces? Tell me more about the experience of being torn to pieces?'

'It's shattering.'

'Suzanne, I'm so sorry. You probably don't understand why I am asking you these inane questions, but it is important to me that you tell me everything and that I don't guess even one thing as to how you are feeling. So, if you were to write a dictionary, how would you describe the word "shattering"?'

'It is like an earthquake. If you are its victim you feel shattered. It was exactly the same way when Edouard's father died. Everyone felt shattered.'

I notice she is biting the inside of her cheek as she speaks.

'Surely, after all that speaking, you must need something to wet your throat?' she asks, with a brave smile.

Rapid change of mental condition. Hysterical weeping alternating with great emotional control and wanting to look after others. She acts out more symptoms from the homeopathic proving of St Ignatius Bean. From the *loganiaceae* plant family. I have a botanist friend who informed me of the other plants we use homeopathically that belong to the same family. If you study homeopathic *Materia Medica* you will find that all of these plants have symptoms in common. Patients who need them all suffer from shock, disappointment and sometimes deception. The nerves of the patient are affected, suggesting to me that Suzanne's is a nervous, hysterical cough.

I prepare a small vial of *Ignatia* 200c and ask her to take the remedy one a day for five days.

'I'd like to come back next week to see how you're getting on.'

'It's not necessary, please.'

'If you take the medicine, I'm sure it will help. The most difficult part of being a homeopathic patient is now over. I am sorry to have caused you distress. I won't ask you these things again. I will only ask about the cough. May I come by on my way home from the hospital next week?

And there it is again, that slight nod of her head that speaks to me of powerlessness to do anything about her situation. It will be interesting to observe how much the effect of the remedy will help her.

When I arrive home to my private practice, the same long line of sufferers greets me on the stairs. My creaking footsteps groan. There are times when my mind and heart become so overloaded that my head buzzes with the problems that have landed at my door. I long for peace and quiet. My footsteps are heavy as I climb the stairs. When I let myself in I don't invite anyone to follow me.

'I'm sorry,' I say over my shoulder.

I go to stand by the window. There are two labourers staggering across the road, no doubt playing truant from work. One whistles at a woman whose hair is too blonde, lips too red. I acknowledge that I am suffering from the symptom of having women on my mind.

Clouds like those in the paintings of the old masters sail past buildings through the sky. I will walk to Blanche's house uninvited this evening and ask her what's wrong. I'll try to make amends, but will leave if she wishes it. On the way I'll walk past La Salpêtrière and administer Bella's remedy, Platinum(*Platina*) 1M, a prescription I am now convinced will not provoke a spontaneous remission … but what about Suzanne?

'Whatever they say, *whatever they say*, is about themselves,' Clemens said.

Do I understand right? That she is grieving for Auguste Manet, Edouard's old man, whilst she lives with Edouard? I only learned recently that the judge died last year. Edouard pursues a bachelor's lifestyle. Perhaps Suzanne is his housekeeper after all and the boy Leon his half-brother. So, why does he sleep in his ancestral home at least three nights a week? The dynamic is confusing and most interesting but I am starting to feel glad that Edouard is a patient of Georges. The remedy must mirror the motives of the man and this man is proving difficult to work out. I look at my watch. I have stood here too long. It is time to invite my first patient into my consulting room.

Bella's First Remedy
May 16th

'I am following Nature without being able to grasp her.'
Claude Monet

In the library, the drama is like something out of an Alexandre Dumas novel. Bella wears the same dress as she wore the very first time I saw her. She walks around like an over-affectionate madam. She places her arm around another patient, kisses their cheek and moves on to the next person. As she moves through the room she swishes the blue cotton folds of her skirt with her arm.

I stand at the entrance and watch her, one hand inside my pocket clutching the bottle of *Platina*. A peculiar sensation like a tightening in my diaphragm grabs me, and won't let me go. I try to ignore it, to physically push it down with a couple of exhalations, but it won't budge. I know all too well what the feeling is telling me. It is an instinctive reaction to my choice of remedy for Bella. Something is wrong. Bella is acting frivolously; there is a softness to her that is not witnessed in the character of *Platina*. *Platina* is misanthropic, contemptuous and hard. Bella needs a different remedy but I don't know what it is.

Someone taps my shoulder. At first I think it is Bella, who a few seconds earlier disappeared behind a column. I turn around and Doctor Ipsen has his face very close to mine. Saliva has accumulated at the corners of his lips and threatens to roll down his chin like a tear. He is unsteady on his feet, no doubt a little hazy from lunch in an inn where he has drunk too much wine. A rank odour blows from his mouth towards mine.

'Eh Gachet, time to give your patient her remedy. Exciting times for homeopathy,' he says, wiping his lips with his sleeve and laughing as if he had just told himself an amusing joke.

In spite of myself, my nerves get the better of me and I stumble over words. 'I'd really ... rather see her in a ... consultation one last time.'

'I'm not surprised you have cold feet. It's up to you. We can easily call the whole thing off.'

'Let's give her the remedy,' I say, with what I hope is an assertive nod.

Ipsen signals to Marguerite Bottard who in turn signals to two other nurses. Within seconds these women are hastening towards Bella. They restrain her. She fights to get away from their grasp and bites one of them on the wrist.

'The bloody cow,' the mauled nurse screams across the room, as she alternately shakes and sucks her hand. The scene makes me smile. Too many times I've seen patients treated roughly for no reason. Perhaps true to homeopathy, like will cure like.

'What is it exactly that amuses you, Doctor Gachet? You don't think it is somewhat perverse to be enjoying the painful injury of an on duty nurse?'

This isn't an argument I want to have, or one I think I can win. I do not enter into the discussion. We follow the nurses, and Bella, out through the corridor to a spare doctor's office, a much more sanitised setting for medical staff than the patient's dank, rat infested bedroom in the basement. I pour one pillule into the cap from the bottle of *Platina* 1M.

I want to say, 'Let her go, let me give it to her straight. I need to build an honest and respectful relationship with my patient.' But I say nothing because I cannot trust Bella not to tear out my hair.

The matron grabs a lock of Bella's tresses and pulls her head backwards. Bella screams and I pour the pillule into her mouth. The matron waits a couple of minutes before releasing Bella's hair. She spits on the floor. Her sputum is clear. The remedy has already dissolved.

'Is that it, Gachet?' Ipsen asks.

'Yes.'

'And don't you want to leave that bottle so the nurses can administer the next dose?'

'There will be no next dose for now. Maybe not even at the next consultation.'

'And this will be when? In a couple of hours? A day, I suppose, at the very most?'

'Next week. We need to just observe what happens from now until then. How much opiate is she having at present on a daily basis?'

'Half the amount she was on before,' the voice comes from behind me. Turning around, I see nurse Morrisot sitting on a chair.

'Sorry,' I say. 'I didn't see you there.'

'I've made sure your instructions have been adhered to, one spoon of laudanum every other hour. Will we be dropping the dosage again?'

She looks at me with a defiant stare.

'No, let's leave it like it is for now, and Nurse Morrisot, come and find me if there is anything to report between now and next week.'

'When I get to my study I will be writing all of this down, Gachet, every sodding word,' says Doctor Ipsen.

'I've also recorded every word of this session, as Doctor Gachet instructed me to do last time,' counters Nurse Morrisot.

'I'm very grateful, very grateful indeed and no doubt Doctor Ipsen is very grateful too because you have saved him a job,' I say, looking back towards him. But he seems, once again, to have mysteriously disappeared.

Premonition
May 16th still

'I've spent my life making blunders.'

Pierre-Auguste Renoir

I have a feeling inside me that something awful is going to happen. It's as if all my nerves have been mangled and my limbs have lost their fluidity. Walking home, I am hardly able to appreciate the crisp Spring light, the trees and their frivolous baby leaves in contrast with stoic old peeling trunks. I wonder if I look closely enough, squint or stare, whether the young foliage already has hints of aged russet, canary and light brown.

'Not so fast Doctor Gachet.'

'Excuse me?'

A hand is on my arm.

'There was a burglary this afternoon in one of the studios in your building. Monsieur Breton said he saw one of your patients leaving the scene of the crime.'

'Impossible, I haven't been here all day'.

The beefy policeman who detained me back in February stands before me, arms folded across his chest like a barricade, screwing up his jagged rock face and pebble eyes.

I have since learned his name is Inspector Fornier. I often see him walking up and down this street as if it is his own, swiping children around the head with little reason and one time when a woman complained of too little space, kicking over the Chinaman's barrel of pickles that stands outside his shop.

'Excuse me,' I say, stepping forward. To my surprise he moves out of the way. 'Good Afternoon, Inspector Fornier.'

118

Patients wait outside my door. Once again, I stand at the window. This time, wondering what Fornier wanted with me – and what is going to happen to Bella? If the remedy is not similar enough it could stir her energies making her madness seem even more exaggerated for a while. If that happened it could be helpful. By highlighting symptoms, a more similar remedy will be easier to find. But I dread such a beginning to her homeopathic treatment, whilst Ipsen is a spy who's poised to pounce. Unable to curb such thoughts, I feel unable to concentrate on anyone else's ailments.

I remember several years ago, my mentor Clemens summoned me to a dinner meeting on one of his rare visits to Paris. On a Saturday evening, I walked into Tortini's, in the Boulevard des Italiens. As I entered, the sound of chatter and laughter spilled out through the door into the street. The restaurant was full and serving staff bustled between tables. I had heard that the Duchess of Berri went there every night incognito and I found myself looking for a woman in disguise. One young waiter, carrying several salvers of boiled lobster in their screaming red shells, caught my eye and motioned for me to wait. I spied gay maiden aunts with young wards, dowagers with chaperones, many beautiful women and several enlarged tables of rowdy male companions. On a table in the corner I even thought I saw Napoleon – but without an entourage, I have to admit it was highly unlikely. Yet, the air was tinged with reverence, excitement and the scent of burnt sugar and roasting meat. Tortini in black frock coat, and broad smile, came towards me clutching menus in both hands.

'You have reserved?'

'I'm with Monsieur Boenninghausen.'

'Ah, Monsieur Boenninghausen, of course. Come this way. I have positioned him at a little table at the back. It is very discreet and very good for meetings. There are three of you tonight?'

I raised my eyebrows.

'Yes,' he remembered. 'There are definitely three.'

We moved through an arch into a more sober space, where the air was relaxed and quiet. There were four tables. One empty, another occupied by a famous actress and her retinue. One of my favourite painters, Gustav Courbet, sat alone at a third. He wore an old ornate shirt, torn at the elbow, and ate hungrily with his large hands. A topaz on his thumb gleamed from the security of its gold setting His features were framed by his long dark hair and obscured by his bushy beard. He is one of a handful of very successful artists in Paris who welcome the moderns. His own art threatens the boundaries of acceptance but also mesmerises with its brilliance. I hesitated. Clemens Boenninghausen tugged at my arm.

'Paul,' he said, rising from the fourth table to hug me and then introducing me to the man in a white suit sitting next to him. The man had marbled skin like coffee with cream and gold wire-framed spectacles.

'Paul, this is Doctor Sharma, he is a doctor in India, apprenticed to Doctor Honigberger, homeopath to Maharaja Ranjeet Singh. Have I got that right?' he asked.

'Yes Monsieur Boenninghausen, your introduction was excellent; you managed to get everything right.'

'I'm very pleased to meet you, Doctor Sharma,' I said, offering my hand.

'The menus were brought to the table. I noticed that whilst Clemens took his pince-nez from his breast pocket to read the Carte, Doctor Sharma simultaneously took his glasses off.

I pulled my chair closer to the table and read through a list of cold pâtes, roast partridge, steamed fish, fried eggs and broiled kidneys whilst Clemens ordered a bottle of iced champagne.

'Doctor Sharma has some interesting ideas,' Clemens said, looking over his lenses with his arms outstretched, palms on the table before him. 'If I had met Ayush as a young man – I hope you don't mind if I call you by your first name,' he said, turning his head towards the Indian doctor. ' – I would have studied under him this philosophical pursuit called meditation.'

'Actually, it is more than that. We have found in India that it is possible to be refreshed quite quickly after practising meditation and this helps during a session that is overloaded with patients. You have to go from one to the other quite quickly as a homeopath. You have to listen very carefully to what everyone says. And you have to come up with the right remedy time and time again, even when you ask yourself "What to do?" You have to be very present in the now. But how is it possible to do this when you have thoughts generated from your previous patient going around in your brain or things from your own life cloying your own mind? We physicians are only human. Categorically, meditation is to be a big a help with this problem.'

The waiter brought over our champagne. With a white cloth around the cork, he prised the stopper off and the bottle steamed. Clemens was still looking at me, drumming his fingers.

'And how do you meditate?' I asked.

'Ayush needs somewhere to stay. If you accommodate him for the next two weeks, I'm sure he'll teach you.'

The waiter poured. We lifted our glasses and drank. The wine was fiercely cold and it smarted on my tongue and at the back of my nose. My eyes began to water. I put down my drink and wiped my lips with the napkin.

'Tell me Clemens,' I said with a broad smile. 'Was it ever to be my choice?'

Ayush ate shellfish with his fingers as if he had been doing it all his life, licking his fingers and twisting them unselfconsciously in his serviette until they were clean. He was interesting and naturally hypnotic. He assured me that Blanche's anecdote about elephants walking across the beach with priests in saffron robes was perfectly plausible.

'They would be giving rides on the elephant for money to make a pilgrimage. This is quite common,' he said. And, 'There are many kings in my country. Many people who are rich enough have their clothes woven in gold and every Raj has a special room full of buxom courtesans. There is real magic in India like the man who cured himself of TB by doing asanas.'

'I'm sorry, Ayush but I don't understand the term "asanas",' said Clemens.

'It is an Indian word. It means making shapes with the body, many are named after animals, and the yogi holds each pose for quite sometime.'

'Like a human sculpture,' I said, quite fascinated.

Ayush's face turned suddenly serious.

'But you have to be very careful. In my country, there are also fakirs,' he warned.

Ayush slept on the floor in my consulting room curled up in a Kashmir blanket. He ate dried foods cooked in spices that he had brought from India and I worried about the pungent smells having an effect on my remedies. During the days, he made himself scarce.

'Walking this lovely city of yours,' he said. 'It is lucky for an Indian to have this experience.'

'Where did you meet Clemens?' I once asked.

'He is a very famous homeopath. I read his books. I wrote to him. He said I should come to Paris because this is where Samuel Hahnemann died. I couldn't be luckier. He met me off the boat and introduced me to you.'

In the evenings we sat on the floor. He remained cross-legged for hours whilst I wriggled on the hard wood with my legs straight out in front of me, my back against the wall. We would begin by humming.

'Listen to your own humming,' Ayush would command. 'Concentrate on the sound of your humming.'

When we stopped my head was so full of a rushing silence it felt like a mountain stream had washed through my mind. With hands held together in prayer, thumbs resting on breastbone, head bowed, he recited words in Sanskrit and then translated for me: *I bow before the noblest of sages, Patañjali, who brought serenity of mind by his work on yoga, clarity of speech by his work on grammar, and purity of body by his work on medicine.*

'Now concentrate on your breathing,' he said. 'Breathe evenly. As the air is sucked upwards make it even in both nostrils. Breathe so the length of time of your in-breath is the same as your out-breath. Breathe so the speed of your breath is even with each breath.'

If my mind wandered to other thoughts, which it often did, I held my breath and Ayush would clap his hands and say, 'All thoughts are directed inwards. Imagine the air filling up and then leaving your lungs.'

When he left two weeks later, I had learned, with great respect for my teacher, the discipline of daily practice. He stood in his white suit with his small bag at his feet, placed his palms together and bowed before me.

'One day I will come back and teach you to meditate,' he said.

'Ayush, what have we been doing every evening for the last two weeks?' I asked, mirroring his bow.

'Preparation for meditation,' he said, wiggling his head.

I sit on the floor with my back to the wall, humming then breathing as evenly as I can. Twenty minutes later, the jangled noise in my head has disappeared. I invite the first person in and am able to lose myself in another's story once again.

Reunion
May 16th, still

'For an Impressionist, to paint from nature is not to paint the subject, but to realize sensations.'

Paul Cézanne

It is almost a relief just to have arrived at Blanche's house. I know that she will probably be out teaching, so I have brought supplies to use while I wait. I set up an easel and canvas and begin to draw her shy house concealed by an abundance of ivy. Then I try to sense the subtle colours and softness evoked by this sunny late afternoon by introducing water based paints. A pigeon marches up and down the windowsill outside her bedroom like a sentry. A red squirrel scurries up a tree. I am captured by my subject. The hours pass. The warm spring air cools. Shadows lengthen and eventually overwhelm. I set up garden flares in old glass jars that I found abandoned by the river and I paint until I can no longer see.

I am loath to pack up my things and leave this spot although night has closed in and Blanche has not returned. I sit on the bench hugging myself with my arms. I watch stars signal as if from a lighthouse to a ship, they mesmerise like Charcot's hypnotherapy, like Auysh's conversation. I fall asleep.

A loud thump wakes me. I was dreaming of sitting in a small restaurant with Victorine. She was speaking but I wasn't listening. I was anticipating Blanche but she did not arrive. The dark mood in the dream greets me as I wake. My hands and nose are so cold they burn. I notice there is an envelope in my lap. It is white, luminous. I shake myself into the present and attempt to open it but the blood in my fingers is ice. I wouldn't be able to read whatever is inside anyway. The flares have gone out. A cloud veils the moon and darkness has swallowed the world. In that moment, I do not care about the neighbours. I bang on the door.

'Let me in Blanche,' I call up to her bedroom. 'I need to talk to you. I've been here since this afternoon.'

I hear no response, so I pick up a stone from beside the tree and toss it upwards towards her bedroom. It hits the window. I do not care if the glass is scratched or broken. I see a small light that can only be from a match and then a larger flare that moves towards the window. I do not know if she sees my face in the glare, if it catches the hint of tears.

'I'm coming down,' she calls in a loud whisper.

When the door opens I am grateful and move quickly inside. The hallway is narrow. Her body is almost touching mine. She puts her palms on my cheeks.

'In the morning we will talk,' she says to my eyes.

I lower my stare.

I see her chest rise and fall.

I'm afraid to move.

'Please, hold me,' she says, and somewhere in that moment I must have dropped the envelope. Reaching out she gasps at my frozen touch but her skin is like a drug.

'Here,' she says, helping me to remove her clothes faster.

The back of my head smashes against the wall as I pull her towards me. Her naked breasts are against my chest. I interlock my hands beneath her buttocks and lift her. Her legs become my wings as she takes me within. She shudders. I do not thrust.

'Please,' she says.

For one chanced moment, I look to the opposite wall by the still open door and our silhouette, a butterfly.

I do not want to move. Blanche brings all the bedding she can downstairs to cover me. I tell her it's a cold night and I need her warmth too and it feels good to hold her whilst we fall asleep. When we wake with the first hint of dawn, I cannot remember a time when I felt happier. We are wrapped in sheets, eating stale bread with crusts that fall like snow from a roof, and ripe, pregnant cheese. Juice from a soft tomato dribbles down her chin. I lick it clean. I want to lick her everywhere. I smooth away a curl of her hair and my lips get lost somewhere behind her ear. Blanche's breath hastens.

Here in Paris, we are taught vaginal stimulation at medical school. It is thought to be a cure for hysterical paroxysms. A condition, we were told, that comes from the womb.

When Canard massaged the clitoris of a young woman in front of a group of students, I walked out. I was told that she fought him hysterically in the beginning but eventually 'climaxed and calmed down'.

'The therapy works,' Canard argued.

'We don't do this to men,' I said.

'Have you ever seen a hysterical man, Gachet?'

'It is hysterical to lose one's temper and want to kill, but men do this all the time. Why don't you test out your theory on such a member of our human race?'

'Can you really not stand the fact that we make these women feel better?'

'Many cry afterwards and their tears are not joyful.'

'They whimper,' he said with his hands on the table and his face too close to mine. 'Where they screamed before.'

'And you expect me to be placated by what you've just said?'

'Doctor Gachet, it's time you gave up your fight. Medicine is medicine,' he said pushing himself away from the table. 'It is how we practise it. Do you want to be a buffoon all your life, or do you want to become a doctor? Because if you do, I suggest you go very quiet from now on. My patience is running out for your ignorance in the ways of the world.'

So, help me God, I am grateful to the education now. I understand the female anatomy in some detail. How it works has been explained to me, graphically. In Blanche's home, the sun pushes its rays through the clouds in the sky. I lift my face toward the window and a beam of light blinds me. Lost in the sound of Blanche's breath, I encourage her to lie then kiss my way down her body.

'Does this feel nice?' I ask, looking up into the sun, hesitating.

'Paul,' she says, 'Please, don't stop, go on.'

The Salon des Refusés
May 17th

'Insults are pouring down on me thick as hail.'

Edouard Manet

Blanche moans and the sun slips behind a cloud. I stop kissing her to look at her face. She is wondrously abandoned upon our eiderdown bed that's still on the floor. I am Hercules. The blood is pulsing through my veins. My heart is big and thumping. I am flying but one second later all my organs are lead weights. I sit on the end of the sheet she'd brought down last night for us and put my head in my hands. Blanche throws her arms around my neck from behind.

'What's the matter?' she asks, with her lips so close to my skin she raises the hairs around my seventh cervical. I shake my head and turn around.

'I've just remembered something. I didn't turn up for Georges de Bellio last week. I'm sorry … I … just lost the moment.'

'Go and see him,' she says standing and handing me my underclothes.

'Blanche, we still haven't spoken about us and I have to know why the other night you told me you don't want me, and now this, which has been wonderful, but … .'

'We can't do this here, not now, when you have to go.'

She has manoeuvred herself around and is kneeling in front of me.

'Tonight then.'

'I am playing at the Bade.'

'Then when?'

Silence.

'Blanche, last week we were practically engaged.'

'Well, maybe that was the problem.'

I look to the tall ceiling, the decorative cornice of grapes on a vine and a square of soot above the mantelpiece.

'Am I supposed to understand?'

'Let's just say it has something to do with the fact that I'm frightened.'

'Of me? What have I ever done to make you feel frightened? Surely not the intimacy, you seem to enjoy that well enough.'

'No Paul,' she laughs. 'I've had other lovers if that's what you think.'

'What are you frightened of Blanche?'

'You wouldn't understand,' she says.

'Please, I am not your enemy.'

'Being left,' she says, sweeping up the bed sheets, walking out and leaving a trail of crumbs in her wake.

It is still early morning. Blanche asked me to leave in the end. I have no idea what happened to the envelope, or what was inside it. I looked for it before I went but it had mysteriously disappeared. I am a little angry that Blanche is so sensitive to being abandoned but not about abandoning me. I walked, of course. Through the damp air of an earlier rainfall that has shined the surface of things. And now, at home, I'm alone dragging out the bathtub from the cupboard again. Cold water will do. I carry bowlfuls from the tap to the bath. My emotions are in control of me. I hope I can wash them away.

I put a foot gingerly over the side. The water is shockingly iced but it feels punishingly good. What must Georges de Bellio think of me? Thoughts come in waves through my mind about Blanche. What do I do with this need to constantly be with her? She doesn't make it easy. If I'm honest with myself, she was coughing again. How can I be the objective observer? How can I treat her? She is frightened of losing me and I have a premonition that I will not only lose her but also my old friend Georges.

I sit on my knees in the bath. My genitals protest. The water stuns, numbs. I splash it on my face. There's a war in my guts and the feeling doesn't go away.

'Nooo!' I call out, disturbing the ghosts in the walls.

As I step out of the bath, I notice the date on yesterday's paper lying on the floor. The opening of the Salon des Refusés is already happening. I have been writing the date on patients' notes all week and I hadn't even realised it was approaching. I don't usually forget things. Perhaps I need a remedy to balance out my energies. Or is it the Phosphorus having its way with me?

There are classes at Père Suisse but he won't be expecting anyone, and as for Georges, my guess is that he will be one of the first visitors standing in line, moustachios glistening.

It is barely 9am and I get dressed for the second time this morning. I must hurry to the Palais de l'Industrie, there's no time to walk. Luckily, I manage to flag down an empty hansom. The coachman raises an eyebrow when I choose to sit next to him.

'Fine morning,' he says, proudly as if this day is his creation.

'The Palais de l'Industrie,' I say, willing the horse to move faster. Exhibition staff will be putting the finishing touches to the hangings. All our paintings are almost ready to show off.

'Would you like me to go quickly?' he asks.

'Thank you,' I say, drumming my fingers on my thigh.

I make my way through the crowd milling on the lawn and up the steps to the entrance, sure that I must be the last exhibitor to arrive. The lobby is dark and sober but a ray of sunlight rushes in after me. I feel a lump form at the back of my throat as I walk through the majestic Salon exhibition that has been hung for two weeks and is now quiet and sombre; through brown and beige marble rooms with highly polished, pink granite columns inset with gold leaf, and a glass roof through which the light falls benignly onto the grateful canvases that cover the walls. Paintings of shipwrecks in thunderstruck seas; swirling grey skies that meet frothing white waves. Paintings of fables in forests, where cherubs fly and nymphs lie naked under the spell of the devil's agent, half man and half goat. A shaft of light is God's kiss upon the scene. Paintings like parables crafted to precision and framed to the fussy prescription of The Académie des Beaux-Arts, works by Ingres, Corot and Rousseau all hang here. And, finally I see it, the doorway and the turnstile that allows patrons to enter 'The Emperor's Salon.'

It is much darker in here, and immediately on entering my sight is obscured but I can see we are many, making history, at the first ever *Salon des Refusés* on varnishing day. I estimate there are over two hundred of us perpetuating an air of expectancy in these grand palatial halls. The catalogue has listed 781 exhibits but already I can see that there are many more. Shoes clack on flagstones. Voices reverberate from the stone walls. Lamplights and chandeliers in every hall throw a measure of imperfect light around. Each painting has entered into a lottery of where they would be hung. An artist has to be lucky that his work is at a good height for the onlooker and that the lighting around his picture does not cast it in shadow, or the canvas deflect a beam.

The section where Camille exhibits half a dozen paintings is immersed in the warmth of sunny-yellow and apple-green farmlands where workers toil in simple clothing. In contrast to the rooms I have just walked through, these paintings are softer, less exacting and full of love.

Père Tanguy is talking to Paul Durand-Ruel. They make an unlikely pair, Pére in his navy blue worker's uniform and Paul formally attired in a black frock coat, but they are drawn together by their communal appreciation of art and their equally strong passion for pipe tobacco.

'Ah, Doctor Gachet,' says Durand-Ruel. 'I have standing next to me the real star of the show.'

A frame can determine how a painting falls upon the retina and many in this room are Pères handiwork. Endless criticism from his wife, no doubt, over the months of sleepless nights, shaping wood with a scalpel, his paintbrush stained in gilt. He draws proudly on his clay pipe.

'And which ones will you take in to sell?' he asks Durand-Ruel, as if his reward is simply knowing this piece of insider information.

The conversation makes my alter ego, Paul van Ryssel, feel more like a commodity than one of the cogs that make a magical event like this one come to be. I move on to find my painting above that of an artist I have never heard of before. Durand-Ruel walks up behind me. 'You've been "skyed",' he says.

'I know,' I reply. The light falls on my work plainly and if you look up, you can only see the texture of the canvas and black outlines – a style that until recently I thought quite odd and have now embraced. In the brochure it says *'Le Haute-Seine'*, by Paul van Ryssel, but at this angle it is *'Le Haute-Rien.'*

There are at least a dozen Paul Cézannes crowding out my work. His exhibits are vivid countryside landscapes. His reds are compelling. His yellows and greens are cooling flames. I remind myself that this is just a hobby for me. It is not my main profession. But it could have been, should have been. Forget it, it is not. I'm uprooted, all over the place, without the safety of home. I need to get some air.

'Painting and homeopathy mixed with your passion is a blessing. You have more than most. The combination will reward you with great joy,' Clemens once said. I can't even complain. It is not as if he never mentioned frustration and disappointment, he did, constantly. *'Everything costs in this life. The only thing you have to decide is whether you are willing to pay the price.'*

My footsteps echo in my ears. Once outside, I pull my cap from my head, push it into my jacket pocket, run down the stone steps and start to walk briskly. The road is full of carriages. Coachmen are arguing as they try to manoeuvre their vehicles to and from a space where their passengers can alight. Reined-in horses attempt to trot in distress amidst the chaos. They remind me of Bella the day she was arrested. There is a long queue, ten deep, snaking its way from as far as the Champs Elysees. There must be thousands of patrons waiting for the exhibition to open.

'I'm expecting a chamber of horrors,' one man says loudly, above chatter that sends a loud clamour up to the sky. At the back of the building I am thankfully alone. I place my back and one foot against the wall. My father was right to insist that I took on another career besides painting. I am not as insightful or as colourful as Camille and Edouard and even they find it hard to make a living. But I can't help wondering if I devoted all my time to artistry whether it could have ever be something more than just a balm for my wounded soul.

The clip-clop of horses and indistinct voices waft over to me, and with them a feeling of hopelessness like a premonition that I know only too well. Tears stab. I squat and allow myself to cry. Looking up at the clouds that mock and jeer, and swallows in perfect 'V' trailing across the sky. 'Oh fuck, fuck, fuck, fuck,' I let loose the curse-word to blow on a wind that slaps me around the ears.

Shunted through the crowd, I show my exhibitor's pass to the attendant. The Salon is opening to the public now. A huge throng force their way forward to either side of me. In high, contemptuous spirit and a jaunty walk, they enter. In crinoline, frilled parasols, top hats, tailcoats, crystal tipped canes, they enter, the lay critics, the sharks. I am a fish pulled along by a wave through the foyer and the antechambers of the Salon with its forsaken art, through the turnstile to our exhibition. Past Degas, Renoirs, Pissaros and Monets. Past Cézannes, Fantin-Latours and one small, skyed, van Ryssel, through a gothic archway, to a room where an enormous painting occupies the length and breadth of the wall in front of me. Frosted windows in the panelled walls above encourage the light to hold it perfectly. It is a masterpiece. Foliage in velvetine dark greens, porcelain skin for a naked Victorine. She sits challenging me, the observer, with her expression. Chin cupped in hand, her brown eyes say, 'So, Doctor

Gachet, Paul, what do you really think?'

Gustave and Eugène Manet are clothed to either side of her, one in a brown serge jacket and the other in an ebony coat. The perspectives are not quite accurate but its message is plain truth with a clarity that is powerful and completely modern. In the foreground a basket has tumbled over and with it go its contents, a baguette and fruit. A young woman in the background wades in a pool. She wears petticoats and her hair is unruly. I get close to the painting thinking it is Bella. Only when I am upon it can I see that it is not.

I sense someone watching me. Prising my eyes away, I look behind to see Edouard standing in the corner by the door like a guard. He leans on his walking stick and appears to be oblivious to the scene. Elbows dig into him as people propel themselves forwards. Then I notice one of Victorine's paintings: a dark portrait of a very young girl, defiant as a street urchin, in traditional style except for the subject matter. It has a very good, eye-level place on the wall, in this, the largest of the halls.

I catch a glimpse of Victorine talking to Emile Zola. She has her hand on his forearm and he laughs at what she has just said. Taking his arm they both turn towards me, not looking at me, but past me to the Masterpiece. Then I notice that everyone is focused on *Dejeuner sur l'Herbe*.

'Outrageous,' someone screams.

Cackles of laughter peel all around

'What a disgrace,' the man immediately in front of me calls out. The person next to him says, 'I can't believe Napoleon has allowed such pornography to be let loose in here.'

'And I've come here with my wife,' another yells back.

A pregnant woman faints. Surely from the hot and stuffy overcrowded room? Three men ceremoniously carry her out. Several ladies dab their yes with handkerchiefs and sob theatrically. There are others, of the gentler sex, led to the exits by their escorts.

'Excuse me, this is no place for my daughter,' a man

addresses me. The crowd, like the red sea, parts. The man and his daughter walk through. I can stand it no longer and follow in his tracks.

A whole gang of artists is already outside. Camille is there, so is Edouard, Paul, Victorine, Claude and Henri.

'Edouard, they scorn you but they're not artists, what do they know?' Camille says.

Edouard stands in front of everyone with aqueous eyes. He leans on his cane with both hands. 'I'm not like the rest of you,' he says. 'Painting has nothing to do with politics, and everything to do with being an artist accepted by the establishment. Today is a very big blow,' he says, walking off, the tails of his caramel frock coat flapping. The rest of us are silent. The bells of Notre Dame chime midday. Victorine chases after Edouard, the clack-clack of her heels moving into the distance.

'Friends are important. He makes it more difficult for himself, running away like that,' Camille says, to no one in particular. 'Ah, well … .'

We disband.

On my way down the steps Paul slaps my back

'It's only the first day. Perhaps it will go better tomorrow.'

'Yes,' I say, 'There is always hope.'

Bird with a Broken Wing
May 18th

'Don't be afraid in nature; one must be bold, at the risk of having been deceived and making mistakes.'

Camille Pissarro

I sit with hope in my consulting room chair, listening to my own quiet breath making the morning's din seem all the more disturbing. It's ironic. Even if I were a professional painter I would still be getting critically stoned for my beliefs. Maybe I am just an inherent revolutionary. What a crazy revelation to have about oneself.

There's a knock at the door. I move towards the sound and lift the latch. The chain jams the door.

'Yes?' I ask.

'It's me, Nurse Morrisot.'

'Please come in.'

I release the chain and Nurse Morrisot's face shatters any hope. 'Doctor Gachet, Bella Laffaire is a lot worse. For the last few hours she's been demonic. She's pulled ancient texts down from the library shelves and stamped them to dust. She's thrown books at lamps, smashing glass shades, and started fights with other patients. The nurses cannot contain her. Her bite is rabid. Please, you have to come.'

I put on my coat and follow her to a waiting hansom. During the journey rain splatters against the windows. We remain silent, only the leather squeaks beneath us. I wonder what this little episode means for the future of homeopathy and I worry that I have let down this noble system of medicine with my mistake.

When we arrive, I delve into my pocket for money to pay the driver.

'The hospital has given me sous,' Nurse Morrisot says.

I walk off swiftly through the rain. A matron and her gaggle of nurses meet me at the door. Doctor Ipsen comes hurriedly towards us. His face is a screwed up rag.

'Good evening,' I say.

He looks straight through me and as he leaves he slams the street door. The sound echoes whilst I follow my entourage down a marble staircase to the basement where the smell of boiled cabbage gives way to excrement. I resist the desire to cover my nose. Bella lies on a straw bed in her cell. She has been bound and gagged. As soon as I walk in, her eyes plead with mine. Nurse Morrisot has caught up with us and stands next to me. She lowers and shakes her head. But to untie Bella now would only reignite the bedlam that occurred before I arrived. For the life of me I do not know what to do for her homeopathically.

'Higher dose of laudanum?' Marguerite Bottard asks.

I hesitate, then decide. 'No, she is safe for tonight. I will be back again first thing tomorrow morning.'

Lost
May 18th, evening

*'It would be very unjust to object to a busy physician, because he,
as a recuperation from his toilsome day's work, in the evening may
drink a glass of wine in company with his friends.'*
Clemens von Boenninghausen, Lesser Writings

I go to the Bade and sit at the bar. As usual, it is heated and
crowded. Blanche drinks at a table in the corner with two of
Charles's cronies. I don't catch her looking towards me but no
doubt she has seen me poking my nose into my glass. After my
second vin rouge, I decide that she is obviously ignoring me.
With alcohol warming my gut I stroll along the busy, balmy
boulevard to the Guerbois.

Everyone who has ever attended sessions at Père Suisse is
there, or so it seems. Another smoky, hot atmosphere, but at least
in this place tonight, I have friends. Camille waves me over. He is
with Julie, and their closest friends Piette and Adèle de
Montfoucault. I wave at the quartet, mouth 'later', and walk on.
I'm looking for Georges. Partisans circulate. Waitresses tiptoe
with trays in the air. There is a man with an accordion making
his way from table to table. Edouard, accompanied by his mother
and two brothers, occupy a table in the corner. He is hunched
over eating a bowl of soup. Eugenie Manet sits proudly upright as
her two other sons look from one to the other.

I crane my head. Victorine is over on the other side of the
room, sitting with a group of people I've never seen before. I see
Georges beside a table positioned next to a wall. He is with Ernest
Hoschedés. The two men look like penguins. They have their

chairs turned outwards towards the room. They drink coffee and smoke cigars. I push and shove towards them, excusing myself along the way.

'Georges, I'm so pleased I've found you. I've been looking for you all day.'

He crosses his legs and inspects his cigar.

'Look, I'm really sorry about last week. I wish I could offer you a good excuse. I know it's unforgivable and I feel terrible but the truth is that I forgot,' I say bending down and whispering in his ear so he can hear me.

'I'm upset with you Paul. We were conducting a proving, a scientific experiment of your own making. The remedy evoked symptoms that were uncomfortable. I didn't want to participate but you cajoled me into it and for what? The greater good of mankind? For nothing, because you didn't turn up.'

'It's not like me. It must be a proving symptom of Phosphorus.'

'Look at you, your shirttails are sticking out and you have madness in your eyes,' he says, waving me away with a flick of his hand. I stand up straight and am pushed back by the *maître d'*.

'Excuse me Monsieur,' he says, bringing a group of new people through to be seated. Georges turns his chair around to face his table. He motions Ernest Hoschedés to do the same. A waitress walks in front of me with her tray held high, 'Excuse me Monsieur, are you waiting for a table?'

'No. No thank you,' I reply, backing away.

In an alcove, there is a strange party going on. A dozen people sit in a line across four tables with their backs to the wall, men and women dressed in expensive clothes that would once have been considered the height of fashion. Their outfits are worn out and faded now, ghostly reminders of a time when their lives were richer, with responsibilities and relationships. Now, they are sorrowful and unseeing. They live only in some dreamlike internal world. I shudder. I've seen it at the hospital, the accidents, the loss of reason, and a future that is doomed by the wormwood in the glass in front of them. The craving for absinthe becomes everything. It is also Edouard's tipple. He calls it his muse.

'Monsieur, perhaps you would like to sit at the bar?' the same waitress asks as she moves back through to the kitchen. 'I think it is your friend, yes, who is waving at you?'

I look in the direction she is pointing. Armand Guillamin sits alone on a stool by the counter. I have met him many times before at Père Suisse. Like me, he has a day job. He works on the railway, I think. It would be good to talk to him. I make my way over to the bar.

'What are you drinking?' he asks, draining his glass.

'Not for me, I've got problems at work. I have to keep a clear head.'

'No my man, you've got that wrong, you have to be inspired. We'll have two more absinthes,' he says to the barman.

I look at the green slime in the glass for quite a while. Armand is already intoxicated. You can see it by the vacancy in his eyes. He's talking but I don't hear him, I'm thinking of Blanche and wondering what the hell is going on. I have fallen for her but our relationship is so strange. I think of Bella and my stomach tugs downwards. I will have to be very present first thing tomorrow. I need to find her a better remedy. I twirl the glass in front of me. The alcohol has legs and slips down the glass like a woman getting into bed.

'I never worry about problems on the railway,' Armand tells me. 'Painting is everything; the railway is just a job.'

I look up at him and try to smile.

'Come on my man, I've bought you a drink, let's drink,' Armande raises his.

In the glass is a river to drown in, some fairytale land. What is it that Edouard once said? 'It opens the mind. Some of my best visions come from absinthe.'

Was he talking about '*Dejeuner*'? Because if he was talking about *Dejeuner*, it isn't just a vision, it is the work of a genius. I'm going to need to find my genius in the hospital tomorrow morning. Like all men who feel doomed I grab at straws.

'A santé,' I say, lifting mine.

Blanche's loving eyes, hardened. Ipsen's supercilious snarl. Bella's warrior expression as she attacks me. Victorine's amusement. Edouard's nearly tears. My face in the glass behind the bottles. Thin lips downturned in misery. Elbows on the counter. Head cupped in hands. Blue eyes never bluer. One more Absinthe.

'To *Dejeuner sur l'Herbe*,' I say.

'To Edouard's cat,' says Armand.

'Does he have a cat?'

Armand laughs, 'He has a blue cat with purple eyes, I can see it and anyway, does it really matter?'

'Not at all, to *Dejeuner*.'

'And Edouard's cat.'

'To *Dejeuner* and Edouard's cat.'

I call for one more Absinthe.

One more.

And one more.

And I am on a cloud watching them have a picnic on the grass by a river under the trees. Small droplets of light swim through the leaves and weave through the air like fireflies. Crickets hum in the long grass at the edge of the water. A finch lands on a patch of ground that is covered with bluebells. The finch says that if you medicate the humours with Absinthe then the spirit is weakened and grows less and less capable of dealing with pain.

Up on my cloud, I feel no pain.

I see Bella playing in a pool of water.

'Hey everybody,' she calls out. 'I've caught a fish.'

Victorine sits naked on the grass staring out at no one. Beside her are Gustave and Eugène Manet fully clothed. The three of them have turned into china dolls.

'You're so unreserved, darling,' it is Victorine's voice.

I wobble on my cloud.

'The fish is a silver slither of pond idiot gyrating and wanting to escape from her pincer hold,' this is the voice of Gustave.

'Waa!' Bella drops the creature and wades through mossy, Absinthe coloured scum, one hand on her belly, the other reaching out to the shore.

'Fun,' she says, when she reaches the others. 'I like to have fun.'

'Girls like Bella are cleverer than you think,' Gustave again.

'I can't believe I had you fooled,' Bella says.

I fall off my cloud. I am falling and falling and falling ... .

'Actually, it is childish. Bella is childish.' This is Eugène.

'Is it darling? Is it childish?' Bella asks.

'Oh, for heaven's sake, I'm going home,' says Victorine without moving her lips.

The four of them are in a boat on the water, with the reflection of sunrays like silver threads of rain. Gliding past cornfields and horses grazing, Victorine leans back against Gustave. Bella sits on the side and the boat rocks wildly.

'Is it deep? I can't swim,' she says.

I am sitting in the stern controlling the rudder.

I say, 'Bella, you are a bloody fool.'

'I'm not. I just want you to save me.'

We both stand. I just manage to save myself from going over the side. Bella falls against me. Her breasts graze my chest. Her hipbones jut into my groin. Her lips are so close I feel the wetness of her breath.

'Well!' she says.

The three china dolls are watching.

'Victorine,' Bella says, 'Don't you know it's rude to stare.'

Found
May 19th

'The artist is nothing without the gift, but the gift is nothing without work.'

Emile Zola

Pincers squeeze my shoulder. I am slumped forward onto a hard surface. Red and black spots colour the insides of my lids, lids that refuse to open. It is darkness that they seek.

'It's time to go,' a male voice chides.

Trying to lift my body up is like pulling a spoon out of a deep bowl of treacle. There is the scent of familiar perfume. With difficulty, I manage to look behind me. All is blurred. A knife like pain cuts through my vertex. I battle to keep my lids open and notice that I'm still at the Guerbois. My body releases itself down again onto the bar.

'You have to leave.'

I nod but don't move. Moments that could be minutes, that could be hours, pass by. Fingers squeeze my shoulder once more. This time I jolt myself upwards and let my feet slide down onto the floor. When I'm standing I wish I wasn't. I am as unsteady as if I was walking away from a fairground ride. All the tables are empty. There is no one around. I fall into a chair. Through the lace curtain in the window I can see a dark street, but what night? Have I forgotten something more?

'Oh my god, you look awful. Hello.'

'Blanche?' I say, glancing over my shoulder, and into the face of the new maitre d' who I don't know well. I can't see Blanche. Where is Blanche? I stand up and stagger back to the bar. My cap

143

has fallen off. I can see it on the floor; a black footprint stamped on its pale cloth. I avoid my reflection and rub my eyes with the heels of my hands. I hear her again, 'Robert, please make him some coffee, strong, with plenty of sugar. After he drinks it I will take him home.'

I swivel around on my stool. Blanche leans back into a chair, hands in prayer, knees and thighs pressed together, calves splayed.

'You look beautiful,' I slur.

'I look tired.'

'Well, I appreciate your concern.'

She opens an imaginary fan with both hands. I seek out her eyes but it is physically painful to do so as she holds my stare. Robert places a cup on the counter behind me.

'I think you should drink,' she says. 'I've been told that to be served out of hours comes at great expense.'

I turn to face the bar. Liquid like tobacco spittle puddles the saucer. The aroma of roasted coffee beans, usually so enticing, does not appeal. I blow onto gold froth until it disperses, lift it to my lips and down it in one. Blanche drapes her arm around my shoulder.

'I care too and it's dangerous for a lady to walk home alone at night. Either I escort you, or you have to stay at my apartment,' I whisper towards her through my burning throat.

She makes a throaty laugh and waves a copy of *L'Avenir National* in front of me, open at the reviews. I try to focus on the text but the letters skip away. 'The sharp and irritating colours attack the eye like a steel saw,' she reads out. 'Not good news,' she whispers, and then in my other ear, 'I'm taking *you* home'

I raise my eyebrows and melt like the sugar in my coffee.

In the absence of a hansom or an omnibus we walk. She props me up as we do so. I'm shivering. We find a bench and sit down. I huddle inside my coat.

'There's a patient at the hospital called Bella. Victorine

brought her in. It's a long story.'

'I have time.'

'Uh, I can't think straight. They gave me permission to treat her homeopathically and I've given her the wrong remedy.'

'Is that why Victorine pulled you over to talk in private at the Manet's soirée, was it about Bella?'

'Victorine wants to paint her. She wanted me to arrange it but I can't.'

'And did you see Georges?'

'No, I mean yes, in a way. He wasn't impressed. Blanche, I don't know what's happening to me. I'm forgetting things. Important things. I almost forgot it was varnishing day for the *Salon de Refusés*.'

'You work at the hospital and you've got a private practice at home. You paint seriously. It's not like it's just a hobby for you. Every evening, you are either out at a café, reading a homeopathy book, or you are seeing me,' she says. 'Do you think you are too … otherwise engaged?'

My eyes close involuntarily. I'm almost asleep but aware that her warmth has disappeared from my side and I can hear her footsteps walking away from me.

'Why are you taking this personally? Blanche. Blanche!'

I try and run to catch up with her but I find myself to be stationary, limbs flagging like a rag doll. Thankfully she returns. I grab outwards for a lamppost to steady me but there isn't one. I stumble and she catches me just before my knees cave and I sink to the ground.

'You do too much. You have no time for anything, Paul. Not really. You skim over everything like a pebble across the water.'

'That's not true. I'm a very passionate man.'

'That's not what I'm saying. I know you are passionate. You're kind and you are good, otherwise I wouldn't be here. But you have more passions than time. Look at us, we're lovers, but the only time we get to talk is at two o' clock in the morning, walking home after you've knocked yourself out with alcohol and fallen asleep on a bar stool,' she says, gesticulating wildly. 'I really don't like to say this but you're going to have to choose. You can't do everything and be everything to all of mankind. You're not bloody Jesus Christ.'

We are in a small enclave untouched by Haussmann, there is no pavement and the stones beneath our feet are rocky. The stench of human faeces overwhelms and a river, of probably urine, runs beneath our feet. A window opens from above.

'Why the fuck don't you go home?' a baritone calls down.

We are silent.

'Make a noise like that again and I'm coming down with an axe,' he says, banging the window frame in its casement, almost shattering the glass.

We walk again. I don't know what to say. When we arrive at Rue Faubourg Saint Denis, we climb the stairs carefully, making as little noise as possible. Once inside, I whisper because the walls in this apartment seem too thin in the early hours. 'I have to be at the hospital by seven.'

'It's all right, I intend to sleep here by the fire,' she whispers.

'Take the bed. I'll sleep here.'

Sleeping in separate rooms is a strange déjà-vu from an earlier period in our courtship, and one that I hoped would not come back to haunt me.

'Do you think you will sleep?' she asks.

'I won't sleep anywhere,' I answer, truthfully, because suddenly my body is a tight springboard for my nerves. My eyes are too dry and my limbs feel bruised.

'My first class is at ten. When you leave you don't have to wake me.'

'All right, and thank you. Thank you for caring.'

'It's not easy.'

'But special.'

'Yes, it is special, I think.'

Haunted
May 20th

'Nothing can be done except little by little.'

Charles Baudelaire

It's early. So early, Madame Lemont hasn't arrived yet. The common parts of the hospital are deserted. There is a cold wind, which happens sometimes, as if the ghosts of past occupants rise up to escort me. I wear them around my neck like an iced scarf. They remind me of the human element that I need to take with me into the consulting room at all times, and especially when I am consulting with those who are compromised. As I make my way down the stairs one putrid smell gives way to another. I feel suddenly fragile and lean over the stairwell retching.

The thwack of a heavy door closes above and light footsteps descend upon me. I look round. Thankfully, it is Nurse Morrisot.

'Good morning, Doctor Gachet.'

'Nurse, I ... .'

'You look as if you've seen a ghost.'

I smile thinly.

'Are you okay?'

'Yes, I think so,' I say, tempted to grab her by the shoulder. 'I've come early to see Bella.'

'A friend of mine was at the Café Guerbois last night and saw you getting drunk on Absinthe.'

I turn around and retch again, when I turn back she is gone and I wonder if she was ever there. The door clangs once more and her footsteps are on the stairs again, this time much faster than before. She has brought me a mug of coffee that she has

147

somehow managed not to spill. We sit on the stairs and I sip the scalding liquid.

'I don't mind telling you that I'm against many of the practices going on in this building. The misogynistic practices are the worst and I'm grateful that you try to help the women in this hospital improve their troubled minds, but homeopathy, Doctor Gachet – it seems to have made Bella worse. Can that be right?'

'I think it is, Catherine,' I say.

We hear a clanging noise like someone in the kitchen dropping a metal plate. Catherine starts.

'I shouldn't be here,' she says, looking over her shoulder.

'Nor I. Doctor Ipsen is meant to be my shadow during all consultations. The fact that he came and went before me last evening was his choice, but if he finds out I have come to see Bella deliberately early this morning ... .'

Catherine Morrisot stares at me for a long time.

'Catherine, I've treated people with homeopathy for years. I have a private practice in my home and I've witnessed many, many cures. I don't manage to help everyone but I've seen these little sugar pills do magnificent work for more than just a few – too many to call it a miracle, or luck or coincidence. Homeopathy heals, Catherine. We don't know enough about it yet and I have no idea whether in practice I can help Bella. It's scientific, built on clearly defined principles, so in theory it absolutely can.

I down the drink whilst still returning Catherine's stare.

'Will you help me?'

'If I thought homeopathy could help I would, but Doctor Gachet, I could lose my job.'

'You could become a homeopath.'

Catherine is not smiling.

'I was wrong about you,' she says, rising.

I rise too and grab her upper arm.

'Please, let me go.'

I release the grip, amazed at my own behaviour.

'I'm still a doctor here. I'd like the keys to Bella's cell.'

She reaches in her pocket and dangles them in front of me. They chime like percussion. She drops them into my palm.

'Thank you,' I say, as she hurries away.

Despite the early hour Bella is not asleep. She is on the floor, covered in straw from her mattress that she has somehow managed to shred. Her hands and feet are still tied. She is perfectly still. Her pupils are not dilating and the stare is not quite so wild.

'Bella,' I say softly. 'We still haven't been formally introduced. I am Doctor Gachet, a friend of Victorine Meurent who brought you here last month. Do you remember that?

Bella nods.

'I want to help you. I don't want you to spend the rest of your life locked up in this place, but you have to be well before you can go free. Mentally well. Do you understand what I mean?'

I wait and just when I think that maybe she is too insane to comprehend me, Bella nods again, more firmly and definitely this time.

'I can't untie you yet. I have to be sure of what I'm doing every step of the way, but I can help you to sit up. Would you like me to do that?'

Another nod.

I move the scrawny mattress against the wall and shuffle her over. She leans against it with her hands tied and appears far more comfortable.

I hear a scuttle and scratching behind me.

'Catherine?'

Heart thumping, I hastily look around, two devilish incisors and a pair of red eyes stare at me. Bella squirms and tries to talk.

'It's all right, Bella, it's just a rat. Look, Victorine is a friend of mine. She was concerned and brought you here because she thought I might be able to help you, and I think I can, but you're going to have to trust me.'

149

I wait again but this time Bella doesn't nod. I go on.

'I would like to take the gag from your mouth. If you scream then you will disturb other patients. There will be pandemonium. You know, you've experienced this before. The hospital staff will hear. Matron will come in and I will lose the opportunity to treat you. Will you be quiet when I take off your gag?'

Bella nods.

I begin to pick away at the strands of string. As the gag loosens sufficiently, Bella lifts her head, opens her mouth and jolts herself backwards. I quickly place my palm tight against her lips. 'If you want to have any chance at living a life outside these walls Bella, you have to help me. We have to be a team. I can't fight the hospital and you as well. You might as well give it a try, because right now, you have nothing to lose.'

I am under no illusion. I know only too well that this woman is manic and violent. It was recorded by Catherine at our first official consultation and must suffice as a diagnosis agreed by a doctor sent from the Faculty of Medicine. I take a deep breath and release the pressure against Bella's mouth. Her eyes hold mine as I walk away and sit with my back against the adjacent wall.

Silence.

'Good,' I say softly. 'We shall start. Would you like a drink of water?'

Bella shakes her head and lowers it. A pearlescent light slips over the wall outside and in through the bars of the high window making zebra stripes on the floor.

'I have to know what medicine to give you. Bella, you're going to have to talk to me. Basically, you can say anything, anything at all, only not too loud.'

Bella says nothing. I look towards the door and a rolling, clattering sound like that of a trolley and also muffled laughter. The noises fade as they move away. I turn towards Bella.

'This place is evil, get me out of here,' she whispers, and spits vehemently to one side.

'Why are you doing that? What are you feeling?' I ask equally quietly.

'You will betray me like everyone else,' she prophesies.

'No, I won't.'

'I was her,' she says. 'No one believes me, but I was her, in another life.'

'Who?'

'Marie Antoinette,' she confirms, with a lift of her chin into the air.

'Talk to me more. What was it like being Marie Antoinette?'

'They cut off my head.'

'Why?'

She doesn't answer.

'Why?'

'Because I was special, not like the rest.'

'Special in what way?'

'I was the fucking queen,' she shouts.

Back at my apartment, I pace the floor. I am frustrated that I was unable to uncover any more information about Bella than that which I already know. I can see the words on the page written by Clemens – *Delusions of superiority; thinks she is a queen* and yet, the remedy is not *Platina*. The books tell me to wait. A homeopathic aggravation leads to improvement. But I can sense that it isn't going to happen this time.

'If you hesitate, if you don't know what to do when you come to the end of a consultation, do nothing. If in doubt do nought and in this way you are a true follower of the Hippocratic oath,' Clemens's words.

'Sometimes to do nothing is to leave a man in pain or in grave danger,' I replied.

'If you know what to do, Paul, you should listen to your instincts but if you do not then your active response is likely to be harmful, do we agree?'

'We agree.'

I have a rough charcoal sketch I made of Blanche on an easel. I have pinned the one I made of Manon onto the wall. Shadows fall on the paper as the sun slowly slips behind the buildings across the road. The light is inked. I am only good enough right now to cover the canvas in vast brush strokes of emotion like sheets of washing against the sky. I do not allow myself the luxury of such bald emotion, but instead drive myself mad with wondering which pursuit of mine I can allow myself to give up.

Luncheon with Edouard
Sometime in May

*'It is the hour to be drunken! To escape the martyred slaves of time,
be ceaselessly drunk. On wine, on poetry, or on virtue, as you wish.'*
Charles Baudelaire

'The most stressful thing in my life is relationships.' This
comment is from me. I am quite drunk, lunching at Tortini's
with Edouard. It is just the two of us at his usual table. We sit
next to each other on a bench facing into the restaurant. Close to
the Palais de l'Industrie, it is safe to presume that many of the
diners have viewed our art this morning.

The sound of laughter and chatter mingles with the clinking
of cutlery and the chinking of glassware. There is a sense of
lightness in the air. I turn towards Edouard and, in an effort to
see him without blurred vision, I pull myself backwards as if I am
longsighted.

'I'm so glad you showed up today Gachet, Paul, Doctor Paul
Gachet, how do you like to be addressed? Oh, it doesn't matter,
because, because if you weren't here today, if you hadn't shown
up, I would have been lunching alone,' he says, sidling towards
me. 'That woman over there with the lilac dress and the neutral
tan gloves and that stupid doily in her hair, look at the way she
sits, poised, so attentive to her companion. I would say she's
beautiful. What about you, wouldn't you say she's beautiful?
Anyway, it's a pointless question whether she's beautiful or not,
the point I'm making is that she thinks I'm a prat. To be honest,
they all think I'm a prat. *Le Dejeuner sur l'Herbe*, let's drink to it.'

I raise my wine. We toast. Pale gold liquid laps my glass and whorls like the ocean, but when the whorls hit my throat, I choke.

'My fucking masterpiece,' Edouard says, not specifically to me. He is looking bleary eyed at the jolly people. 'Let's talk about you. You were telling me of relationships.'

'Yes, right now, relationships worry me more than art.' I splutter and hiccough.

'Are you all right?'

A diamond at a woman's throat catches the light.

I rub my eyes.

'I'm all right, yes,' I say when the spasm has calmed down.

'What of relationships?'

'Difficult.'

'Difficult?' he says.

We both watch a pretty girl walking back to her table. She is fresh like the spring blooms in Camille and Julie's garden: platinum hair in a chignon with a mother-of-pearl comb, skin like cream, and jade-green eyes. She walks tall, turning this way and that way, as if she's dancing past the waiters. Edouard has lost himself and is smiling.

'I'd like to paint that,' I say.

'It's a Renoir, definitely a Renoir.'

'No, not that, the grey mother-of-pearl disappearing into … into a metallic lustre, of, of rainbow colours.' I have my elbow on the table and I lean my head on my hand.

Edouard turns towards me and looks me in the eye. 'Paul, I want to thank you for what you have done for my family. Leon's grown. He's tall now. Not sickly like he used to be. Must be something to do with the homeopathy,' he says, tapping his forefinger against his nose. 'And Suzanne's cough is gone in just a week.' He slaps my thigh. 'Although she has been a bit tearful,' he whispers in my ear.

'Family,' I say.

'Family,' he confirms.

Suzanne is not his housekeeper then, and the boy Leon … .

He sits back and hangs his arms inside his knees like a little boy, taking a deep breath and blowing outwards. 'Doesn't work for me,' he says, as he straightens his back. 'You have to believe and I'm too much of a realist. You heard it here first, Paul. Oh, but why can't they accept *Dejeuner* as just another piece of art, something new to admire like a *bite de luxe.*'

What doesn't work for him? Is he talking about relationships? It seems to me that on a personal level at least, he seems to sail through those like a yacht on a calm sea. His art, perhaps?

'If only there was a pill to make a man less sensitive.'

Then I realise, he is talking about homeopathy.

'It doesn't work like that,' I say, suddenly sober.

'What?' he asks, and shakes his head.

'You don't have to believe in homeopathy for it to work. It's not a religion. It's the most scientific system of medicine that we've got.'

'Well, doesn't work for me, all the same.' he says, turning away from me.

'The minimum dose. Potentisation. Infintesimal amounts of a substance too small to have an affect. It's impossible. It can't work. You might be cured by it but you, sir, are definitely a fool if you have ever believed in it.' I shout.

Conversations are curtailed on the other tables. Edouard stares at me. I lower my voice so that only he can hear me. 'We have proof that homeopathy works. Scientific proof. Jean-Paul Tessier ran a trial at the Hospital Ste Marguerite.'

'Please … .'

'I need to tell you this. Over 8,000 patients were studied and the conclusion was homeopathy works best and at 1% of the allopathic cost. They once thought the Earth was flat, Edouard. Now they think a nude in a painting has to be shrouded in fantasy.'

'But my gammy leg is still my gammy leg,' he says.

'You haven't received the right remedy yet.'

155

'Do you think I should come and see you?'

'No.'

'Why the hell not?'

'I don't think I would know what to do any better than Georges.'

A waiter drops a salver on his way to the kitchen. The noise pinches my face and lifts my shoulders to my ears. The world seems suddenly harsh.

'Right then, I'll get the bill,' he says, looking directly at me and putting on his top hat that rested with his frock coat on the seat beside him. 'This afternoon I'm going to visit Courbet in his studio. Come along if you like, I'm taking Victorine.'

I ride the omnibus. It's not a busy time and I manage to get a seat by the window. I refused Edouard's invitation to attend an afternoon chez Gustav Courbet. I have more pressing things to do. But as I sit here and gaze at the eerie reflection of my own face in the glass, I have time to imagine the scene:

A very large space with a glass roof and sunrays pouring down like an umbrella of light. Courbet holds court in the centre. An overlarge easel for his overlarge canvas, he paints *Basket of Flowers* in somewhat smaller proportions to the original. A dark background with a big white border, the light from within the picture is a luminescence for the petals and a trigger for their almost-scent. He paints with abandon, talks and laughs with his assemblage, but all the while, he remains focused and his brushstrokes precise. His sycophants marvel at the magic of it all.

Victorine and Edouard stand to one side. Out of reverence she is subdued in her attire, wearing black, although the dress is cut so low on her chest that her breath is visible. Attention is drawn to a jet broach where the fabric meets her flesh. It has limp beads hanging down to humour the onlooker.

Edouard has his arm possessively around her waist. He wears the same cream frock coat that he had on at lunch with a mousseline cravat and matching suede gloves. One hand is pressed upon the pommel of his stick, one foot neatly poised behind the other as he entertains Courbet.

The bus stops and I push my way to the front. I had not anticipated that I would alight here but I have just noticed we are in rue Hotel de Ville and decide to pay a visit to Suzanne Leenhoff.

The entrance is open and I step into the coolness of the hallway with its stone mosaic floor. A gilt edged mirror hangs on the wall. I climb the plush red-carpeted stairs and knock on a highly polished wooden door. Suzanne answers immediately with a smile that on realising who it is dissipates quickly. She pulls a shawl tighter around her shoulders. 'I'm so sorry,' she says, as if she'd done something wrong. 'I was expecting someone else. Edouard said he wasn't going to be painting this afternoon.'

'I've come by to see how you're getting on.'

'Please come in. I haven't been good,' she says.

'Thank you,' I reply, removing my cap and following her through to the salon. I sit down on the sofa with my cap in my hands. She sits primly in the armchair opposite. A slight breeze comes through the windows and the cut glass crystals of a lampshade make an otherworldly tinkle.

'Please, tell me how your cough has been since I last saw you. It's worse?'

'No, it's not worse,' she says. 'It's gone.'

'I'm relieved. I thought you said it's worse.'

'I am worse, Doctor Gachet. In myself I am worse. I used to have an uncontrollable cough and now I can't stop crying all the time. Your medicine hasn't cured me, it's just moved things around.'

'I see. Has this ever happened before?'

'Never,' she says, emphatically, raising her voice. Clamping her hand to her mouth she starts to cry.

'Suzanne, I think you are grieving. It has to come out.'

'How do you know that?' she asks.

'From our last conversation, it seemed to be that way.'

157

'What way? What way?' She stands and starts to pace the room. 'What way, Doctor Gachet? You mustn't presume because I *know* that I never told you that.'

The room goes quiet. I look towards the ground. I can hear the rustle of crinoline as she sits down.

'People cry when they're unhappy, mostly,' I say.

'I'm not unhappy,' she almost screams. When she speaks again her voice has lost its hysteria and is soft like a summer breeze. 'I have lost someone,' she says. 'Not a relative, a friend.'

'Suzanne, you don't have to tell me.'

'I think I need to tell you Doctor Gachet, if you promise me that my words will be received in the strictest confidence,' she says, once again her voice rising in tone.

'Of course, but you just need to give yourself time. It's the same for everybody. Grief is not an illness. It is part of life.'

'It is a man. Are you surprised?'

'No.'

'I was beautiful once.'

'You are beautiful now.'

'You don't have to lie. I like to think he loved me. I like to think I don't delude myself. It's just that lately things appear very different to the way they did before and they make me so upset.' She cries into her fist. 'Edouard and Leon hardly talk to me. They move stealthily around me like cats waiting to be pampered but I don't know whether I'll ever be able to cater to their needs again and be myself in the way that I was with them in the past. Am I making sense, Doctor Gachet? Please tell me that I am making sense?'

'Can't you talk to Edouard and tell him what you're going through?'

'Of course not.'

'I see.'

'But do you understand?'

'It is more complicated than just grief.'

'Exactly, it's so hard to admit even to myself.'

158

'You will grow stronger.'

She stops crying. Her lace handkerchief is balled in her fist and she looks aimlessly to one side. 'I think this is worse than the cough and I've said too much. I feel like I've betrayed him.'

'Honestly, you've said nothing except share your feelings and whoever the man was, or is, he has not been betrayed.'

She walks me to the door.

'Oh!' she says. 'I nearly forgot. Edouard has asked that you drop by the studio. He wants to settle what he owes you for both Leon and myself.'

'Please tell him I'll drop by.'

An Unexpected Patient
May 22nd

'Chamomile in the smallest dose seems to diminish in a remarkable manner over-sensitiveness to pain or the too acute sufferings of the organs of the emotions from excessive pain.'
Samuel Hahnemann, *Materia Medica Pura.*

The window in my kitchen/dispensary is open, voices sweep through to me from the well outside.

'*Merde!*'

A woman's laughter.

'Don't you even ask if I hurt myself?'

'Monsieur Breton, God did justice when you tripped up, ha, ha.'

'I won't tolerate you living here a moment longer.'

'Oh, but Monsieur Breton, you do have to. A few days ago we paid you in front of your policeman friend, enough for a whole year.'

'My policeman friend doesn't have a good memory.'

'That may be, but my husband would think nothing of causing a small accident and you are very clumsy, as we can see today, *n'est-ce pas?*'

'Madame, you are despicable and that man, I understand, is not your husband.'

'That's not the case in the eyes of our Lord.'

'And your Lord also has eyes for when a man breaks his ankle and a woman just stands there and laughs.'

'I have to go; I have a slot at the wash shop.'

I go too – downstairs to help the man.

In the well, the walls rise up like a chimney to the sky. Monsieur Breton lies on his side, on the damp, mossy paving stones and lifts one leg in the air supported by his free arm.

'Doctor Gachet, come quick and help, I think it's broken,' he says. 'Oh, my God, this is so painful.'

Monsieur Breton scrunches his face like a baby with colic, squeezing out tears that dribble over his cheeks. On one knee, I carefully examine his ankle. My touch makes him wince even more.

'Tell me what happened and try to fill me in with as much detail as possible.'

'Look, I don't have to tell you anything. I am in agony, I can hardly talk.'

His ankle has puffed out like a pudding but there's no hint of a break. A ligament tear is every bit as painful as a fracture and, although I can't be sure, this is what I diagnose. The treatment for a minor crack in a bone and a sprain is relatively the same.

'Monsieur Breton, I'm going to go up to my apartment and get a chair for you to sit on, then I will strap up your foot, all right?'

'Yes, all right, but be quick.'

I fetch the equipment and help him into the chair. Sitting cross-legged on the floor before him, I wind a bandage soaked with witch hazel around his ankle. He cries impatiently, 'Do you have to do that Gachet? It's fucking cold.'

'Monsieur Breton, I have a remedy for you. I think you need it.'

'What does it do?'

'It's *Chamomilla.*'

Chamomile, a flower from the *compositae/asteraceae* family, along with Arnica, Calendula, *Bellis Perenis* (daisy) and *Echinacea* are all remedies that hasten the healing of injuries.

'But my daughter gives it to my grandson for teething. It's for babies.'

'Precisely,' I say, slipping one under his tongue.

The Homeopaths Convention
May 23rd

'An artist, under pain of oblivion, must have confidence in himself, and listen only to his real master: Nature.'

Auguste Renoir

Maybe I need *Chamomilla*. I have just emptied a dozen boxes on the floor, kicked the contents and banged my fists upon the wall like a tempestuous child. I've been through every piece of correspondence from Clemens. I've read every aphorism in the Organon of Medicine and still I don't know what remedy to give Bella. Hastily, I undo the buttons on my shirt and tear it from my body, toss it away from me and watch as the cotton flares amongst the flaming logs in the grate.

I sit on the sofa I have drawn up close to the fire. My face smarts and burns and I'm happy for the discomfort. I recognise that I am in desperate need of good advice. I don't have time to write and wait for a reply from Clemens and even if I did, his answers are often illegible these days and not filled with such great wisdom; he is a very old man. And then it comes to me. I prod the fire maniacally with the poker separating the logs so that soon there will only be dying embers there. I put on my coat and walk across town to the Hospital Ste Marguerit, where Tessler finished his studies in 1851. I have no logical reason to go there. Instinct is taking me, an instinct that I am starting to question. Just the other day Charcot stopped me in one of the corridors.

'Don't you think, Doctor Gachet, that when a human being thinks differently from the rest of society that it is time for that person to start questioning himself?'

It is early evening. The air is comfortingly warm. The sun has already slipped down from the horizon and the fading light is true to the season. The hospital is still open to visitors although I get the sense that the porters are going through some ritual in preparation to close the doors. I report to the concierge.

'Name?' she says quietly, seemingly a softer woman than Madame Lemont.

'Doctor Paul Gachet.'

'You work here?

'No, I ... .'

'That's funny, I've seen your name, where is it?' she says, flicking her way through well-worn pages in a ledger.

'No, no,' I say, wondering what to do when this conversation finally gets to the point.'

That's right, you've come for the meeting?'

'The meeting.'

'Yes, The Homeopathy Conference, it's been going on all day.'

'Yes, yes, of course,' I say, clapping my hands. I received an invitation to this gathering a while ago. My peers are here to discuss the future of homeopathy.

'Ward four,' she says, pointing with her pen down the corridor.

I lean against the doorjamb. Jean-Paul Tessler is long gone. Outside Ward 4 there is a plaque on the wall that reads *The Samuel Hahnemann Ward* but the large oval room is empty of beds and patients. The air is dusty and rough like pumice in my throat. In the centre there are a dozen chairs placed in a circle. Men in dark coats occupy them all. When I enter the room no one turns around, no one looks up. They are all engrossed in a heated debate.

'No, no, no, don't you understand, you *must* give a single remedy that corresponds to the whole picture of the disease. It is impossible to cure the patient otherwise. You can palliate. You can suppress symptoms. But as Hahnemann said in the Organon

163

you have to give 'a medicine which among all medicines has the power and the tendency to produce an artificial morbid state most similar to that of the case of disease in question'. He said 'a medicine', not medicines. One medicine. I rest my case,' said a man of about my age.

Another responds, 'Well, there you are, you see, you haven't understood a thing. In later writings, even Hahnemann himself used more than one remedy to affect a cure and that bears true in my practice. *Rhus tox* helps with the pain in the majority of cases of rheumatoid complaints. Mercury cures syphilis even for the allopaths. Belladonna, scarlet fever, I could go on. If someone came to me with rheumatic symptoms and syphilis, I'd give two remedies. If their symptoms improve I will be pleased. I don't know why you have to make it any more complicated than that.'

Someone else stands up. 'I agree, but what about our colleagues in the Faculty of Medicine? If we explain this remedy is for this and that remedy is for that they will understand how it works. The methodology will be familiar. They'll stick a label on the bottle and sell our cures in a shop and then who will come to us?'

'It won't matter,' the original voice intervenes and rises to his feet. Because what you are practising Sir, might be in the name of, but it is *not* homeopathy.' He points his finger theatrically at his opponent, who responds.

'Your way is too complicated, too elitist. And how many cures do you actually manage to facilitate whilst you're messing around being intellectual and searching for the one, elusive, curative remedy?' He looks round, obviously proud of himself. Another man stands and then everyone is standing.

'Homeopathy has rules – the law of similars – like cures like – the most similar remedy to the complaint must be given.' The original speaker moves forward, pushing his adversary backwards as he emphasises each set of words. His opposer falls into a chair, slides backwards and clunks to the ground.

'It really does depend how you apply the law of similars,'

someone says.

'A similar remedy doesn't have to be exclusive, doesn't have to be the only one,' someone else replies.

Someone hits someone. There are shouts of 'Hey, hey hey.' More chairs fall on their backs. Two dozen fists fly seeking a target. Ha! A homeopathy brawl. I have seen enough. I doubt they will hear it – they don't seem to hear anything outside their own fixed ideas – but I let the door slam loudly anyway, hoping that they do.

Montmartre Night
25th May

'By adding to this the state of the mind and disposition accurately observed by the patient's friends and the physician himself, we have thus constructed the complete picture of the disease … .'
Samuel Hahnemann, *Organon of Medicine.*

A grown man hiding behind a tree seems absurd. And yet here I am. It is eight o' clock. Dusk, the in-between time that always sparks excitement within me. Fresco style clouds fade into darkness. The workday mood is over. Even the birds are silent now.

I wait to catch Catherine as she embarks on her journey home. Every few minutes I take a chance to peer out from behind my post. Charcot's light is on in his office. Ipsen has already left. I saw him sauntering off, swinging his satchel.

Now Catherine stands in the doorway. Perfectly poised, she sniffs the air like a gazelle. A shadow moves across the wall in Charcot's office. He could come to stand by the window at any moment and I have to make a choice. Catherine starts walking away from her job towards her private life. I make my decision and run across the green, my breath like a hurricane in my ears. My legs and chest ache, reminding me how lacking in wellness I am. I feel as if even the trees are watching me. I don't look up to see if Charcot has observed me. I keep my head ducked and watch the ground moving rapidly under my feet. When I reach Catherine I grab her by the arm and pull her to the side, up close to the building, where I know we can't be spied from the inside. Her eyes scream alarm. I place my hand over her mouth. I am desperately trying to catch my breath.

'One chance,' I pant. 'One chance is all they're going to give me. I need to work it out, Catherine. The remedy Bella needs, I don't know it. I have to do some research. Help me.'

'How?'

Some phantom life form is breathing down my neck. I look around, no one's there.

'By making an urgent appointment tomorrow morning to see Charcot. Then tell him you have word from me and that I am sick. Extend my humble apologies to Ipsen about a further delay in Bella's treatment. Tell him, I am using homeopathy on myself and have every faith that I will return to work within the next few days.'

I turn my head again and see Charcot. His belly precedes him. He stares ahead as he walks out of the door. Too fiercely, I push Catherine around the corner, use my body as her shield.

Helped by the driver, he climbs into a waiting hansom and settles himself inside the carriage facing the horse. There is no way that I won't be seen if he looks this way at the pertinent moment. I hold my breath. The preambles reveal themselves to me in sound: crunching of pebbles, snorting of horses, whip cracking. Then hooves start to take on a rhythm. Rusty wheels moan.

'Gee up there,' the coachman sings.

And the carriage is in front of me, black and shiny with plush, red leather, seats. Charcot keeps his focus ahead. The coach turns down the long driveway. I expect him to twist his neck and look behind. He doesn't, at least not until the hansom is out of sight. I let go of Catherine.

'I'm sorry,' I say, drawing my hand across my mouth.

She moves a few steps away from me, nods her head tentatively says, 'I have to go home.'

'Will you make the appointment?' I call, as she walks away.

'I will,' she calls back, running now towards whatever awaits her. My chin is down. I look up but it is already too dark to see her on her way. I explore my jacket pocket and pull out a match and strike it against a stone. From the other pocket I take out the piece of paper given to me by Victorine. The writing is unclear. I think it reads:

Père Laffaire,
1, Rue Marceau,
Faubourg Montmartre.

The flame dies. There are no lamps to light these grounds. I stub my toe and stumble on the rocks that surround the lawn. I hold my foot and hop to the end of the driveway.

'*Merde!*'

After several attempts to put my foot down, I eventually turn left, limping towards Montmartre.

Although sinister things do happen in its shadows, Faubourg Montmartre has its own pulse and it welcomes with vivacity. It is the land that Hausmann forgot on the outskirts of the city. Many labourers of Paris and poor romantic fellows of the art-world live and conjugate here. Narrow winding streets, many built on an incline. Buildings squashed together like prisoners in a cell. Small houses that are crumbling, home to two or three families sometimes more, and the rents are very low. Such a contrast to the broad haughty newness of the tree lined avenues of Champs Élysées, Bois de Boulogne, Ave Clichy and even Pigalle. But as I approach the first narrow street my heart is warmed by lamps burning behind stained glass windows that in the moonlight throw smudged colours across pebbles on the ground. The sound of an accordion floats down from the courtyard at the foot of Rue Ravignan. Before me a hill of winding lanes, I begin to climb.

I guess that rue Marceau is right at the top, close to a spate of gardens lovingly nurtured by ambitious growers. Wheat – hence the big windmill – grapes, vegetables. Camille's partner Julie once grew flowers on this land that she sold on the main streets in the centre of Paris. Also close is the beer garden, Moulin de la Galette. The sound of gaiety from there is magnetic. I find myself taking off my hat and dipping it in my pocket, whilst walking faster towards the promise I have made to myself of just one beer. But on such a balmy evening the place is overcrowded. There is not a seat to be had.

Here, even the poor dress up in finery: seamstresses especially; off-duty prostitutes; flirting househusbands wearing their one good suit. I people-watch for a few moments. A girl twists around on a bench laughing with a group of boys. A couple buy beer for an elderly woman whilst their children scrabble for coins beneath their wooden table. I wonder if Père Laffaire is here somewhere. He could easily be that portly man with a woman on his lap. I am jostled. It doesn't take long for me to decide that the beer will have to wait.

I have to ask several people if they've heard of Rue Marceau as there are a number of streets around here that are not even marked. At the same time I enquire if they know either Père or Bella Laffaire.

'Ah,' a woman says. 'Of course I know. It is the street of the cobbler Marceau.'

They are all corner buildings in this enclave. Not one of them is attached. Built crudely out of wood, the twenty or so dwellings are little more than huts. The first house has its door open and lamplight splashes out from inside. I walk up to it, hesitantly, crunching brittle grasses underfoot. A woman sits on the bare floorboards. She has four children around her. The party of five eat food with their hands. A boy of ten or maybe twelve is the first to look up. He has rounded cheeks, a frown and large deep-set beseeching eyes. He is wearing a double-breasted coat with large silver buttons, and his nose runs. So, this is the right place. The woman looks up.

'What do you want?'

'I have news of Bella.'

She looks down again, and scoops a wedge of mashed potato in her hand.

'Bella Laffaire? He said he went looking for her. Some woman paid her bail, he said. He's spent nights crying out there. Not in here. He said he can't stand it that she's disappeared. I told him not to come back until he's over it because I don't care about Bella Laffaire.' The woman stares me out whilst popping something small and round into her mouth. She chews then swallows. 'Where is she then?' she asks.

'Look, can I come in? This is a little delicate.'

'I'm not sure,' she says. A thin stream of oil glistens in the lamplight as it dribbles down her chin.

'I have your husband's note here,' I say, uncrinkling the piece of paper, holding it out, leaning forwards through the doorway although still too far away for her to take it from my hand.

'Now let's get one thing clear. He's not my husband. I would never marry him. He doesn't deserve it. And that Bella used to help him out, feeding the brats whilst I earned a few sous at the launderette,' she says, slapping the hand of one of the children who grabs something off her plate. 'The tart helped him out in other ways too.'

'Was she living here with you just before she disappeared?'

'That one live here! You'd have to kill me first.'

'Forgive me for asking, but I'm a doctor at the Hospital Salpêtrière and I need to find Bella's family.'

'He *tells* me he's her family.'

'What's she like, Bella?'

The woman spits. A fountain of saliva sprays the children's food and nearly reaches me at the door. I take a step backwards.

'If you see him, will you tell him that I called?'

I turn around. There is a man standing directly behind me. His fingernails are grimy. His lips are plump inside the edges of a shapeless beard. He carries a lantern that he holds up to my face.

'Monsieur Laffaire?' I ask.

The man laughs. His breath has the same smell as the fiery

alcohol in my dispensary.

'Naaah,' the man replies and walks on like a liberated scarecrow, the grass breaking beneath his feet. A little shaken, I make my way along a narrow beaten path back towards a cobbled road. It's early in the year but I can hear the crickets hum. My mouth is dry. I decide to go and have that beer.

The man with the accordion has come to Moulin de la Galette. His music brings a sense of abandon as couples leave their tables for the dance floor. Over at the marquee I order my drink.

'I'm looking for Père Laffaire.' I say to the bartender.

'He's heard you've been asking around. He's been waiting for you,' he replies, cocking his head towards a young man that I vaguely recognise from the cafés in the Boulevard des Italiens. He has long hair past his shoulders, gripping cold eyes and an athletic physique. His clothes are a gentleman's but there is a frightful scar on his left cheek and beside it the skin on his chin is puckered as if from an old burn. I surmise he is a wrestler brought up on the streets. He makes his way towards me all lightness and smiles.

'We can talk over here,' he says, paying the bartender for our drinks then leading me over to a table whilst the froth of my beer cascades over my glass soaking my hand.

'I know who you are Doctor Gachet,' he says, sitting opposite. 'I've always wanted to meet you. You're a great doctor. I admire your work. I've heard all about your cures. Alfred Pissaro, Suzanne Leenhoff, Gustave Bonnet.'

'Who told you?'

'I get around,' he says, leaning back in his chair, the scar on his forehead twitching slightly. 'I know a lot of things. For example, I know you give Victorine Meurent a special medicine to ward off syphilis. Now there's a lucrative business I wouldn't mind getting involved in.'

I get up to walk away.

'Please,' he says. 'You haven't finished your drink.'

'Who are you?' I ask.

'I consider myself a relation of Bella's.'

'But you didn't write the note and give it to Victorine?'

'You are very astute doctor. No, that wasn't me. But I did have it in my diary to pay you a visit. La Sâlpètriere isn't it, the hospital where you work? Do I speak to you, or is there another doctor I need to talk to about Bella's homeopathic treatment?'

I sit down again, a little stunned.

'That's better,' he says. 'The evening is fine. It's early. Relax.'

I stare at my glass. A trail of bubbles swim to the top.

'I'll come straight to the point. Bella at the hospital ... .' He looks at his nails and sucks on his teeth. ' ... is costing me money. Oh, and I forgot, I happen to know your lady friend, Blanche Castets. Not normally my type. Too difficult to deal with.' He takes a pipe from his pocket and stuffs it with tobacco. He strikes a match and puffs red sparks. Fragrant smoke rises in strands. 'But we had a nice meal together. If she had her way she won't be seeing me again, I think she finds me a little fierce. She likes the ballet by the way. Oh don't worry, I'm not going to hurt her ... as long as I get what I want.'

'I'm starting to find you offensive,' I say, rising to my feet.

'And I'm finding you trying,' he says banging his pipe down onto the table. 'I can't speak any plainer.' His face is reddened and very close to mine. 'I don't make requests, Doctor Gachet. You can have Bella but you have to pay for your little experiment. Think again about what you find distasteful because life can get a lot more distasteful than this.' He downs his liqueur in one, scrapes his seat backwards and walks away. He is gone in a second, past the trellis and the early jasmine. I watch after him as he slips between foliage and a white shop front fascia, remembering I've seen him before, with Bella, in a café, a long while ago.

Someone tugs at my sleeve: the snotty boy.

'Hello,' I say.

He approximates a smile and shuffles from foot to foot. I

search in my jacket pocket for a coin which I flip into the air, catch it and slide one fist over the other. I hold out my clenched hands, which tremble slightly, in memory of that last encounter. He points, guesses right. I try the trick several times until he looses then I give the franc to the boy. He shakes his head.

'Go on,' I say. 'You won it fair and square.'

He snatches the coin quickly but he doesn't run away.

'I want to help Bella,' he says.

'Can you read? Is this written by your father?'

He shrugs.

'Can I get you a drink?'

He shakes his head.

'How about a dance?'

He laughs.

'Will you talk to me about Bella? Tell me how you find her, that sort of thing?'

He nods.

'Come,' I say, leading him away from the café into a narrow street where we sit side by side on a doorstep.

'If she's happy with you then I think you should keep her,' he says with liquefied eyes.

'What's your name?'

'Paul.'

'We have that in common. I am Paul too. Pleased to meet you,' I say, extending my hand. We shake. 'Paul, Bella is in hospital. She's very sick with strange thoughts. I want to help her too. So, that's another thing we have in common. I need you to answer some questions. Is that all right?'

He smiles weakly.

'Tell me some stories about Bella, anything that you remember. It will help me to understand the problem a bit more.'

'Can't she answer your questions?'

'No,' I say gently, shaking my head.

'I won't get her into trouble?'

'I have nothing to gain except Bella's cure.'

Paul thinks for a long while. I wait for him and stare at the moon.

'Bella looked after me better than my mum. My dad loves her like a daughter, he says. But I caught him doing things to her, grown-up things. She used to boast a lot, and she told us about her wonderful apartment in Boulevard St Germaine with silk sheets and satin curtains. Robert used to say, "Yeah, right, so why are you still here then?" He'd get a swipe across his head for that.'

'Yes,' I say. 'Carry on.'

'She always had a story about people like the Emperor's wife. "Ooo, she's not as pretty or as cunning as yours truly," she'd say to the mirror whilst she put on her rouge. "I'm better than your mother," she used to tell us every day. "Never you forget that,"' he says, wagging his finger and puffing out his chest. 'And then she ran away.'

'Did she talk about the past, before she looked after you?'

'Her mum died. She always said, "None of this would be happening if my mum was alive".'

'None of what? Do you know what she was talking about?'

'Looking after us when she should be "out there lording it instead of scrubbing dishes in a hovel",' he says, holding his stomach and spitting the words out.

He talks on for a while more and when he finishes I notice he sits straighter, and his misty eyes have cleared.

'Did anyone ever tell you that you are a magnificently eloquent young man and a wonderful mimic?' I shake his hand again with emphasis this time.

He looks perplexed.

'You've just helped Bella,' I say.

He is still angry. I ruffle his hair. 'Go on, it's late. I'm going home now, thank you for your help.'

He hesitates.

'Go on,' I encourage further and watch as he runs off.

I make my way downhill towards the centre of Paris. My descent propels me forwards with hurumphing breath and legs that do not wish to carry me. The streets are dark with only a slight relief of intermittent moonlight squeezing through gaps between the rooftops. I'm trying to hold onto Paul's description of Bella but I can't control my cogitations.

'Bella at the hospital is costing me money ... I happen to know your lady friend Blanche Castets. I think she finds me a little fierce.'

I am angry with myself. I'm not usually a fighter but I should have knocked him senseless. The weasel, the pompous pimp.

I have arrived at Boulevard des Italiens. It is late. Somehow the whole evening has passed by. Only a couple of old sops sit on the pavement. They have empty wine bottles at their sides. Propped up against a shop-front, legs straight out before them, they sing some made-up aria without a tune whilst looking directly at each other's eyes. Three or four carriages with drivers line up outside the cafés on the other side of the road. The street lamps are lit here; the night is no longer sinister.

I stand outside the Bade. Blanche is there. She wears a floral dress, one I haven't seen before. She sits alone at a table facing the street. Her eyes are downcast. Her violin lies before her. It has one string curling up into the air.

At the back of the restaurant there are a group of doctors from the hospital. One stands with his glass raised. His colleagues sit beside him, having backed away to give him space. They hold their hands outwards ready to applaud. In a bucket of ice are several bottles of champagne. How very new.

I move behind the door to one side. I have to peer around a panel to see her. A man and a woman leave. He wears white gloves. There are shiny buttons on his shoes. She has a large magnifying glass hanging on a ribbon from her wrist. They push past me as they walk out the door.

'It's not like the Bade to have strange men loitering in the doorway,' he says, as they walk away.

A waiter brings Blanche a balloon glass with a wave of

liqueur – I think it's cognac. He lifts it off the tray onto the table and puts a small coffee before her. She sips. I imagine the liquor leaves oily deposits on her glass. She turns her head towards me. For one second I think she has seen me but there is no sense of recognition in her eyes.

The medical men are all sitting down now. A waiter brings the bill on a silver tray. He stands at ease and averts his gaze while his patrons sort the finances out between them. I bring my fist to my mouth and turn around, homebound.

I change my mind and move back to the window. Blanche's body trembles and I know she is coughing. Failure wells up in my throat. The doctors are standing, putting their coats on, kissing goodbye. I move around the corner facing the kerb but my back can still be spotted through the glass wall. The door creaks open. Male voices full and throaty in the air. The temperature has suddenly dropped. A cool north-easterly wind sweeps through the streets again and again. I imagine them in a gang, collars up, stamping feet. I hear their farewells of 'Goodnight,' and I suppose their hands are waving whilst their little crowd disperse.

'Where are you going? My man can take you,' I hear.

'No, that's fine. I'm happy to walk and clear my head – too much champagne,' another says, and in reply, a laugh that stabs the air.

'Let me take you home. You've got to be up early in the morning.'

I know the voice. It belongs to Doctor Beaune, a handsome senior medical man in his fifties with white hair and a neat precise cut to his clothes. It is well known that he lives alone and his camaraderie with orderlies is spoken of in hushed tones.

'I'm very grateful. Very grateful for your concern but it is precisely because I have to be up early tomorrow morning that I must walk to tire myself out and, as I have already said, clear my head.'

No more words. Just footsteps. It's hard to discern their direction. I place my hands in my pockets, stand on the kerb, face the road and hope for the best. It is hard to keep my head down when the pounding of leather on stone makes its way towards me, but I dare not look up. Instead, I cross the street. When all is silent I turn around and run back towards the Bade. I pull at the locked door handle then peer through the glass. It is darker than dark.

'Blanche,' I call, running through the empty streets in the direction of Quai d'Orsay. My heart thumps and bangs against my chest wall, paining me, for the second time in a day.

'Blanche.' I call repeatedly. I don't have the stamina and stop in the middle of the road, panting. There's no oxygen in my lungs with which to call out further. I stumble to the side, grab onto a lamppost in an effort to stop my legs from buckling. I imagine myself on my knees in the dirt having lost it all.

As my breathing slows and my legs recover, I contemplate walking the rest of the way to Blanche's mews. I hear laughter from an alley behind and footsteps coming towards me. I wonder if it is one of the doctors from the restaurant this evening, the pompous pimp – or heaven forbid – Inspector Fornier. It is Blanche. She has a black silk coat on with all the buttons undone and underneath it her floral dress. There are no pins in her hair. She makes me smile.

'We can't keep holding discussions on the street at night like this, as a couple we'll get a reputation.'

'But you have to tell my why you were screaming my name,' she says, walking hypnotically towards me.

'You heard?'

'Someone told me.'

'We're near the river. There's a bench there. At least let's go and sit down.'

She encourages me to take her arm.

'They told me you sounded desperate.'

'I am.'

'To see me.'

'I am concerned. There's a woman named Bella at the

hospital. I've been given permission to treat her homeopathically. I think I've told you about her before. I went to Montmartre to visit her family. To help me establish her remedy, I needed to find out more about her history and so on. Anyway, I got pounced upon by her pimp at the beer garden, he said he took you out to dinner and that you like the ballet.'

'Pardon?'

'Do you know who I mean? He said you find him fierce.'

'Oh, him.'

'You do know him then.'

'He's sometimes at the Bade. He always sits at the bar and and earwigs on everyone's conversation. I told him to stay away from me when he grabbed hold of my arm. No one talks to him, not even Victorine.'

She shivers. I put my arm around her shoulder and we watch the moon's reflection in pieces upon the water.

'Did you?' she asks, through a yawn.

'Did I what?'

'Find out what you need to know for that girl's remedy?'

'I'm not sure yet, but yes, I think I did.'

She whispers in my ear. I am conducting a homeopathic proving. The remedy is something people say to each other. I have just learned that 'I love you' are the most potent words. I close my eyes and cover her cold hand with mine.

The Medical Detective
May 26th

*'Now, in order to act really in conformity with nature, the true
physician will prescribe his well-selected homeopathic medicine.'*
Samuel Hahnemann, *The Organon of Medicine.*

I stand by the window. Blanche sleeps. She told me that she's not
coughing as much and no haemorrhages since she took the
remedy.

'It's come back again, but Paul, it's really not so bad.'

I've instructed her to take the remedy daily. If the cough
goes, to stop. If it starts again, to pick up the daily dose.

Looking out onto the river, I can't see their bobbing
movement, but I can just about discern the shapes of barges
docked on the other bank and a bird floating across the darkness
– no, I think it's a bat.

There's a pattern of shadows thrown across the bed made by
the lace curtains awash in moonlight. Blanche stirs and I hold my
breath. I don't want to wake her. I move towards where she lies,
stand over her, kiss my fingers and place them on her parted lips.
I feel the wetness of her mouth. Is it the way the shadows fall, or
do I see a faint smile widen her cheeks?

Already dressed, I leave. My legs ache from all the walking I
have done in a day, especially ascending Montmartre. You often
see old widows dressed in black clutching the very walls of the
houses as if life has conspired to throw them down the incline.
For me, I just wish I had some Arnica, Leopold's Bane, a plant
that heals bruising from injury predominantly, but also aching
from over exertion. You don't have to be a homeopath to

prescribe it, it always works well. I've heard anecdotes about men in brawls who have been given this remedy at the time of their incident and not manifested a predicted black eye. And in my experience, postpartum women heal in half the time. A small bottle of Arnica 6c used to be in my pocket the whole time, until I thought about the theory that if you carry it about with you, you are tempting fate in some way. Now I leave it at home. I regret doing so now. There will be no transport on the streets at this hour. It's a long walk home and it's dark. The moon has slipped behind a thickening cloud. Many of the roads are unlit. I have an idea for a painting. Midnight blue landscape, black shadows – from afar the two colours blend completely and any form is indistinguishable. Up close you can see the configuration. I will title it 'Night'.

When I arrive home the air in my apartment is chilled and saddened. Tomorrow I will check the walls for damp. I boil a pan of water on the stove; drinking chocolate will warm me.

Even at this time there are muffled voices coming from the well outside like whisperings in a bad dream. I take a chair to the window, sip the thick, sweet liquid and stare at the sky. I am tired but won't rest until I find Bella's remedy. Back at my desk I light a lamp and open my two *Materia Medicas*. Big tomes both of them, leather-bound, pages edged in gold and almost as thin as a layer of skin: *Materia Medica Pura by Samuel Hahnemann* and *Characteristics by Clemens von Boenninghausen*. Pulling up my sleeves as if about to dig a ditch, I abandon them and sit back in my chair to think. Five remedies come to mind:

First is a medicine for delusions that I have tested on myself. My experience of this drug is that one feels better than in normal humdrum life. Colours seem brighter. Music has more depth. Simple foods taste glorious. There is a sense of lightness that came over me both in body and mind like walking on air. Things felt so pleasurable, even ecstatic, so much so that tears can be produced from laughter over nothing funny at all. For me all it took was dropping an onion into the sink. There was also some sense of omnipotence, a feeling that my artwork was significant and as important as Manet's. But I felt like I was being dropped from a great height as the effect wore off. The true, blunt world was hard to endure. Yet, I had never before experienced such delight, and since then only with Blanche, for the primary effect is a feeling very much like being in love. I look in the books. Hahnemann says of Cannabis, *Sometimes a furious mania, so that he spat in the faces of those around him.* And yes, I can imagine Bella doing that but her overall state is not mirrored by the essence of Cannabis.

Next, I consider Phosphorus. What is it that I associate most with Phosphorus? It's compassion and sympathy almost to the point of pathology. Maybe Bella is sympathising with the historical figure of Marie Antoinette. Ah, but this is conjecture and the link is too tenuous for me to take seriously. It is almost as if I have created this association to feed my own laziness and to solve the problem quickly.

Forget Phosphorus. Belladonna then. Bella-donna. This poison must be the remedy. At last, my nerves are all sitting to attention even though my energy reserves are completely depleted. I rub my eyes. Belladonna is the remedy I associate most with the word congestion. Dry fever. Inflammation. Pulsation. Like a boil that comes to a head. Delusion and violence. The books say: *spitting and biting, fantastic illusions, frightful pictures before the eyes, frenzy and madness, chattering like a mad person, insanity, talks madness and folly, great restlessness, restless with anxiety.* Yes, it is entirely possible that Bella could need this remedy but there is nothing specific enough in the remedy description for me to shout 'Aha, I have the cure'.

Then there's *Hyoscyamous* (Henbane) that I know to have mania of an exhibitionistic nature. I read in Boenninghausen: *loquacious insanity, shamelessness, lasciviousness, kissing mania, furious, jealous, fear of being poisoned, unhappy love with jealousy, phantasies.* Added to that in Hahnemann: *extreme fury, he rushes at people with knives, he strikes and tries to murder those he meets, foolish acts, performs ridiculous antics like monkeys, sings love songs and ballads, insanity.*

How I wish I had been able to take notes when I was with the boy Paul. I am desperately trying to recall what he said, something about Bella boasting, a sense of superiority. That's right, when he was wagging his finger he was mimicking Bella saying, 'I'm better than your mother, never forget that.' And, 'None of this would be happening if my mum was alive.'

I recall the scene on our protest day. The man at the window with the caved-in face shouting that he was not going to pay her because he couldn't get an erection and Bella's response, 'The devil will have his way with you; what about the first time?' She is feisty. I will give her that. Her main delusion is that she is a beheaded queen. I think that I need to ask her more about Marie Antoinette. But for the purpose of finding her remedy, I have to believe that what I know now is the essence of it and if so, jealousy and unhappy love don't seem to come into it. In my mind I toss this remedy aside and recall the last one on my mental list for insanity, *Stramonium* (thorn-apple) – another plant. People who need this medicine are violent, they fear violence, so much so that they cling to people and things. I do not even bother to read the books. Bella is not in that state. The road to cure will not be found by using *Stramonium*. Of these five homeopathic preparations, the most similar is Belladonna but Bella needs a remedy with the expression of boastfulness and feelings of superiority that do not reflect the lowly life she leads. It is 4 am. Just for a few moments, I will rest my head on my desk. My bony arms will suffice as my pillow.

Falling asleep on a counter or a desk is becoming a bad habit. I can see by the light tumbling in and climbing over me, warming me up, that it is already morning. Time to get going although, unusually for me, I don't have to be anywhere soon. For a few seconds I think how nice it would be to begin painting that night scene and I contemplate a stroll to Père Tanguy's to buy midnight blue, royal blue and bitumen. Or pastels. I shall have to decide. But not now. Whether I like it or not, today is set aside to find the *Simillimum*, the most similar remedy, for Bella Laffaire.

With one hand on my lumbar and a stiff gait, I move like an old person over to the kitchen. Chocolate is congealed in my one and only cooking pot and I curse myself for not rinsing it out the night before. I put one hand through my hair, contemplating the job that at this moment appears to be beyond me.

'Pitiful,' I tell myself. 'Gachet, you are truly ... .'

I catch my reflection in the curved side of the pan. The image is a little distorted but not too much of a lie. The margins of my eyes are inflamed. I have the untidy beginnings of a beard, an unruly mustachio, wild hair that looks as if it has never been brushed. I stick my tongue out. It is thick and white. What a fright. I run the tap. The water trickles, then spits at me viciously. The rude pipes gurgle and grind. With a pumice stone I scrub the metal blind. The atmosphere of a dream is haunting me. Dogs. I was dreaming of dogs, dogs from my childhood that I learned didn't really die but have miraculously been projected into my adult life, lying on the floor looking up at me with their take-notice-of-me eyes. The room is filled with other dogs, not my own, curling around my legs, licking their wounds, or standing before me anticipating love. Then it came to me that they were all my dogs, although I hadn't fed them or walked them for years. The realisation of this hit me like a bout of self-loathing and this is what's haunting me. I scrub my hands clean.

I try meditation, focusing on a burnt orange disc against a coffee background like a planet in my mind. In the past, the answers to many questions have come to me this way. Nothing happens this time and I still don't know Bella's remedy. Maybe it hasn't been proved and so doesn't exist yet – what a bleak thought.

At my desk, with the *Materia Medicas* open, I count down the remedies in the index of both. Hahnemann has described more than one hundred substances in a thousand pages. Clemens has written up nearly one hundred and fifty preparations in equal space. I feel like I've been kicked awake only seconds ago, my eyes smart from lack of sleep. Rubbing my lids to clear my vision, I sit down, resigned. One of the *Materia Medicas* is open at page one in front of me. I begin to read. Only two thousand pages to go.

Page two hundred in *Materia Medica Pura*. All symptoms merge into one. I've contemplated the different characteristics of over twenty-five remedies. I like to think I have discerningly eliminated medicines from the 'possibles' pile, but the truth is that substances lost their individual expression over one hundred pages ago when my brain became a desert.

At dusk, I do not recognise myself in the shaving mirror. The candle in the soap dish by the sink flickers. My face is gaunt. There are definite lines around my nose and my mouth. Life seems to have aged me recently so much quicker than it ever has before.

What would Blanche think of me if she turned up now? I'm hypnotised by my bed and am thrown into it by some invisible force. Pulling the blanket up to my chin, curving my back, knees into abdomen, chin on breastbone, I become a mollusc. The cotton sheets beneath me feel cold and damp. I am desperate for a world where there are no expectations. It is what I hope to give myself when I fall asleep.

Day or night? Time is losing its relevance. There is a big notice on my front door:

Dr GACHET EST MALADE.

I ask a neighbour passing by in the hall, 'Please, tell Monsieur Breton, on your way down, that Doctor Gachet is sick and will knock on his door as soon as he's better.'

'You're right.' The neighbour wears a woollen hat that looks like a sunken syllabub. I wouldn't recognise her again except that her shape is incredibly round. 'You look like death and you wouldn't want to pass that on to anyone else,' she says reproachfully, folds of her skin wobbling under her chin.

Blanche arrives at 8pm with a simple supper of bread, wine and cheese. I have no appetite. We sit down to eat. I tell her how grateful I am that she's come round, but as she speaks I am tapping my knees with my knuckles.

'I feel that this is a decisive moment for homeopathy,' I tell her. 'Maybe I shouldn't have opened my big mouth, because I think I'm going to fail.'

'That's why you need food to keep you going. You have work to do and I have a book to read.'

The evenings are still cold. I light the fire. Work. I sense Blanche looking at me every so often. Eventually, she falls asleep and the fire, starved of wood, dwindles to embers. Having already read and re-read one hundred remedies I am still no wiser. I suddenly wish I had never heard of homeopathy, and also that I wasn't such an idealist but an ordinary doctor, enthralled by the mesmerism classes run by Charcot.

I carry Blanche to my bed and undress her. In her slumber she sprawls happily all over my side. Hovering at the edge I fall asleep with ease.

May 27th

When I wake Blanche is gone. I can tell from the position of the sun outside my window that I have overslept. A nervous shudder jolts through me. This is day three of my supposed illness. I must finish reading the *Materia Medicas* today. Tomorrow is Monday. I'm well aware that the pressure is my own.

Blanche has left me a fresh croissant – an innovation from the baker up the road, or so he says. Blanche assures me that every baker in Paris is claiming the same thing. There is a curl of fresh butter in a dish, slightly clarified by the burn of the sun through the window. There is a whole pot of coffee and a jug of milk without even one floating strand of hair from a cow's udder. A small vase of freesias with their overwhelming sweet scent intoxicates me. And a paper, L'Avenir, to keep up with the enemy. She knows me well.

Another dusk. I am almost at the end of Boenninghausen's *Materia Medica*. In Hahnemann's there are only two remedies to go:

Valeriana

Excessive mental excitement, with hallucinations of vision, hearing and the senses in general, as in pyrexial fevers. Uncommonly rapid change of ideas. Anxiousness. Fearfulness in evening in the dark. Hypochondriacal restlessness or excitability with trembling. Despondent mood. Morbidly excitable and irritable. Hysteria, with tremulous over-excitability of the nerves and very changeable moods and ideas … .

I turn to Hahnemann. He has not recorded notes on Valeriana. His penultimate recording is:

Veratrum album

… She is inconsolable about an imaginary misfortune, runs about the room howling and crying out, with her looks directed to the ground, or sits absorbed in thought in a corner, lamenting and weeping inconsolably; worst in the evening; sleep only till 2 o'clock. He pretends he is a prince and gives himself airs accordingly. Boasts she is pregnant. He searches for faults in others … .

The word 'boasts' catches me. I go back a bit and read again. *He pretends he is a prince.* Then I skip to the last line. *He searches for faults in others.*

I turn back to Boenninghausen, turn over several pages to the next medicine.

Veratrum Album

Mental confusion, deliria of insanities, mostly mute, religious or with pride … .

With pride, yes, with pride. My heart bursts with pride.

Monsieur Breton
May 28th

'Art is not what you see, but what you make others see.'

Edgar Degas

I'm outside Monsieur Breton's apartment. The last time I was here I was taken captive and tied up by the words of the policeman Fornier. Taking into account the sustained injury to Monsieur Breton's ankle, I am prepared to wait quite a while. Holding one foot off the floor, he finally answers the door.

'Doctor Gachet.'

His grey hair, usually combed neatly to one side flops over his eyes. His face is sallow and thin.

'You received my message.'

'You're a doctor; you're not allowed to be unwell.'

'It was selfish of me I agree. I will try and do something about my humanness in future,' I say, making a slight bow. But my words do not prompt even a vague smile.

'Would you like me to have a look at your leg?'

'How much are you going to charge me?'

'How much do you think such a service is worth?'

'I suppose you'd better come in then.'

He hops through the narrow, windowless hallway, holding onto the wall for support. I offer to take his free arm to help him but he shrugs me off. Where the hallway widens is a plain wooden chair.

'We can do it here,' I suggest.

He sits down gratefully. I open the doors to the adjoining rooms for more light and kneel to examine his swollen flesh. The

188

bruising has decreased and there is no inflammation. This is a very good sign.

'What happened to the bandage?'

'I took it off.'

'It would have been better if you had kept it on.'

'Pah.'

'Well, there's no point in my doing another one then. Can you put your foot down?'

He tries, his face blanches and he immediately lifts his foot up into the air like a balloon. Then he tries again and this time it rests lightly on the parquet.

'Good.'

'Have you taken the remedy?'

He shakes his head.

'Look, you have definitely torn a ligament. It's going to mend with or without a remedy. I have something upstairs that will make the healing much faster and will strengthen any weakness left in the joint. You may also have a slight crack in your bone. This too will mend by itself. Again a remedy would accelerate the healing process.'

'No thank you.'

'You should sit with your foot up, resting it on another chair.'

'I'll do what I please.'

'Right then,' I say, standing up. 'As you are taking the advice of your own internal medic, I don't think that it's necessary for me to call again. Don't get up. I can see myself out.'

I start to walk towards the door.

'Doctor Gachet?'

I turn around. Monsieur Breton is waving a ten-franc note in the air.

Relief
May 29th

'When you've got it, you've got it. When you haven't, you begin again.'

Edouard Manet

I only had *Veratrum Album* in stock in 30c but I need something stronger. Something strong enough to push a very sick vital force in the direction of wellness and so I've been diluting and succussing for the last ten hours. Now, as I walk towards the river, feeling as light as if I have just taken a dose of Cannabis, there is a sensation in my diaphragm that confirms I have the correct remedy in my pocket. As I enter the hospital, the chill of the high stone arched walls is palpable. Half a dozen statues look down on me with a frozen expression. Who cares? I sing 'Bonjour' to Madame Lemont.

'I have a message for you,' she replies, her voice slicing through the atmosphere. My footsteps and my heartbeat amplify as I make my way towards her. I expect an envelope containing my dismissal or a withdrawal of homeopathy from the list of treatments for Bella.

'Doctor Ipsen has been waiting for you. He wants to know as soon as you arrive.'

'Do you know where he is now?'

'With Doctor Charcot, of course.'

'I will find him. And Catherine Morrisot, do you have her timetable there?'

'She's in the library.'

Catherine is wiping down the shirt of a patient.

'Catherine!' She looks around. 'Look, please carry on with what you're doing. I just wanted you to know that I'm back with a remedy for Bella. When will you be available to take notes?'

'I'm not sure; I'll have to ask nurse Fontaine to take over my post. There's plenty of gossip. Doctor Ipsen's been drinking coffee all week with Doctor Charcot in his study and he has repeatedly come to me for news as to when you will be back. I would guess that they will want you to see Bella as soon as possible.'

In the reverberating hallway, she says, 'Samuel Hahnemann's "The Organon" is very interesting.'

'You've been reading the Organon?'

'Yes, I found a copy in a bookshop on my way home.'

As we arrive the door to Charcot's office opens as if it was known in advance that I would be standing there. Catherine waits for me in the corridor whilst I go in and talk to Charcot.

'You are better?' Ipsen asks, sitting princely in a high backed chair.

'Yes, thank you, I am.'

'And what was your self-diagnosis?'

'I diagnosed Bryonia.'

'Bryonia, how interesting, I have never heard of this ill. Is it catching?' he asks, his lips twisted into a supercilious smile.

'So you will be able to identify it when you see it: symptoms are better for stillness and hard pressure. There is irritability especially when disturbed, a fear of the future and a constant preoccupation with one's work. Bryonia is the Latin. Wild hops, the common name. It is also the remedy. And here's *Veratrum Album*, my diagnosis for Bella Laffaire,' I say, taking a vial from my pocket and displaying it in the palm of my hand.

'There is a nurse outside?' asks Charcot.

'Nurse Morrisot.'

'You seem to have found some attachment to Nurse Morrisot. Isn't she also the one who delivered the news to me that you weren't well?'

191

I don't answer him.

'Very well, tell her to bring that Laffaire woman in here. I want to be a spectator when your homeopathic remedy is administered. I'm giving a talk at the Faculty next week and will be happy to tell them all about your treatment. It will make very good after dinner entertainment, I feel,' he says waving his arm at me from behind his big oak desk.

When Bella is dragged in, supported around her shoulders by Catherine and Marguerite Bottard, so that the tops of her feet slide along the floor, I say nothing. When she lifts her head I notice she has a black eye and a broken nose, I say nothing. When her eyeballs roll upwards behind her lids from too much laudanum, I say nothing. When she slumps backwards in a chair and I pour a tiny white pilulle from the indented cork into her mouth and watch as the lactose dissolves against the wet flesh of her inner lip, a sense of relief washes over me. Catherine rests the ledger on the corner of Charcot's desk. He leans over to watch her record an entry.

'Record the time, Nurse Morrisot. Please don't forget to record the exact time and date,' I say, fixing the stopper back in the vial.

Doctor Ipsen looks from myself to Catherine several times. When she finishes, she and the other matron haul Bella up again to carry her out.

'Doctor Ipsen, you're not writing anything down. Don't you want to keep your own notes up to date?' I ask.

He looks bemused.

'You can rely on Faculty men not to forget anything.' Charcot comes around his desk, puts a hand on my shoulder and is ushering me out. 'It comes with the territory,' he says.

Different Perspectives
August 29th

'Work lovingly done is the secret of all order and all happiness.'
Pierre-Auguste Renoir

In the end, it is a thin line that divides between health and sickness especially when involving the mind. The process of recovery is not to be found, necessarily, in changes of organic material in the brain but in behaviour, whilst the impetus to act in an irrational way becomes slowly overwhelmed by sanity. It is incredible to see. I am witnessing this process now in the case of Bella Laffaire.

In a consulting room with Bella and Ipsen, he stands by the door as if fearing infection. She sits on a wooden chair in the centre. I sit on a bed by the window facing everyone. Catherine Morrisot is in a corner taking notes.

I admit to the discovery of one-upmanship and the enjoyment of disarming my competitor. Drawing out the moments that he has to endure watching the success of Bella's treatment, I sketch her face. Bella, who only four months ago was as wild as a beast, is in this moment beautifully composed. She is not drugged. For the last three weeks she has only had one teaspoon of laudanum each day before sleep. Bad dreams still haunt her. Have her up in the night attacking monsters, so I'm told.

Ah, but look at her now. The hard lines on her face have disappeared, replaced by smooth skin around her mouth and eyes, and her forehead has un-puckered. I can see that she is much younger even than we had at first presumed. It saddens me that I did not have the opportunity to sketch her some months ago, or for Victorine to paint her, for to have such a visual contrast on record would have been amazing.

'Bella? How are you doing today?'

She rubs her left wrist with her right hand and gives me a twisted smile.

'The string that they tie you up with at night is cutting into your skin?'

She shuffles in her seat. I put my sketch aside, take out a pot of Calendula from my pocket and rub some gently into her wrists.

'I'll make this part of your prescription.'

She stares at the floor.

'She is eating better, Doctor Gachet, and the other nurses report that she hasn't had any violent outbursts in the drawing room for several months. In the words of Marguerite Bottard …' Catherine shuffles through some papers until she finds one which she extracts from the pile and reads, '… helpful, that's how I'd describe her recently. No more talking nonsense. No more prancing around. I don't know why she's still here, actually, do you?'

'I told her I didn't, Doctor,' Catherine says, with the vague hint of a smile.

'Thank you, Catherine.'

I glance over at Ipsen. He has his hand over his mouth and his fingers are playing the accordion on his cheek.

'Bella, I'd say that things are improving for you then, but how do you feel?'

One tear bursts free forming a rivulet down the left side of her face.

'As soon as you are better, Bella, the hospital will dismiss you. Do you think you are better now? Please talk to me and tell me what you're thinking.'

'I'd be frightened to leave here,' she says, softly, with her hand over her mouth as if ashamed of the words seeping out. She quickly glances over her shoulder at Ipsen and just as quickly turns back towards me.

'You're afraid?'

'Yes.'

'What are you afraid of?'

'Of him.'

She glances over her shoulder once again.

'Doctor Ipsen?'

'Really Gachet, this is just ridiculous,' Ipsen says. 'Anyone can see that the girl is just making this up.'

I decide to continue with my sketch that I abandoned some moments ago. For several minutes the room goes quiet save for the sound of charcoal marking paper. The light has slightly changed, grown darker, the air heavier as if it might rain. Bella's cheeks have dropped slightly. Her lower lip trembles. It feels as if the room is filled with melancholia.

'Not the doctor,' Bella says.

I place the drawing beside me on the bed. The charcoal makes a grey stain on the sheet.

'The one that always comes here to see me and says I am his property. That I will always be his property.'

Ipsen stands with one leg crossed over the other. His elbows are crossed too. One hand holds his chin as he looks over at Catherine who scratches in her ledger with a fountain pen.

'Who is this man? Does he have a name? Are you sure he comes to visit you?'

'He is a very bad man.'

'What does he look like?'

'The devil.'

August 29th, late afternoon

Blanche and I are on the Island of La Grande Jatte. But for us, the place is abandoned. We sit on damp grass, our backs supported against tree trunks, looking up at the sky over the water.

'I can't see anything,' she says.

I check my watch again.

'You will. Only a few minutes now according to Le Moniteur.'

'I thought you didn't believe a word they print in that paper.'

'I believe this.'

'Why do you believe this and nothing else?'

'Well, why would they lie about this?'

'I don't know, why would they lie about anything?'

'Because it suits them for the public to believe lies about some things.'

'And not others.'

'Exactly.'

'And you really think Napoleon is behind it all?'

'Well, of course he is, he's running the country, isn't he?'

'Oh, my God! Look, Paul, look, I can see it!'

As the water stops lapping the bank near us, and the birds sit in the boughs as motionless as Degas' statues, there's an eerie quiet and a darkening without clouds. The sun's reflection on the lake has gone out and it isn't slipping under the horizon. It is halved. The moon, like an ancient Roman coin, has rudely placed itself over the face of that wildly burning star. Quashed, its rays squeeze out sideways. I stand. Turn around. The light is not exactly like dusk or dawn but something else, and the atmosphere ominous but peaceful, as I have never known it before. Blanche and I, are also silenced by this phenomenon. We are taller within its aura. Time is of no consequence until the spell is broken by the sound of flapping wings as a dozen birds ascend and then settle into an arrow in the sky. Ordinary light has returned but I am still moments away from myself, a mere shadow, blending into my surroundings, newly disturbed.

Blanche says, 'Paul, tell me, what you are celebrating?'

'Celebrating? Oh yes, Blanche,' I say, arriving back in my own body, like a traveller coming home. 'We're celebrating Bella, my patient at the hospital. She's getting better. The remedy is working.'

'That's wonderful.'

'This case is going to pave the way forward in medicine. Imagine, sufferers of mania, melancholia and hysteria, all being treated with homeopathy and recovering in hospitals all over the world.' I'm a figure pacing through light under trees freshly green. 'Going back to their real lives instead of sinking deeper into their madness. Becoming citizens of the world instead of locked up like prisoners in cells with rodents for company and their joints disintegrating from the damp and their rotting straw beds.'

There is a strange shape on the grass by the water. I move towards the bank, shield my eyes with my hand and look up then come back to finish what I was saying.

'Ipsen, the Faculty man who is watching my every move, can't stand to see it. It is like a competition for him, my medicine against his. He is tied to the past and the old way of doing things, but the case has been meticulously recorded and there are witnesses, Blanche: Catherine Morisot, and even that old flagship of Salpiêtrière, Marguerite Bottard.'

'How does it work, then, your homeopathy?'

'Have you ever wondered what propels the earth to spin on its axis? What turns the tide? What makes the moon cover the sun? Or spermatozoa collide with ovum? What makes you and I alive and different from a dead person? Hahnemann termed this

197

force, this energy, this something-other living inside us, as the *dynamis*. It is to the dynamis that homeopaths direct their remedies. They are messages, which if correct, instruct the body to heal itself. How about that for an answer?' I say, warrior-chested.

Blanche cocks her head

I take a few more paces. 'What?' I say, offering out my hands to pull her up.

'How will we celebrate?' she asks, a little huskily.

I lead her towards the clearing.

'How about the sighting of a solar eclipse?'

September 1st

It felt like a holiday. I took Blanche to visit Camille and Julie in La Varenne. We stayed for the weekend. On Sunday, whilst Blanche and Julie tended to Lucien and prepared a meal inside, Camille and I sat in the garden drinking *vin blanc* and smoking cigars.

'It's about time you showed them how that medicine of yours works. If it wasn't for you, my brother Alfred wouldn't be alive today.'

'I'll drink to that,' I said, raising my glass.

'I'll drink to that too,' Camille said. 'A santé'

Our glasses clashed and wine spilled over the sides.

'Come let me pour you some more,' I said, tipping more alcohol into his glass. 'Never before has "a santé" been a more appropriate toast.'

'I'll drink to that,' Camille said.

'I'll drink to that too.'

We went on and on like that the whole afternoon, becoming quite drunk and immune to the scenery: nature's palette of yellows, reds and greens – poppies, daffodils and grasses. What will soon become a mass of skeletal trees, a climbing frame for squirrels and a bald elevation for old bird nests is now in full bloom – breathtaking, all of it, especially when drunk, even on a stern day with a hidden sky.

And that is why I am nursing a sore head as I sit with Catherine on a bench in the grounds of the hospital. If the weather is fine, we meet there once a week at lunchtime for a picnic to discuss homeopathy, in which she seems to have developed a particular interest since reading the *Organon*.

She has finished eating and bends down towards the grass.

'A simple daisy,' she says, pulling the plant up from the root and twirling it between finger and thumb. '*Bellis perennis*, a homeopathic remedy.'

'Well, not quite,' I say, and she looks at me quizzically. 'It only becomes homeopathic because of the way it is prescribed, otherwise it's just a daisy.'

'And when it's potentised?'

'Then it's just a substance that's been potentised, until it's given to the patient according to the law of similars. *Bellis perennis* is a remedy for bruising and injury to the soft tissues. I think the common daisy has a soul too. Think of where it grows, so vulnerable to getting trampled underfoot.'

'I like the idea that a flower has a soul.'

'Now let me tell you something else. The law of similars can be applied to anything, not just remedies that we potentise. For example, if you burn your finger you will find a better balm in soaking it in hot water than cold. Cold will give instant relief but will hurt more when you take your finger out and it will not stop the skin from blistering whereas hot water will.

'Some time ago, I watched Bella bite a nurse's hand in the library – a particular nurse who I will not name, although you will probably know who I mean when I say that she always treated patients roughly. I've been observing her ever since and I can tell you, she's a little bit more wary and restrained these days. Like cures like, wherever you find it in life, that is homeopathy.'

'What happened to you when you took Cannabis? I've got an aunt who has a urinary problem. I matched the symptoms by looking in the book you gave me and it's significantly helped but now I want to understand more about this remedy.'

I look at my watch.

'That's a long one. Ask me another time.'

We usually end our conversation with a brief discussion of Bella. Time is running short but Catherine's observations are important to me and I don't I want today to be any different.

200

'The case of Bella Laffaire – how do you think it's going?' I ask.

'Three months and she's almost off the laudanum. Her speech seems to be less and less deluded. I think it's going well, don't you?'

'Are you sure?'

'Am I sure of what?'

'You don't think this very bad man is just another of her delusions?'

'No,' she says, shaking her head and twisting a serviette around her middle finger.

'What is it Catherine?'

'He comes every week. He spends half an hour with Bella and he always has an appointment with Doctors Ipsen and Charcot.'

'You never mentioned this before.'

'I'm always asked to escort him to her and wait outside. At first I thought he was a member of the Faculty. Then Doctor Charcot said that he was Bella's brother.'

'What does he look like?'

'Evil. Controlling.'

'Right.'

I do not knock or announce myself. I do not take into account what he might be doing, who he is with, or if he has an appointment to demonstrate his genius. I do not care. I walk straight into the study of Doctor Jean-Martin Charcot.

'How dare you, Gachet,' he says, rising from behind his desk.

'The man that comes every week to see Bella Laffaire. Who is he and why does he come here?' I demand.

'I don't know what you mean.'

'Don't you? I really thought that when Bella told me of a man who comes to see her, it must be another of her manic delusions but no, I've since found out that he really exists.'

'Gachet,' a red-faced Charcot screams, 'At least shut the door.'

I accede to his request.

'If you must know, he is Bella's brother, a gentleman and a very astute businessman. He has agreed to look after and care for Bella when we proclaim her well. You are going to cure her Gachet, isn't that the idea?' Charcot says, trying to be calm and sitting down behind his desk.

'He's not her brother. He's a man who earns money from her by immoral means.'

'That's a very serious claim. Do you have any proof?'

'It's obvious; I can't believe you don't see it.' I bang my fist upon his desk.

'A doctor of your standing surely knows the difference between hypothesis and fact. Now I'd like you to get out,' he says.

I sit in a café on the left bank and order Beaujolais. Outside, it is raining. The sky is a mass of lead cloud. On the opposite wall hangs what I think is a Degas, in a very dim light. I get up to inspect the ballerina sketch on a lime green background. There is no signature but the attention to detail of the dancer's calves is unmistakable. The plain, thin wooden frame is coming apart in one corner. Not one of Père Tanguy's. I miss it; I haven't painted for months.

'I will put the wine on your table, Monsieur?' The waiter asks, a full carafe and a glass on his tray.

'Yes please,' I say, turning around.

'And Monsieur, that lady at the entrance, she requested me to ask if she can join you at your table.'

'Yes, of course,' I say, looking up.

'Doctor Gachet,' Suzanne says, her coat and hat like a suit of armour as she sits broad between the arms of the narrow chair that's instantly wet from her clothes. 'I saw you through the window and realised I have some important things to tell you. It's not just because I wanted to get out of the rain.'

'I'll get another glass,' I say motioning to the waiter

'No, please,' she says, waving both her hands. 'Leon told me that you've dropped by a few times when I've been out and well, I just wanted to say that I'm back to my old self again.'

'And no cough?'

'No, no cough for quite a few months.'

'The magic of homeopathy.'

'I don't want to mislead you. I'm not sure that homeopathy had anything to do with it but I am better, so thank you, and at the last visit your words were very comforting.'

I manage a quarter-smile.

'Anyway, more importantly, Edouard often asks why you haven't gone along to his studio to collect your fee. I do tell him that I haven't seen you for quite a while.'

I hit my forehead with the base of my palm.

'I keep forgetting. Please tell him thank you and I will try and get there soon.'

Master of the Art
September 15th

'There is only one true thing: instantly paint what you see.'
Edouard Manet

The bell to the little shop tinkles. Père Tanguy and I both look up from the mixing bowls where he has been making some pastel paints for me. He's asked me to come back in a few days but I'm so fascinated by the process, I have stayed to watch him blending a pigment with clay and Arabic gum. He moulds it into sticks and leaves it to dry. The interesting part for me is the deftness of his hands and the way he instinctively knows how much pigment to add to the clay, and how wet the clay must be, which seems to somehow vary with each colour and shade. I ask him, 'But how do you know?'

'I just know,' he replies, shrugging his shoulders and carrying on oblivious to Edouard who saunters forward, leaning on his stick a little more heavily than I've ever seen him do before. Tanguy is also oblivious to the crowd of around twenty people who now stand outside his shop – adults making a frame around their eyes as they peer through the window and children with their noses and tongues pressed to the glass. Their bodies must be making a shadow across his sightline but the lack of illumination doesn't seem to bother him.

'Hello, hello,' Pére says, flattening out four sides of a stick of midnight blue with the pad of his thumb.

'I'm sorry about the entourage,' Edouard replies, though judging by the amusement on his face he's not sorry at all.

Since the Salon des Rèfuses, caricatures of Edouard and his

work have appeared in the papers on an almost daily basis. Now, I'm told, he hardly has time to lunch at Tortini or to turn up later at his precious de Bade because of the society lunch parties and soirées that he is constantly invited to. I also hear he is in negotiations with Paul Durand-Ruel, who will sell, and apparently pay for, some of his paintings in advance. No other modern artist can claim such notoriety, such fame.

'Ah, Paul, I'm so pleased I've seen you here. Perhaps you will walk back with me to my studio when I'm done? I'd like to pay you. This man is a genius,' he says, turning to Tanguy who nods absently as he gets on with his work. Edouard carries on speaking regardless. 'He has cured two members of my family. Two. With people dying from coughs all over the city, it's a bloody miracle, that's what it is. Hey Tanguy, don't you agree?' he asks, inspecting the artwork all around the walls.

'I agree. I agree.' Tanguy answers, still engrossed in his task.

'I didn't know. Gustav Courbet comes here too. We should all feel a little humbled to be in the holy man's company on this wall. And Monet, Monet, Monet. What's your name? They ask. I tell them, Edouard Manet. Is that the same as Claude Monet? No!' He swivels around from his inspection of the wall and nearly falls. I reach out to steady his arm.

'Thank you.'

'You're welcome.'

'And so, Doctor Gachet, how does it go?'

He doesn't wait for an answer.

'I've come for emerald green, blood red, light, light pink, whitest white, earth brown and a pot of Cézanne's black, all in oil.'

Someone bangs a fist upon the door. In seconds there is the drum roll of a multitude knocking. Père Tanguy drops his stick. It disintegrates into a messy mound.

'My word,' Edouard says, 'Is that all for me? And you haven't even locked the door. What restraint shown by the great Parisian public. Or do you think they are all too stupid to notice the entrance is not barred to them? They could all be with us having a party whilst Paul and I purchase paint.'

Edouard turns towards his audience and with one finger underneath the brim of his hat, pushes it away from his forehead so they can see his face. Seconds later, he turns his attention back to us.

'I can come back for my pastels tomorrow,' I say, feeling a little hemmed in by the crowd and thinking I can leave through the back door.

'What are you? A man or a wimp?' Edouard asks. 'Take your paints and go if you must.'

'They are not ready yet,' I say.

'Have you been drinking?' Tanguy asks Edouard.

'Yes. So?'

'It numbs the senses and that mob is making a terrible noise,' Tanguy says, and in his haste drops a block of resin, which bombs onto the table.

'Don't worry my friend, through your colours the world is recreated. Take your time,' I say.

Edouard cocks his half-turned head and examines me keenly.

'Very good, Paul. Eloquent. I wish I'd thought of that.'

'You're lucky. You don't have to. Your art says it all,' I reply.

He displays his palm for me high up in the air. I grab it and feel like a musketeer.

We walk through the throng. I'm behind Edouard, watching as grubby hands reach out to touch him. Within moments the heavens roar and the rains cascade. The rabble disperses in a myriad of directions. Both Edouard and I pull our coats over our heads. Edouard holds his walking stick high up off the ground, which causes him to falter. I reach out to steady him.

'You can never get a bloody hansom when you need one,' he shouts.

I see one on the corner and run to hail it down. Once settled inside, Edouard speaks:

'I can almost taste the colours in my pocket. Sometimes I crave their smell. It's all part of the experience, like a sensual dream. I spent the whole morning setting the scene for my next painting – inspired by the greatest of Muses – Victorine. She should be there waiting for me when we get to the studio. I hope she managed to persuade her African friend to come along.'

'I haven't seen her for a while.'

'She gets away with it. I don't know how she gets away with it. She can get away with anything, that girl. Not to capture her I-don't-know-what on canvas would be criminal, don't you think?'

Edouard looks out of the window at the rain then all at once his attention is drawn to the interior of the carriage. He stares straight ahead. 'It will be my Olympia,' he says and a flame from his fire leaps up inside my throat.

I am transfixed. Edouard has Victorine naked on a bed, propped on bone-white pillows and lying on a deeply cushioned bedspread. She wears only a leather thong in a bow around her throat. Her left wrist suggestively covers her vagina and holds her right thigh. Every time Edouard looks up from the canvas they lock eyes. She's a swirl of pink and creamy skin that enfolds a perfect female form.

'Victorine, my lovely naked champion, we conceive together like making a baby. You inspire me, you … .' He waves his paintbrush in the air and spots of emerald-green land on the wooden floor like an indoor pyrotechnic. Beside the bed an African woman stands holding a bouquet of flowers. She wears a maid's uniform of bold fleshy pink.

'Vivien, Vivien, please, look at Victorine!' Edouard shouts, as a black cat leaps up and walks across the foot of the bed.

'That's brilliant,' Edouard exclaims. 'It has to go in. At Tanguy's I was thinking, why do I need a pot of Cézanne's black? Paul, are you all right sitting on that broken chair?' He affords me a slight glance.

'When a man is in the right place at the right time then

207

everything goes right for him. I am in the right place now, my darling Victorine.'

I look around at the enormous high ceiling as if the whole of an upper floor has been cut away. This space was probably once used by a blacksmith or was a stable for horses or both. Even now there is the odd stray strand of hay upon the floor.

Edouard's art is stacked against one wall, including *Dejeuner sur l'Herbe* facing outwards, still unsold. On the other side of the room is a painting of Suzanne sitting on a sofa in their living room with the boy Leon standing behind her. Suzanne is portrayed with the face of a young girl whilst Leon, standing behind her, is seen as a young man. I look away from this picture to what Edouard is painting now, an unashamed courtesan, a common fantasy for the average bourgeois male.

At Père Suisse the talk is all about Edouard. It is a very small class: just Camille, Armand, Henri and myself. We have a female model, one dressed rather primly, sitting upright in a chair. We all sketch her, concentrate on her body, gauging the strength and shape of muscles beneath clothes.

'Did you say as you came in that you bumped into Edouard?' asks Camille.

'At Père Tanguy's this morning before I came here.'

'You were there all morning?'

'No, no I went along to Edouard's studio to watch him paint for a while.'

'And did you get paid?' Camille says, grinning widely. 'Let me guess: by cheque, signed Madame Manet.' I do not say anything, although he is totally correct.

'We don't see him. He no longer sits with us at the Guerbois,' says Armand.

'Things have taken off for him,' says Henri.

'He's painting Victorine nude again, I hear, and this time the scene is set in a bordello. Yet when I talk to him he is absolutely certain that he is not one of our gang. He really believes he does not need us and that the establishment will enfold him in their tender arms, not just for his character, but for his work as well,' says Camille.

'I can't see this happening when the Salon constantly refuses him. He is not Courbet,' says Armand.

I swallow hard and say nothing. My sketch is sagging. Henri's seems to be vital even with such a dull poser. Camille's is elusive amidst an aura of clouds. For me, everything is too solid, too weighed down: the body, a bland vehicle; the chair, just an object that allows the model to sit down. Everything lacks sensuality. And I'm acutely aware that Victorine is not here with the gift of femininity that she brings to the room.

Melancholia
October 26th

*'There is no doubt that when, in an effort to know the man, we
compare Manet's paintings with the curiously unsatisfactory
chronicles written by his friends – Bazire, Proust, Zola, Duret and
others – we are faced with an inconsistency that leads to the
conclusion, difficult as it is to accept in view of the artist's
legendary worldliness, that Manet was secretive, that much of
what puzzles us was intended to do so, that much of what appears
enigmatic is indeed rooted in mystery – in short, Manet cultivated
the disturbing character of his pictures.'*

Charles Baudelaire

A Père Suisse outing to the Louvre: creamy pox-marked stone
walls; majestic, mosaic-tiled floors; light pouring in from all
sides. Here is every artist's history – on plinths, hanging from
walls, in the very structure of the building, even absorbed by the
molecules in the air. Every time I come here tears prick the
corners of my eyes. I arrive at the room exhibiting marble
sculptures amid the faint timbre of visitors' muted words.
Victorine sits lonely on a bench. Opposite, Claude and Henri sit
and sketch frantically. She stares ahead in exactly the same way
that Edouard portrays her. Usually her spine is a bamboo rod.
Now she slouches. As her physician I am concerned.

I sit beside her.

'You're not inspired?' I ask.

'Oh Paul, Doctor Gachet,' she smiles and looks up into my
face and I can see that she has been crying. She laughs nervously
as I read her deep emotion.

'You're going to ask me if I'm all right. I am,' she says, sniffing. 'You're a good friend and a caring physician but please don't ask me about this. I'm just a little sad.'

I don't say a word but take a leaf of sketch paper, charcoal and a wooden board, from my portfolio. Placing the board on my knees with the paper on and the charcoal on the bench at my side, I fix upon *Captif*. Three centuries in the past, Michelangelo captured the male form like a living image with muscles that stretched and flexed. His statues breathe feelings. I notice *Captif* wears a shadow across its feet.

Victorine speaks again. 'They're all in the Batignolles having a celebration, the Manet family. I saw them through the window on my way here. Edouard saw me and came out. He had a letter in his pocket that he pressed into my hand.

' "I was going to come by later and give this to you," he said.

' "What is it?" I asked.

' "Take it. Read it later. It's a pledge."

' I asked him what he was talking about. I was angry. There was something in the way he was addressing me.

' "I think *Dejeuner* and *Olympia* are amongst my best works. You inspired them. The note is signed by me to say that when I sell my work for a decent price you will be rewarded," he said.

' "I don't need this." I told him, but he closed my hand into a fist with the letter inside it and put a finger to my lips.

' "Yes you do. It's an insurance policy. One you might need to call on."

' "Why now?" I said.

' "I'm going away tomorrow to Holland. I'm going to marry Suzanne," he said.'

She stops talking. I study the sculpture.

'I wasn't going to tell you and now I have,' she says.

'It will remain confidential,' I say, gazing at her tearstained face.

'He doesn't love her, not sexually, he told me that, but he'll marry her anyway with Madame Manet's blessing. She is giving him a gift of 10,000 francs. It's an advance on his inheritance. Have you seen how she treats Suzanne? It's hard to believe, isn't it?'

Could Leon be Edouard's father's son? Is this why Madame Manet both resents her future daughter-in-law and blesses the marriage? A family scandal kept secret by an arrangement amongst all players. But it is only supposition, and as Clemens has demonstrated, it's an unreliable explanation. It seems the more I get to know Edouard the less I know him. He is like a puzzle with a thousand tiny pieces; each one that's found and put into place represents only a fragment of the whole, a picture that as yet I can't determine.

I shrug. Start to sketch. But can I reproduce on paper such perfection as *Captif*? Of course not.

'Oh, I don't know. I don't understand my reaction myself,' she sniffs and laughs and holds a handkerchief to her nose. 'Look at me. Why am I doing this? I'm an expert in seeing men come and go.'

I do as instructed and gaze at her face. The confident, dynamic Victorine is nowhere to be found. She seems smaller, fragile, broken. A cold draught sweeps over us. She shivers. Her lips are tinged with blue. I put my wooden board on the floor and place my coat around her shoulders.

'Come. If you're not going to sketch today then at least let me take you home.'

'Don't you wish to sketch, Paul? Claude told me that he bumped into you and you've been looking forward to coming here all week.'

'It's all right, really. I can come back another time and so can you. I'm meant to be meeting Blanche soon anyway. It's fine.'

We walk down rue de Rivoli, past Père Suisse, through Hotel de Ville where Edouard stays with Suzanne, over the bridge with ribbed, moss-coloured water trembling beneath us. A vicious wind blows our hair from our faces. Notre Dame looms to our left and we walk towards it. Every time I pass this gothic cathedral I have to look up. Metallic green figures walk up and down from the spire: a fiddler, a priest, a dancer.

'Do you ever pray?' I ask her.

'No, do you?'

'No, but I consider myself to be a religious man.'

'I don't understand.'

'I have my own religion based on wanting to be an asset to the universe.'

'Do you mean being good?'

'Yes, I suppose I do.'

'Honestly, why don't you just say what you mean then? You always make things more complicated.'

'That's how I am.'

We arrive at her front door in rue Maître Albert. She places her key in the lock, enters the dark corridor then hugs the door. A black cat curls itself around her calf.

'What will you do for the rest of the day?' I ask.

'I don't know. Probably buy a bottle of cognac and write a song. Thanks, Doctor Paul, for bringing me home,' she says and her voice is low. She waves her fingers at me, I open my mouth but before I can say anything she closes the door.

I have time, but not enough to make it worth returning to the Louvre, so I go back to the café where I had breakfast this morning. I sit facing the window and the Seine. Henri walks towards me. I stand and wave and he joins me.

'That's good. I've been looking for you. I'm pleased I found you. I guessed from the way you went off and didn't say goodbye that something is wrong with Victorine.'

'Did you know Edouard is getting married to Suzanne?'

'Oh, really?'

'You don't sound surprised.'

'How can I be? Whenever he's drunk and morose he's always moaning that one day he'll end up wed to her, and if you'd ever spoken to Antonin about his friend, he would have you thinking that Suzanne and Edouard were once Romeo and Juliet. Surely,

Victorine must know she's not marriage material. What did she expect?'

'Not to be affected by the news,' I say, a little stunned, certainly I hadn't been expecting yet another twist in the tale.

We order coffee.

'Has Claude stayed at the Louvre?'

'A messenger brought a letter. He's been summoned by his father.'

I nod.

I know Claude is dependent on his father for money and that he bears a grudge about it. It seems that somewhere along the line we all have a price to pay. As if reading my thoughts, Henri says, 'I'm planning to go to London to get away from this place where not one of us, with the exception of Courbet who never paints outside, is considered worthy. In England, they withhold their emotions and appreciate the avant-garde. I've been told that my work will sell really well there and I'm more than ready for a bit of that.'

At this moment, it seems inconceivable for me to be anywhere other than France and more specifically Paris. London has a reputation for being without passion, grey and cold. Paris, as harsh as she can be, makes me feel alive.

'And what about love?' I ask.

'A handicap in the present clime. Look at Camille: painting night and day then walking the streets in his old Russian hat looking for a buyer. Too many times he's gone cap in hand to his mother who treats him like the door-to-door salesman he has become. Are you seriously asking if I want to live my life like that? No thank you. You're a doctor, it's different for you.'

'Everyone has their problems.'

'No,' he says. 'You paint, you have a profession, you earn your own money, get on well with your parents – who are both still alive – and you have a lovely lady friend, so I hear. No, you are definitely all right.'

I am with Blanche in the Tuileries. It is inclement, hardly the well-to-do scene that Edouard painted last year. The wind whistles and slaps our faces. I put my arm through hers and hold both her hands in my own. We walk through the trees under an umbrella of russet and yellow leaves, whilst a brown carpet crunches underfoot. The gardens are almost deserted. A few solitary gentlemen fix us with strange stares that make me wonder who is odd – them or us? A nanny pushes a squeaky perambulator. It is the first time I have ever seen one that is not a sketch in a newspaper. We stop and ogle at the sight of this recent invention.

'Do you think in wanting more of you I am being selfish?' she asks.

'I agree, we never have enough time together, just us two, but I am miserable when I'm compromised in the things that I do.'

'I think I'll write a symphony, and when you want to be with me I will tell you I can't.'

'No, seriously, I think you should do that. You're a brilliant musician and composer.'

'You say that because you love me.'

'No, I say it because I think it. And I love you. They're two separate things.'

She looks at me quizzically but her smile is broad. She squeezes my hand.

We start walking again. Two figures stroll towards us. One is tall and thin wearing a navy coat with a white lace collar. The other is shorter, slightly more rounded, with black stockings and scuffed shoes peeping out from under a black cloth coat. I recognise their conjoined gait long before their faces become clear. I have seen them walking off together many times, one woman towering over the other, holding onto her ward as if at any moment the shorter of the two will slip away. I am taken aback. I start walking faster to reach them quicker. I intend to make a fuss. As I pull on Blanche's arm, she asks, 'Do you know those women?'

At that moment, the taller one tightly shakes her head as the two stroll past.

'Paul, I asked you a question,' Blanche says.

'Yes, from the hospital,' I answer, looking over my shoulder so that now it is Blanche pulling me forward.

'What's the matter? You've gone white.'

'Something must have happened. This is not good news. Nurses don't have permission to take patients outside the hospital grounds.'

'Who are they?'

'Nurse Morrisot and Bella.'

Blanche nods knowingly and takes a big stride.

'She doesn't look as if she is insane,' Blanche says.

'You couldn't tell in passing but she isn't, not anymore, not in my understanding. The homeopathy is working. I don't believe in coincidence, Blanche. There must be a reason why we should catch them here. Obviously, whatever's going on I'm meant to know about it. I'm going to run after them.'

'Do you trust her?'

'Who?'

'The nurse.'

'Strangely enough, I would have said one hundred per cent until now.'

'She seemed to indicate that whatever's going on she is handling it.'

'Yes, she did. But I'm the doctor. I'm responsible.' I look over my shoulder. Catherine and Bella are walking through a gate into the street. They are heading in the right direction for the hospital. I reflect on Catherine's part in Bella's treatment. She has proved herself to be intelligent, responsible and caring. She has been an ally. I don't know what she's up to now but I decide to award her my trust.

'If you want to run after them ... .'

'No, it's all right, Catherine knows what she's doing.'

'Are you sure?'

'Yes. Yes I am.'

'Then tell me about your morning?'

'I went to the Louvre to sketch.'

'And I wrote a melody. For you.'

'For me?'

'Yes, but it's not finished yet. What about the Louvre?'

'I was with Claude, Henri and Victorine but no one stayed long. Claude was summoned by his father. Victorine was upset and I walked her home. Henri came to look for me. It was all a bit chaotic, really.'

'Oh, what was wrong with Victorine?'

'Edouard just told her he is getting married to Suzanne.'

'How awful. For her, I mean. So, what's she doing now?'

'I don't know. She said she's going to buy a bottle of cognac and write a song.'

'I think we should go there.'

'What? Now? To her home?'

'Yes.'

'Why? She made it perfectly clear that she wants to be alone.'

'I just want to see how she is.'

'You hardly know her.'

'She's a friend of yours and a fellow musician.'

'This is our time together. Are you sure?' Blanche tugs strongly on my arm and clutches the cloth of my jacket as she propels me forwards. We head in the direction of the rue de Rivoli where Blanche accosts a woman with a wheelbarrow.

'Madame, I'd like to buy some vegetables.'

'You should have come to the market, I'm on my way home.'

'I will take the rest of your onions, peas and mint.'

The woman drops the handles of the wheelbarrow with a thump. Hands on hips, she huffs, bending her back into the beginnings of an arch and revealing a white apron beneath her coat tails, stained by greenery, mud and tomato juice.

'Only if you take the potatoes and the onion flowers as well,' she says.

Blanche lets go of my arm and elbows my chest.

'Yes,' I say, as a matter of course. The truth is I was miles away in the land of Sâlpètriere and meditating on what I will say when I'm confronted with the abduction of Bella Laffaire by Ipsen and Charcot. My absence costs me a franc for vegetables and another twenty sous for the bunch of alliums. I do not question the robbery. I trust Blanche to have evaluated, whether under these circumstances, we are paying the right price or too much.

As we walk across the bridge and the wind sweeps my hair from my face like a deja-vu of earlier in the day, Blanche berates me, 'She charged us a fortune. Why didn't you say anything?'

'I don't know. Why didn't you?'

I acknowledge to myself that this is our first domestic argument.

'Why are you smiling?'

'Because I love you,' I say.

We are silent until we reach rue Maitre Albert. The door to Victorine's building isn't open. She might have gone out. I don't even know if she is still there. There doesn't seem to be a bell-pull. I look around for a pebble on the cobbled street. Blanche stands looking up with her hands on her hips. I find a stone on top of a muddied leaflet on the floor of an advertisement for a café concert at the Guerbois. The stone is too heavy. I fish in my pocket for a coin to throw at Victorine's window. It misses. I pick it up and throw again. I do this several times like a circus clown till I feel a hand on my shoulder and turn around.

'She's not here or she doesn't want us to come in,' Blanche says, and at that moment Victorine appears at the window. She wears only a chemise. She calls down,

'What is it Paul, what do you want?'

'I told Blanche that you were feeling low. She wanted to come by and see if you're all right. She's brought you some flowers and some vegetables to make soup.'

'Wait,' she says, 'I'll come down.'

218

The door opens slowly as if someone is having trouble pushing it. I grab it to help and eventually a child squeezes out and runs past me.

'You may as well come up,' Victorine calls from the top of the stairs. The common parts of the building are circular and dark. They feel damp and smell of napthaline. I take the wrapped plants from Blanche's arms. She picks up her skirts and begins to climb the spiral staircase. I follow behind. When we are half way up she loses her footing. I catch her in my arms. The paper crackles and the flowers snap. When we arrive on the second floor, Victorine stands in her doorway, she has a long silk shirt thing over her chemise, the two sides of which she holds together in her fist.

'Hello, Blanche,' she says, leaning forwards to kiss the two of us on both cheeks. As she moves towards me, there is a whiff of alcohol on her breath and the scent of pipe-tobacco clings to her hair. 'It's very wonderful of you to think of me in this way, but I'm all right.' As she speaks she looks over her shoulder into the apartment. 'I have company,' she whispers, turning back.

I hand Victorine the squashed vegetables and the dead blooms. Potatoes fall on the floor like a broken string of pearls. Blanche bends to pick them up.

'Victorine, darling, are you coming back to bed,' a female voice calls out.

Blanche looks to me.

'We're so sorry to have disturbed you,' I say.

'It's nothing,' she says. 'Thanks for these. You can disturb me anytime.'

I bow my head.

She turns away and shuts the door.

'I think she's so exotic,' Blanche whispers and I release my suffocating breath.

It's very late – or early, depending upon which way you see it. I can't sleep. It gives me a thrill to say it, so I whisper it to myself several times – Blanche is sleeping in my bed. It doesn't change; every time she sleeps here I feel the same way.

I sit at my desk and unfold my sketch paper, a little troubled that I have allowed myself to run out of good writing equipment. As I raise my pen to start a letter to Clemens I'm aware of an eerie silence coming from the well. It feels as if my body is draining itself of blood. I am chilled and start to shiver. Looking towards the bedroom I see only the bottom of the bed. From the doorway I can hear Blanche's breathing as a concerto. My heart pumps wildly. I'm aware of something both sinister and ridiculous. She doesn't even have a hint of a cough. I stay to listen whilst her music grows softer and mingles with mine.

Dear Clemens,

I hope you don't mind me saying but I miss your letters so much these days. I used to have a friendship with Doctor George de Bellio, a Romanian homeopath living in Paris, who also loves modern art. He no longer speaks to me. It sounds awful to say this and I wish you were here so that I could explain. I don't think I can, adequately, on paper.

So many things have been happening in my life. I have met a wonderful woman who has captured my heart. I've become very much a part of the drama that is 'modern art'. I am also a dedicated homeopath. My cup runneth over, as a friend reminded me just today.

Clemens, my mentor and friend, I have things to say that only you will understand. Please forgive me, I don't wish to burden you with what is contained herein and I don't want you to feel that you have to do anything. It will be enough just to believe that, even for one instant, someone else understands this very isolated, homeopathic, point of view.

You know that I am employed as an allopathic doctor at the hospital La Sâlpètriere. I am treating a patient there who suffers from acute delusions of grandeur and who was admitted to the hospital. I have been granted the permission to treat her homeopathically. I made my initial prescription four months ago and now monitoring her progress I anticipate that she will very soon have the stability of mind that should allow her to survive as an independent person in the outside world. She is now quite well, with the ability to join in society, in the day-to-day running of things, I believe. With a diagnosis of mania the change in her mentality in so little time is quite remarkable. But to gloat on homeopathy's success is not why I write.

The thing is that since taking on this case, I have become increasingly concerned about my own state of mind. The Faculty have sent men round to the hospital to spy on me. I feel as if homeopathy is their blood sport, and I have been manipulated, like a bird reared for shooting. When I think this way, I do not feel safe. Is this merely a symptom of melancholia? I cannot be the non-judgemental observer here.

I have also had other experiences. I treated a boy in my private practice for mild choleric symptoms and the remedy seemed to work well where allopathy failed. I had them queuing around the block!

Two boys came to get me from Père Suisse's art classes. By the time I got back the crowd had dispersed and I almost got arrested. A policeman accused me of trying to cause an uprising!

Wait, I haven't finished. Bella Laffaire, my patient at the hospital, the one who I was telling you about. I needed to speak to her family as part of the case-taking. I traced a possible relative to Montmartre and was threatened by her pimp at the Moulin de la Galette ... .

As I write I realise that I cannot send this missive. I smudge the ink with my left hand, my pen-hand, right across the page until the writing is a blur and spend the rest of the night in my bedroom, standing by the window, watching Blanche's white reflection in the darkened glass.

We Men
November 4th

'In painting, as in the other arts, there's not a single process, no matter how insignificant, which can be reasonably made into a formula. You come to nature with your theories, and she knocks them all flat.'

Pierre-Auguste Renoir

I have begun my love affair with physical exertion. In the same way as overeating swells your guts and you have to move for relief, anxiety expands inside me, and so I run. The pursuit is hard on my clothes but Victorine has negotiated a good frequent rate for me with her mother, the laundress. I do not have such a good arrangement with the cobbler for my battered shoes and my feet are constantly sore but my nerves are calmed. I run every morning at dawn through the dark grey streets of Paris that are expectant with the promise of light, sometimes sliding on cobbles or pummelling modern pavements, down to the embankment. I seem to grow stronger, stamping my jealous demons underfoot.

I run next to the Seine with her cold, wrinkly skin. Past the bobbing barges filled with fruit and coal and covered with tarpaulin. I run with the sound of my own heartbeat in my ears and quivering vision. I run towards sunrays like seedlings growing on the horizon. I run until my lungs threaten to burst and I must stop with my hands on my thighs panting like a dog. I run to the rising sun.

This morning has already burst open with sunlight and although my breath is accelerated and my body sweats profusely, I am much calmer than I was before I started.

Home again, I lie next to Blanche.

'Hello,' she says, huskily, sleep filled, squinting like an artist perusing her work.

'Hello,' I reply.

'What are you doing lying on top of the covers fully clothed?' she asks.

'I had a bad night.'

'I do worry about you,' she says, reaching across me to the bedside table where she reads the time on my watch.

'*Merde!*' she says and slides herself over me so she can get up.

I make a mountain of our pillows and lean against it, cross my legs, and watch as she stands naked at the sink to wash.

'*You* worry about *me,*' I say.

'You don't have to worry about me anymore. You've cured me,' she says, although I know I haven't. Firstly, if she were truly healed it would not have been I but the remedy that cured her. Secondly, she would not have to keep taking Phosphorus every week, which I know she does. Her symptoms are merely palliated and although this outcome would have the druggists advertising success, I, as a homeopath, have encountered real cures, where the patient does not have to keep taking any more medicine and the symptoms don't come back.

I say nothing.

She has twisted her lips to the side and is rubbing some cream into her cheek. She watches herself in the mirror, mesmerising me. I have a sudden urge to stand behind her, press my body into hers and hold her breasts, but I don't. Such behaviour is reserved for leisure times only.

'Should I be worried?' she asks, bending over slightly to view my reflection in the glass.

'No,' I mouth, shaking my head.

Midway, she stops making circular motions with her fingers on her face and waits. I do come to stand behind her but hold her hips away from mine whilst I kiss the cheek that she has pointed to the ceiling.

'You're not going to tell me?' she says, eventually.

'Tell you what?'

She puts on her clothes whilst I relieve myself of mine then go through to my kitchen/dispensary. I fill a pan with water. Blanche comes in with her scent of patchouli.

'Coffee?' I ask.

'Yes,' she says, sitting down on the stool at the counter.

'I don't want to make you late,' I say, head bowed, running my fingers through my hair.

'I don't care.'

'I care. I don't want you to lose your job.'

'I won't.'

'You might.'

'Paul, this is absurd, you have to tell me.'

'I don't know what you want me to say.'

'Something, anything, whatever it is that's bothering you. I thought Bella was doing really well.'

'It's all become more complicated. Of course I will tell you. Over dinner in a little place I discovered at the foot of Montmartre and I promise I will tell you everything. It's getting late, go to work.'

Reluctantly, she stands and swaggers forward like a child who has been told to go to their room. She kisses me and turns away.

'Bye,' she says huskily, disappearing from sight, slamming the door.

I am alone, noticing the lack of sound from the well again, watching goose pimples rise on my arm.

Two hours later, I am still in my kitchen dispensary. It is a Wednesday, my painting day. Yet, here I am naked, sitting on a stool, idle, wasting time. I intended to have a bath but, despite the low temperature in the room, I have not moved.

In contrast to my stillness, rue du Faubourg Saint Denis is alive. Horse-drawn carts outside squeak from their rusty wheels, horse's hooves pummel the road, peddlars call out their wares, and vagrants roar messages of doom to the world.

I watch as the light pours through my red medicine bottles and turns into scarlet arrows in mid-flight across the room. A harsh wind thumps the window followed by a thud against the front door.

'Gachet!' a voice calls. 'Paul, open up!'

'Camille, are you alone?' I call back, suddenly alert and making my way towards him.

'Of course I am, why do you …?'

I open the door.

'Oh, are you modelling for someone?' he whispers, looking over my shoulder into the room. 'Ah, then there must be a woman in the bedroom,' he says when he can see no one.

I hear the street door open and close. A cold draught intrudes and leaps up the stairs. I hug my bare body with my arms.

'I'm freezing, please come in. Is everything all right? Julie? Lucien? Your mother?' I say, pulling him inside.

'Everyone's fine,' he says, walking over the threshold twirling his Russian hat in his hands. 'No one's going to Père Suisse today. We're all at Café Guerbois. What are you doing naked at this hour? No, don't answer that, it will ruin my image of you as a piously good man,' he chuckles.

'That needed to be challenged.'

'Well quite.'

* There is silence

He continues, 'Come on man, we need to go.'

He is right. Everyone has turned up to this intimate restaurant with its panelled walls where strangers often jostle elbows and make new friends. It's certainly very early in the day, even for this place, to be crowded. All the tables have been pushed together in the centre of the room and every seat is filled.

The owner's wife is young and precocious. She places a clay pitcher of water at either end of the table and a half a dozen tumblers around each one.

'What's it to be then?' she asks this crowd of high-spirited men, these revellers, for whom she seductively smoothes her apron with her palms.

'Is that an offer, Clothilde?' asks Edgar, looking around to appreciate the effects of his wit in the expressions of others.

'I've heard you were the saucy one,' she says, taking a crumpled piece of paper and a pencil from a hidden pocket in her dress and standing poised to write. Edgar stares back at her with his soulful, droopy eyelids, a motherless child, a moody man-boy.

'Better luck next time Degas,' shouts Armand from the other end of the table, raising a tumbler in a toast, water slopping over the sides.

Edouard sits back and lights a cigar.

'It's Cézanne that she's looking up and down,' says Claude.

'Hey, Clothilde, sit on his lap. You can be *his* model. As long as you like to be outlined in bitumen and have your privates turn up like purple rolling hills,' shouts Edgar, perking up.

'Let's drink to that,' Henri calls out.

Everyone stands and water is poured and handed around at each end of the table. Clothilde suddenly turns from fey to matronly as she taps an empty tumbler with a spoon several times. The room waits in a silent hush. I look to the pools of water on the table already bleaching the colour of the wood.

'Right then,' she says. 'Are you going to order? Do you want food? Or just drinks?'

'Bring wine Clothilde,' says Edouard, who never rose to partake in a drink at Clothilde's expense, but stayed in his chair puffing and re-lighting the brown crêpe-like tobacco that keeps going out. 'Several pitchers of your impressive house red for the boys. If anyone wants beer, they can order it themselves. And bring menus. I, for one, want to eat.'

'Hey,' says Clothilde, poking Edouard's arm. 'I wouldn't mind modelling for you.' Words that award her a collective 'wooo!' as she walks off into the kitchen, slamming the door behind her.

'I'm not eating, Julie will have prepared a meal for me for when I get home,' Camille tells Edouard.

'You're being ridiculous, that's hours away. You're up in Paris for the day and besides, this is my wedding party. I've just got back from Holland. I'm a married man.'

'Oh, you didn't, you didn't, you didn't marry Victorine,' Charles calls out, with his hands covering his face in mock despair.

'No, don't be ridiculous, I married Suzanne like I always said I would'

Everyone is quiet.

Eventually Camille talks softly, swallowing first as if his mouth is dry. 'I remember when you first introduced me to her. It was obvious you were very much in love.'

'Love … yes love … ,' Edouard says, staring at the volcanic tip of his cigar. 'Anyway, enough deviation away from the main event, where are those menus?' he asks, standing and looking around. 'I don't know about any of you but I'm starved … . Ah! The beautiful Clothilde.'

She smiles as she places baskets of bread on the table and hands out the menus from under her arm.

'Venison. Goose. Is this compliments of the groom's maternal parent?' asks Henri.

Claude throws a bread roll at him. Henri picks one up.

Camille shouts, 'Hey, hey, hey, we're in a restaurant. Henri, put that down.'

I gaze at Edouard above my menu. An intriguing thought comes to mind. Could Suzanne have been courting Edouard at the same time as having a love affair with Auguste, his father? Edouard catches me staring and lifts his eyebrows. I quickly look down at the list of dishes.

'You look like you've seen a ghost,' Edouard says in a low voice, leaning across the table towards me.

' I've had a very stressful time at the hospital.'

'But you're a brilliant doctor, everyone knows it, I've seen those crowds outside your front door.'

'Well, it's a bit more complicated than that.'

'Look, if there's anything I can do to help … ,' he says, sitting back and calling to the rest of the group, 'Is it venison and goose all round?'

Clothilde's husband and brother come through from the kitchen like rustic soldiers. They set wine and glasses down. Clothilde stands and watches with her hands on her hips.

'We'll have goose and venison all round,' Edouard tells her.

She nods her head decisively. Everyone helps themselves to wine. There are an abundance of toasts. Our host holds an empty carafe above his head and calls out for more.

'We need to stick together, Edouard,' Camille says, his eyes full of sorrow and wisdom. 'We're the old men here.'

'You speak for yourself.'

'The others look to us. We could bring the whole thing together.'

Edouard's eyes shine like those of a dog who has been kicked too many times and now doesn't even like to be stroked. He turns violently towards Camille.

'Look, I understand that you need an alternative. I might paint outside. I might present work that the stupid world does not seem to understand but my sole ambition is to have my paintings exhibited at the Salon. I am not a rebel. I am not, what's that word I hear bandied around everywhere these days? … a realist.' And despite a very obvious attempt to keep his emotions under control, Edouard is shouting now. 'I am not a realist!'

It is 11am and already my friends have all had quite a few glasses of wine. Auguste stands up, handsome in his black jacket, fawn trousers, and well-trimmed chestnut hair. He sways slightly from the wine.

'United we stand, divided we fall,' he says. 'We can all help each other.'

'Here, here,' from the rest of the group.

'And I'm not a socialist. Now, you can celebrate with me or

drown your own sorrows, I don't much care, but can we please get on with the business of getting drunk, and eating? Which, the way I see it, is the reason we're here!'

Clothilde and her henchmen bring in the food. A fat goose, with sprigs of cranberries and scented with oregano, cut into portions and sliding off the bone. Pale venison, lean, deeply blushing, and tender. Potatoes, carrots and leeks roasted in olive oil with rosemary, sage, and garlic. Steam rises from the banquet and silences the gang.

'So good,' says Armand.

'Yes, lovely.' Camille.

'Quite wonderful.' Paul.

The door opens and two men walk in.

'This is a private party,' Edouard says.

The two men stand in the doorway as if they haven't heard.

'Look, we have all the tables here and there is no room for strangers.' Edouard waves his arms in the air as if he is conducting music.

'That's all right, we'll go and sit at the bar,' the taller man says.

'Do you know who that is?' I interrupt Charles and Emile.

'His name's slipped my mind. He's the one who wrote that article, the worst one, about *Dejeuner sur l'Herbe,*' says Emile.

Edouard stands and sways over to the bar. His walking stick marks each step.

'There is no overflow to this party,' he says.

The journalist turns towards the bar. Edouard grabs his jacket collar in both hands. 'Listen here you little parasite, don't think you can write disparaging articles about my work when you clearly know next to nothing about the ins and outs of my profession. And don't come in here when I'm with my friends so you can spread your voyeuristic filth all over the front page tomorrow.'

'Now, come on, I know you're feeling a little sensitive about your nasty little painting but I have every right to be here and have a drink with my pal Pierre,' the man says pushing Edouard away.

Edouard falls backwards, steadies himself, and marches forward. With the pommel of his stick he hits the man fairly hard upon his cheekbone.

'Maybe now you understand,' he says, shrugging his shoulders and walking away.

The man reaches out for Edouard and clutches his arm as Clothilde and her henchmen come through from the kitchen.

'Get out of my restaurant!' she shouts, clapping her hands. 'Get out, get out, get out!'

The reporter lets go of Edouard and holds his cheek with one hand whilst lifting the other in the air. 'All right, all right we're going,' he says.

On his way out he sidles close to Edouard. 'Why don't you fuck your own grandmother,' he profanes, through gritted teeth.

On their way out, the intruders hustle a group of women in the doorway. Three models walk in laughing at some previously told joke. They immediately lighten the tainted atmosphere, help themselves to wine and warm the knees of Henri, Armand and Edouard, until Blanche walks in with Victorine.

'Edouard,' Victorine says, standing before him, pulling off her lace gloves finger by finger. 'You're having a painter's party and didn't invite me. I met Blanche in the Boulevard Saint Germaine and she agrees that it has to be a mistake,' she says, her cleavage heaving just above the lap-girl's face as she leans over to kiss Edouard on the cheek. Straightening up, she snatches the glass away from Edouard's lap-girl and drinks the contents in one swallow. 'Congratulations,' she says.

Edouard's mouth hangs open.

Blanche quietly seats herself beside me. She watches the scene wide-eyed whilst puffing out her cheeks. 'I'm pleased you came,' I whisper in her ear. 'I thought you were working.'

I am conscious that my breath smells of cheap alcohol whilst she is wrapped in the scent of something far more heavenly. I look at the food on the table congealing on white plates.

'My pupil isn't well,' she says.

Blanche and I slip away from the alternative wedding party that is missing its bride. We leave unseen, I hope, and I know I will swear to Camille that we were still there when such and such happened – the invisible couple.

I take her to that little restaurant in Montmartre with only three tables, each one lit by a diminishing red candle around its flickering flame. We are the only patrons in our private dining room. We eat oysters, and feed each other until we both confess that the aphrodisiac actually causes slight nausea. She is working in the evening and keeps checking on the time. I, on the other hand, choose to forget it. Or maybe, all the alcohol I've consumed makes that decision for me.

'So tell me what you were unable to tell me this morning,' she says.

It is a rude awakening. I am in a good mood. I don't wish to be drawn back into my problems.

'Oh, I don't know, it's just work,' I say, turning my beer glass around and around.

'Paul, I can't stand this, I want to be your friend.'

I am wilting. My shoulders are hanging over the table now. I might even pass out. I purse my lips and shrug.

'*Merde!*' she says.

'It's Bella,' I say.

Blanche nods. I notice her eyes are glazed and I look down at the table.

'You know I used to worry that I wouldn't find her a curative remedy. Now I am afraid for what will happen when she's well. She has a visitor that Doctors Ipsen and Charcot entertain. I'm sure it's her pimp. Blanche, I think I'm going mad with it all.'

'I thought I was going mad when my parents died, but I didn't. I think it's because I didn't let myself.'

The tears she harbours are infectious now. She offers me her hand across the table and I take it. We are framed in this moment.

'Phew!' I say, opening my shirt collar 'It's very hot in here.'

Outside on the pavement we embrace and I desperately try to feel her flesh through her many layers of clothing.

'Please, don't work tonight,' I request.

'I have to.'

I impose my lips upon hers and search with one finger for the spot at the back of her neck that makes her shiver.

'No you don't,' I say softly.

'Don't do this,' she pleads.

I pull away, hurt, and say, 'What?'

I walk Blanche to the Café Bade and watch her go in. It's early. She wants to rehearse. With my attempts at seduction failed, I decide to go home and have that bath that I never managed to have this morning. I feel the roughness of my beard with my palm. With foaming soap and a sharp blade, I will raze, spruce myself up, then return to watch Blanche perform.

Dusk has come and gone. The world is in darkness. I find myself walking the wrong way, towards the embankment, watching a bitter chocolate glow fall over the Seine, and a moon slither, white and bony, a scythe-blade behind a cloud. I turn towards Notre Dame, so overwhelming and large. Behind me the silhouette of the Louvre is low-lying with understated importance. To have permission to sketch and imitate the old masters is a validation in itself, but to have work on exhibit there must be better than receiving sainthood.

I think I can just make outwhere de Concorde with Cleopatra's needle pointing to the sky. And across the bridge, l'Ecole des Beaux Arts on the other side of the river, behind iron railings, a 'keep-out' reminder from the ones who rule.

I sit on a bench donated by the parents of some unfortunate young man. I lean forwards and put my chin in my hands. Before me a row of Haussman's creations with floor to ceiling windows, slated roofs, balconies like coats of armour or cast-iron lace. Paris. Despite its shortcomings, I'd rather be here than anywhere else.

Before I let myself in through the street door of my humble dwelling it feels strange. Everything remains visually the same but it appears to me as if something has intrinsically changed. The whiteness of the external walls seem more luminous and, in comparison, the shutters more grimy from the smoke heading over from the factories in Montmartre. I stand in the courtyard looking up at the interminable moon with its posse of stars. All is silent.

It takes too much time but I prepare myself a perfect bath anyway. On the stove, metal pans of water produce steam. The warmth will melt my joints and arouse my skin, so that when I lie there every cell in my body will be revived. This is the theory. I am out of kerosene, so no lights, just candles and the fire to entice relaxation. I give into it with the will of a laudanum whore.

'Ahhhhh,' I let out one long, most audible breath wishing Blanche was here to claim me or that I could just be happy to be here by myself. Is this why Camille married Julie, and Edouard, Suzanne? They teach at l'Ecole des Beaux Arts that women are a distraction to one's art. In the world of medicine, they are an accoutrement. In life they are vital when the right one comes along. Above the splash and plop I hear a tenor in the street below.

I never wanted to leave you
It was far too soon for me to go
The pale light of morning came much too soon
I should have told you so.
I should have told you so.

I'm late. Time gets eaten away by mysterious predators. They chase me. My hasty footsteps clunk down the stone stairway and rebound off the walls. Another tenant bumps into me and I catch a fright. The hallway seems hollow and empty. I place my hand on his wool coat to check he's really there.

'Another quiet night,' he says, lifting his hat to me.

I watch him enter his apartment on the ground floor. Then I run up one flight to apartment number two.

I knock.

No answer.

I knock again and again.

I bang my fists.

Monsieur Breton, let me in,' I call.

Perspective
November 16th

'No art is less spontaneous than mine. What I do is the result of reflection and study of the great masters.'

Edgar Degas

The voices in the well have gone and, as I would an annoying brother who has come of age, I miss them. Even though they were a scandalous intrusion when I was with a patient and my concentration was stolen away from my work, I wish them back. I did not appreciate it before, but the melodrama and thrum of community life comforts. Instead, a preternatural silence prevails. My private practice hours have been affected too. Officer Fornier has told me that our concierge Breton is away on an extended holiday.

'And the other tenants?'

'Some have left,' he said.

The street door is no longer left open or shut systematically. Whether my patients can get inside the building or not is now a random affair. For example, there is a knock on my door but I am not expecting anyone.

'Yes,' I say pulling back the barrier between myself, and a couple with a girl of around twelve. Her father carries her.

'Doctor Gachet?'

'Yes.'

'Sorry for disturbing you outside of your consulting hours, but every time we arrived here within the times written on the plaque outside, we could not get in.'

'Yes, we seem to have a serious concierge problem, but I have

236

some time now if you'd like to come inside'

'Thank you.'

I usher them in to sit at the other side of my desk. The girl sprawls with one arm around her father's neck and her head on his shoulder. One leg has fallen between his knees, its foot lying dormant on the floor. The father lifts the heavy limb and places it next to its twin across his thighs.

'Please, tell me, why are you here?' I ask.

'I'll say it quickly … .'

'No,' I say. 'I want to know details. Take as long as you like.'

The parents look at each other. Lifting her chin, the mother turns to me and says, 'We can't afford to pay a lot more.'

'It will be the same price. Please go on.'

'It started with pain in her stomach, diarrhoea, and vomiting. My mother-in-law agreed to pay for a doctor. He prescribed this,' the father says, reaching into his pocket and pulling out a brown corked bottle. He leans forwards and hands it to me. I study the label: Doctor Landry's bowel cure. The main ingredient is lead acetate.

'You are giving her this?' I ask.

'Yes, two spoonfuls daily.'

I put the bottle on my desk.

'Can you describe her symptoms now for me?'

'Well, as you can see she has no energy to do anything. She can't move her legs. She describes them as 'dead'. Florette, tell the doctor how it feels.'

Florette lifts her head slightly and then lets it drop down again onto her father's shoulder.

'She keeps falling asleep and everything you ask her, she says she can't remember.'

'Either that or she can't be bothered to talk,' adds the mother.

'And stomach pains, vomiting and diarrohea?' I ask.

'They're cured.'

'She doesn't go at all now, just lumpy black bits in her knickers.'

The father looks at the mother accusingly.

'Well, I have to tell him,' she says.

I have seen similar cases many times. It is common practice to give derivatives of lead for spontaneous purging, although ironically, not long ago the practice was to give emetics, sudorifics or bleed the patient dry. Now that is considered barbaric and dangerous. Lead, in my experience, does seem to alleviate rapid ejection from the bowels, but the physical cost is exhaustion, constipation, paralysis and in extreme cases, even death.

'If you are to prescribe for Florette, where is your strange, rare and peculiar symptom in this case?' I can hear the voice of Clemens in my ears.

I walk around my desk and sit on the edge of it.

'Florette, can you hear me?'

The father shakes her awake. 'Answer the doctor,' he says.

'Yes,' she says, weakly.

'That's good. In a minute I want to turn your chair to the window. I need you in strong sunlight. I'm going to pull down your lower lip and lift up your upper one. That's all I'm going to do. Is this all right with you?'

She doesn't answer. Her father shakes her again.

'Yes,' she says again.

With difficulty, we manage to turn the chair. I perform the examination. There is a distinct blue line along the margins of her gums. It is the strange, rare and peculiar symptom that as far as I know is only produced by lead.

Whilst I'm dispensing her remedy, I can't help but give myself the permission to be angry. Mercury for syphilis, heroin for coughs, cocaine for dentition: all poisons in their crude form. Whilst regular doctors pat themselves on the back for curing relatively superficial symptoms, their patients grow sicker, suffer more and often die. And they call us homeopaths murderers and charlatans.

The spirit of Clemens is with me again. He stands beside me, tall and upright with a shock of white hair that he pushes affectedly to one side. '*You are what you accuse others to be,*' he says with an amused smile, appreciating the irony.

I make up the remedy for Florette. It is one that does not formally exist in the homeopathic pharmacopoeia, one that I have made up myself and used many times in cases such as this: lead, in Latin, *Plumbum.*

Similia Similibus Currentur. It causes and in the same way it cures. My medicine is not toxicum. I am confident that in its dynamic heavily-diluted form, it will encourage Florette to become well.

As the family leave my practice, the postman is at my door. He hands me an unusual-looking envelope. I flip it over many times then tap it against my thumb. The paper is thick, smooth and grey with a crest as a watermark. By the shape of it, I guess it is an invitation.

I sit down on my stool in my kitchen/dispensary to open it. It is from Ernest Hoschedé. He is having a party at his home and requests the pleasure of Mademoiselle Blanche and Doctor Paul Gachet to join him. I am amazed. The last time I saw Monsieur Hoschedé was in the Café Guerbois. He was with Georges de Bellio, the two of them very obviously ignoring me. But should I be surprised that he has chosen to invite us? Probably not. I have learned that, unlike homeopathy, the game of life has no measured outcome for any of its rules.

Catherine waits for me by the bridge at the bottom of rue de l'Hopital. It is a sombre and dark morning with a marbled sky and a wind that comes from behind us, biting our ears and whipping our clothes.

'How are you Catherine?'

'I am well thank you, Doctor.'

'Shall we walk? I have something to say.'

'I already know what you're going to ask.'

'Even to take Bella into the grounds is impermissible. To take her outside the hospital is folly, complete folly. If I can bump into you then so can anyone else.'

'It was my decision and I was prepared to take the consequences should I have been caught.'

'Why did you? – And how did you do it?'

'The man Bella is frightened of came to visit. After he left she was gagging for breath and clutching her throat. I instinctively knew that she would be better for some air, so I borrowed a coat from Nurse Fontaine and took a chance in smuggling her out.'

'But to the Tuileries, that's miles away.'

'I know, but it seemed to do her so much good.'

The rural road is unlit and we both carry lamps. Their effect is being slowly annihilated by the oncoming watery daylight. The wind assaults us from all sides.

'Do you think I can make a living out of homeopathy?' she asks.

'Why do you ask?'

'I am getting married,' she says. 'Please, Doctor Gachet, don't tell anyone.'

You can't be a nurse and a wife in Paris. Sâlpetrière expects the complete devotion it received from the nuns. And if those women in winged hats hadn't overruled doctors' decisions in the name of Our Lord then no doubt they would still be employed today. Instead, modern nurses are ordinary, humbler folk. That is, except for Marguerite Bottard.

'I don't make much money from homeopathy,' I tell her honestly. 'Most of my patients are poor and I treat them for next to nothing or free. But there are others who do make a living from it. So, yes, I do believe you can.'

'I am a woman, Doctor Gachet. Do you think I will find myself pinned to a stake if I do?'

'They don't do that anymore Catherine.'

'I've seen them Doctor Gachet. It's in their eyes when they look at you. They would have your head rolling off a block if they thought they could get away with it.'

240

Sâlpetrière stands before us like a holy place, wide with three central arches and a big black dome. The building casts the illusion of righteousness and the doctors inside are the illusionists who perpetrate that thought. I turn to Catherine.

'Congratulations on your engagement. Your secret is safe with me. I will see you inside.'

I have somehow managed to persuade Ipsen to come down to Bella's cell for this consultation, partly because I want him to experience how Bella has to live, and partly because I believe her personal surroundings will put her most at ease.

'Hello Bella,' I say jauntily, as we walk in the door.

She is dressed in a long, grey, calico nightgown and sits on the side of her straw bed.

'I'd like you to tell me how you think you are doing?'

'I'm all right,' she says.

Ipsen and I sit on chairs, side by side, like a jury. Catherine stands behind me by the door, notebook in one hand, pen poised in the other, making her customary notes.

'Tell me, why do you think you are all right?'

'I can see myself now and what I have done,' she says with her head bowed.

'What do you mean by that?'

'That I've sold my body to men,' her voice is barely a whisper.

'And, in your opinion, what is wrong with that?'

'Nothing, only perhaps it shouldn't be so.'

'Why shouldn't it be so?'

'There is no reason. Only I know that there are those who think that it shouldn't be so.'

'And what do you think?'

She lifts her head and shakes it.

'I wish it wasn't so.'

She looks at me directly with liquefied eyes.

I swallow and ask, 'And who are you?'

'I am ... .'

241

'Yes?'

'I am ... .' She closes her lids and opens them. 'Bella Laffaire,' she says.

'This is ludicrous,' Ipsen says, through his teeth.

I sit forward and put my hand on his knee.

'Carry on, tell me about Bella Laffaire,' I say to Bella.

In the chapel, an alternative exit to the building, Ipsen stops me by pulling on my arm.

'Doctor Ipsen,' I say, above the droll sound of the organ. 'If I didn't know better I would think you were being aggressive.'

'Don't ever do that again, Doctor Gachet.'

'Do what?'

I look around. A woman in black with a lowered veil kneels on a cushion in one of the pews. A dozen candles flicker on a table in the corner and a palette of colour is thrown on the floor by light coming through the stained glass window over the altar.

'Put on that spectacle as if you are a producer in a theatre. It is my opinion, and I represent the Faculty here, that you are making a mockery of a very serious profession.'

I look up to the rafters in the high ceiling, then to the far wall where a porcelain Jesus looks down at me full of melancholy as he hangs crumpled on his cross.

'Doctor Ipsen,' I say. 'I did not put on a spectacle. I merely asked the patient questions, which she answered eloquently. If you saw drama, then it is in the nature of her cure.'

'There is no cure. We don't have a cure for madness,' he spits.

'And is it your opinion that a madwoman can get better without any medical intervention at all?'

'You're wasting your time Gachet, Bella Laffaire will never get better.'

'Then how do you explain what you saw?'

'I saw nothing,' he says loudly, stamping his foot like a spoilt boy.

The organ music grows louder. I walk off for I can stand no more, but on second thoughts turn around. The organist strikes one long irritating chord then the music suddenly stops. Ipsen and I stand there locking horns. I wait for the sound to dissipate.

'You miserable bastard, you saw and heard everything,' I call out.

My words resound off the walls. The mourner stands up, and looks at me accusingly. Ipsen raises his chin. The angry sounding footsteps heading for the door are my own.

I refuse to let Doctor Ipsen provoke a bad humour inside me, but I have lost all power to remain calm and collected. There is tension in every cell of my body and bile rises up into my oesophagus like the fire of a terrible dragon. I take large strides then break into a run. Feeling awkward, because my work clothes are not suited to this exercise, I push myself to run faster on legs that would rather collapse beneath me. I run, panting, lungs strained and bruising. I run with a stitch in my diaphragm and blisters swelling on the pads of my toes. I run to the river that has been whipped by the wind into a crocodile skin. Along the embankment, past the Louvre, through the Tuileries, left at Place Concorde, across Pont Neuf to Quai d'Orsey, I run behind the Palais de Justice, through the winding streets to her. I run to Blanche. I arrive puffed out, but have only half-exhausted my anger. She opens the door.

'Come on, we're going out,' I say.

I don't know what she sees but she does not question the command. Silently she goes to get her coat. I wait, huffing, one hand on the doorframe.

'Where are we going?' she asks, shutting the door.

'We're going to celebrate the efficacy of homeopathy,' I say.

She takes my arm. I am already feeling better. 'I can't even begin to tell you what it was like,' I say. My strides are wide and fast, so that I am sweeping her along. 'Bella was like a different person. All that manic behaviour was completely gone. She was

243

rational. But it was more than that. She'd worked it all out for herself: all the emotions that she couldn't face before. She said, "I've always been my mother's little princess whatever happened to me, whatever I have done," I wanted to get up and dance.

'Of course, I should be celebrating with my medical colleagues, but who wants to celebrate with a bunch of beaurocratic dinosaurs anyway, especially when I can buy you champagne and watch as it wets your lips?' We have stopped in the middle of the street. I smile but she stares at me with concern.

'I worry for you,' she says.

I look up to the sky. 'I know.' I bunch her fist in mine and we cross the river and walk towards Tortini's and every few moments Blanche glances in my direction. There is a false bounce in my stride as she glides along beside me.

'Doctor Gachet' is a whisper on the wind – a ghost in the air – words in my head.

I turn around.

A blast of cold air punches me in the face.

'What is it?' Blanche asks.

'Oh, nothing,' I answer.

We turn down a street lined with clothiers, a chemist, and a wine shop.

'Let's go in here,' she says, as we look at our reflections imposed in the window, behind it a display of bottles with expensive price tags.

'Why?'

'They sell very fine champagne.'

'I want to take you ... .'

'Home and besides I'm uncomfortable in these clothes.'

I wanted to feed her potent bubbles on a spoon. I wanted to hear her laughter and make love to her as a celebratory rite. Instead, we have abandoned the bedroom. She wears a shirt of mine, sits with her feet up by the fire and listens to my wrath.

'How can Ipsen do this? And why, Blanche, why? Why would he want to pretend that there has not been a significant change in

Bella? Do you think it is personal? Do you think it's less about homeopathy and more about having taken a dislike to me? That's perfectly possible I suppose, but why deny humanity a beneficial medicine? Surely he's above that, don't you think?'

Blanche looks up at me, sipping from her glass as I pace.

'Look, it's not conclusive, I agree. One patient doesn't prove anything, not really, but it should pave the way for more test cases, more investigation. I just can't believe that he has taken this attitude. And where does this leave me?' I look to my glass and the wine going flat. 'I need a plan.'

I wake up with a start, on the floor, with my head on the sofa, next to a sleeping Blanche. There is an empty champagne bottle on the table, the sharp odour of alcohol on her breath. I stroke her arm, put my ear to her mouth to check her breathing, then go to sit on a chair facing the window. Silk veils of clouds sail across a darkening sky.

I decide to create a document, a scientific paper worthy of appearing in a medical journal: 'The case of Bella Laffaire'. Copies will be sent to every medical society across the globe. It shall contain Ipsen's diagnosis of the patient, my hypothesis and conclusion, all the detailed case-notes with my observations, a long explanation as to the homeopathic process and how I came to my prescription. A well-scripted accompanying letter will be proofread by my father. I'm sure he will oblige. I will use the most professional approach to present the evidence. I can see myself in the future, lecturing in medical schools all over the world.

I sit down on the floor to meditate for as long as it takes. When she wakes, I want Blanche to see me tranquil. I need her to know that I can work it out – for both of us – and that she doesn't really ever have to worry about me.

The Pinch of the Game
November 23rd

Tell me, do you think I'm going mad? I sometimes wonder, you know ... .'

Paul Cézanne

I have my own ideas about why Ipsen denies the efficacy of Bella's treatment but do not wish to assume anything. So, I have taken to following him. In the evenings he returns home to a buxom wife and three well-built children, which is surprising because he is so thin. Perhaps it's his conscience disallowing him to put on weight.

He employs two liveried coachmen, owns two ornate carriages, and always makes sure that he is dropped outside the hospital gates so that he can walk into work. He lives by the park in l'avenue Hoche.

He accompanies his wife to the Opera, to dinner parties in well-to-do parts of town, to gown shops on a Saturday, and at least three times a week in the early hours he frequents a bordello in Place de Clichy. He takes coffee in Café Filou, a small establishment opposite the Seine.

I visit Charcot. His office at La Sâlpètriere overlooks the sincere beauty of a natural landscape – a grass plain of some acreage, scattered trees and a barely diminished horizon, here on the outskirts of urbanized Paris.

'Come in Gachet, come in,' he says, with one arm casually draped over my shoulder and guiding me towards a chair. 'Sit down'.

Such a welcome far from pacifies but instead makes me

slightly overcome and I at once forget what I have come to say. 'Bella Laffaire,' is all I manage to get out before he speaks again.

'I know.' He stands next to his desk, his arms behind his back 'I want you to know that personally speaking, I have the greatest respect for you and homeopathy. I mean it must be an intellectually stimulating pursuit to have at first attracted and then seduced a man like you.'

He takes a breath.

'Doctor Charcot, do you believe that a case of manic insanity can be cured without any medical intervention?'

'Actually, Gachet, I don't believe that mania or insanity can be helped at all, as with all nervous disorders at this point in time, they are incurable. An insane moment might pass, but the predisposition to insanity? No, that remains to overwhelm the patient at any time.'

'If I said that there is some reason to suspect that underlying emotional issues are being addressed in the case of Bella Laffaire, would I have your interest?'

'My personal interest, yes. But I don't make the rules.'

'Doctor Charcot, with the Faculty's permission, Catherine Morrisot and myself have meticulously written up the case of Bella Laffaire for only one reason: to demonstrate the effectiveness of her treatment. I need to have the opportunity to present it to someone who does make the rules.'

Charcot bites his bottom lip. He comes to stand beside me with one hand on the back of my chair.

'Come to my house on Sunday for lunch. It is in the best interests of everyone concerned that this matter is resolved quickly. Do you prefer partridge or goose?'

I stand outside Charcot's front door eying the varnished heavy oak panelling and signal my arrival using the brass lion-head knocker. A tall, slim, grey-haired woman, dressed in black comes to the front door and although she smiles, her face betrays a bad smell in the air.

'Good afternoon,' I say, taking off my cap.

I try to hand over a small cardboard box tied up with ribbon but she does not take it from me.

'And you are?' she asks.

'I'm Paul, Doctor Paul Gachet.'

'I see,' she says, grabbing a piece of paper from the top of the sideboard. 'Yes, I have you. Jean-Pierre is serving aperitifs in the sitting room. You know the way?'

I shake my head and then as an afterthought she says, 'I am Madame Chanterel of 'Le Delicieux'. My waitresses will be serving you lunch.'

Doctor Charcot's apartment is probably the same size as Madame Manet's but with a very different décor. The carpet is plush, the colour of fresh blood. A cast-iron dog sits upon the floor. The walls are wood panelled. A number of pen and ink drawings in black frames hang here and there. I lean over to inspect Charcot's taste in art: a Paris street, La Notre Dame, La Sâlpètriere. All unremarkable and unsigned.

'Doctor,' Madame Chanterel says.

'I'm sorry, yes, please lead the way.'

The sitting room could be an extension of Charcot's office but for its heavy velvet drapes drawn against the day. Every light is lit but all are shaded with frosted glass that hardly brightens the atmosphere at all. The fire is paltry: two skeletal logs and a single flame like a tongue between them.

Doctors Ipsen and Quackenetre sit at either end of a sofa smoking cigars. Doctor Charcot comes forward from his stance in front of the fire.

'I bought chocolates for your wife,' I say, handing him the small cardboard box.

'She's taken the children over to friends. But thank you, I'm sure she'll enjoy them,' he says, placing the box on top of the mantel.

A middle aged man in a tuxedo approaches me from out of nowhere.

'Sir,' he says. 'What can I get you to drink?'

'We're all having Pernod,' says Charcot.

'Then I will too,' I tell the man and turn towards Charcot. 'The chocolates will melt if you leave them there.'

He takes them away and puts them on an occasional table barely two feet from the fire. Ipsen squirms slightly and with one finger pushes his glasses further up his nose. Quackenetre leans forwards, eyes twinkling with anticipation, as if he is about to witness a horse race or a duel. I place myself in the leather-studded armchair opposite the fire. An interesting painting of a ship in a very stormy sea is badly lit on the wall in front of me. It looks like a reproduction of one of Edouard's earlier works and I find myself wanting to take a closer look.

'I was just saying that you would be bringing your notes on the case of Bella Laffaire.'

Ipsen and I exchange a brief glance.

'Yes,' I say, reaching down to the floor to pick up my portfolio.

'I would like to take a look at that,' says Doctor Quackenetre, reaching out towards me with one hand.

'Of course,' I say, passing him my work.

He puts his cigar down on an ashtray and opens the folder. The first page is an index. He seems to read it with some attention. Then he whips the air with it as if to shake the paper free of creases, and deposits the sheet on the floor by his feet. Everyone looks at him as he thumbs through the rest of the papers, closes the cover and replaces the ribbon.

'I suggest,' he says, holding it out towards me. 'That you do away with this.'

'Did I hear you correctly?' I ask, taking it from him.

'Oh yes,' he says. 'You absolutely did.'

I look at Charcot who is in his usual lecturer's pose, hands behind his back, and Ipsen who intently stares at nothing. The Pernod arrives as green as I perceive my face to be. I wait until the waiter walks out of the room.

'Doctor Charcot, what is going on here?' I ask.

Quackenetre says, 'Doctor Ipsen has changed his mind about Bella Laffaire's diagnosis. He thinks we have all been a bit too brash in labelling this patient manic, or deluded or even needing help. You see, a relative of hers has come to claim her. A rather forceful and somewhat powerful man whom the police have advised us to placate … .'

'I can't believe this,' I say to no one in particular. Combing my hand through my hair, I start to pace.

'He claims that Bella has always been a little highly strung. In fact he called her "my darling little shrew" a number of times.'

'I know who he is. That man is a pimp,' I say.

'Come now, Gachet,' Quackenetre says forcefully, coming to stand.

'Doctor Ipsen are you sure? Are you really sure that you will lie like this to appease a pompous cunt who thinks he is above the law?'

'Thank goodness your wife and children are not here Jean-Martin,' Quackentre again. 'Doctor Gachet, this is totally unnecessary, this obscene language from a doctor, my God!'

Doctor Ipsen remains sitting. His eyes harden, magnified behind myopic lenses. He looks at me and says, 'Doctor Gachet, Bella's relative is circumstantial, but after the fiasco of your last consultation, I can't let your little homeopathy experiment go on. I feel morally compelled to render it null and void. You are lucky that I am not hauling you up in front of all the directors of the Faculty for a hearing. And I don't believe I've lied, I have simply changed my mind.'

'Good day, gentlemen,' I say. I pick up my portfolio and walk out into the hall.

Charcot comes after me. He grabs my arm.

'Gachet,' he whispers, 'I have always liked you, and in some ways respected you, but don't you care? Can't you see it? Are you really such a fool? Think quickly man, what good will it do and what will it prove if you walk out now? They have talked about it and they will rescind your membership of the Faculty. You won't be able to practice medicine officially and the scandal will be humiliatingly written up in all the newspapers. Do you really want that?'

A lump of bile rises in my throat. I feel like I'd just been sick all over the man's shoes. I wipe my mouth as if I had just done so and follow him back into the room.

The scene is quite surreal. At least it is in the way that I experience it. They say the effects of absinthe can come back to haunt you during stressful times. Maybe that is what's happening to me now.

We are in the dining room: an oval space with an oval table and a glass domed roof. The walls are the colour of a mossy pond. Doctor Ipsen and I sit in the middle of the table, facing each other. Doctors Quackenetre and Charcot are at either end. There is stilted conversation and much silence interrupted by the scratching and chink of cutlery against china. At first I thought I'd get drunk, but in truth, the wine is not worth risking a headache. So I watch them when they do speak, each of them in turn, attempting politeness, asking for salt to be passed or if nurse Morrisot has been employed a long time. They seem to be strangely comforted that I actually came back to eat with them. Do they really think I'm obliged to take on their politics without further ado?

'Doctor Ipsen is travelling to America on Monday. He will be there for three months on Faculty business. With his special interest in medicinal drugs, he is the best to perform the link between us doctors and pharmacology. We're lucky we have someone so accomplished. So, on Friday he'll be winding things up for the Faculty in Salpiêtrière,' Quackenetre says.

I have a chimera: I stand up, walk over to Quackenetre, lift his plate full of food and crash it over his head, then swipe my fist upward beneath his jaw. I then turn around and walk casually to the other end of the table. 'The paintings on these putrid walls are pure crap,' I say to Charcot.

251

Back in reality: 'That's fine,' Charcot agrees with a forkful of food midway between his mouth and his plate.

I smile to myself.

'It's a real shame about homeopathy, Gachet. We were all rooting for it even if we did already know that it couldn't possibly work.' This is Ipsen.

In a fancy again: Ipsen's on the floor, his chair fallen over behind him. I'm straddling his body and repeatedly pummelling his bloody face with my fist.

Then reality seeps in. The door opens behind him. A very elegant young woman enters. She has two small children, a girl who is trying to keep her balance in her mother's wake and a boy, a little older, buttoned to his chin in a thick woollen coat.

'Jean-Martin, I'm sorry to disturb your lunch, I've had to come home early, Genevieve is not well. She is burning up a fever. I thought, perhaps, you might attend to her right away.'

'Genevieve is our baby. Excuse me gentlemen.' Charcot says, and leaves the room accompanied by his family.

Neither Quackenetre nor Ipsen speak, although both have clearly finished their food. Waitresses bustle in and remove our plates, so efficiently I barely have time to thank them. Moments later Charcot bursts back into the room. 'Doctor Ipsen, we need an anti-pyretic,' he says.

'Willow bark, of course. If you don't have any here we can hail a hansom to the nearest hospital.'

'Her age makes her too delicate. I saw abdominal haemorrhage time and time again at the Hospital for Sick Children after giving willow bark,' I say.

Ipsen does not reply but purses his mouth and drums his fingers on the table. The waitresses bring our ice cream.

Madame Chanterel asks, 'Is everything all right with the catering?'

No one answers.

'Jean-Martin, Jean-Martin, come quick,' Madame Charcot calls.

Doctors Charcot, Quackenetre and Ipsen run towards the sound of her voice. I follow behind. When I arrive in the nursery, the doctors are standing by the door in conference about what therapeutic step to take.

'None of us are experts in infant diseases, I'm going to take her to the hospital,' Charcot says.

'It's November, she'll die of cold on the way,' Quackenetre says.

'Willow bark, willow bark,' Ipsen says again. 'Doctor Charcot, you should listen to me.'

Madame Charcot is sitting on the floor by the crib. I go to sit beside her.

'I have three homeopathic remedies for fever in my pocket. My suggestion is that we give her one of each whilst your husband makes up his mind. The worst that can happen is that none of them is the right one. They cannot cause even one iota of harm.'

I see her silhouette nod in this darkened room.

'Do you have two spoons? I must crush the pillules into a powder first.'

'Jean-Martin,' Madame Charcot calls.

Her husband makes his way over, wearing the light from the hallway like an aura.

'Doctor Gachet wants to give Genevieve something homeopathic,' she says.

'Just while you're making up your minds what to do,' I say.

Charcot looks towards his colleagues and nods.

'It will do no harm,' he tells his wife.

'He needs two spoons,' she says.

'I'll go and get them.'

Just by chance I made a home visit this morning to another baby with a fever. I brought Aconite, *Chamomilla* and Belladonna with me in my pocket. Rare is the infant fever that is not brought down by one of these.

Doctor Charcot hands me the spoons. I decant one pillule of

each remedy onto one of them and crush them down with the convex bottom of the other. Then I pour some of the granules between the infant's lips. A powdery white moustache glows above her mouth.

'Let me know how she gets on,' I say, coming up to stand and then, seizing the moment, in a loud voice, 'Doctor Charcot, you'll have to forgive me. I must look in on a patient and so must be leaving now. Thank you for lunch.' I nod to the other two. 'Doctors Ipsen, Quackenetre.' and leave, not at all sorry to be gone.

24th November

It is Monday. I am restless. I leave early from Blanche's home. I have my portfolio of the case of Bella Laffaire under my arm. I am wondering what to do with it – what can I do with it?

This morning Blanche has a private client who lives on the rue de Rivoli, a woman in her early twenties whose fiancé wishes to marry a woman who plays the violin – a challenge, according to Blanche. When I tried to speak to her at eight o'clock, she could not think past what to wear and not being late. So, I have breakfast alone by the river in Café Filou, in the Boulevard des Augustins. I've bought a copy of the Gazette des Beaux-Arts. I intended to read it over coffee and croissants with honey but find myself staring out at the unwelcoming waters made choppy by a blustery wind. Boats sway and threaten to lose their cargo to an iron-grey and greedy Seine.

At the table behind me, two men are having a whispered conversation. I'm sure that if they were talking normally, I would be deeply engrossed in the long essay about Courbet by now and would not have heard a word. But as it is, my curiosity is piqued and, in spite of myself, I can't help but listen.

'A generous offer but I can't accept,' says a voice that I recognise. 'My colleagues wouldn't approve.'

'Then how else can we pay you?'

'My wife is most taken with last year's gift. She is in the South right now with a team of people she's employed. She tells me every room will be a different colour. It should be ready by next summer vacation time. Maybe a yacht and a crew for the season?'

'Every year for as long as all the hospitals in Paris keep ordering our laudanum. Of that, you can rest assured.'

'Very generous. Very generous indeed and most appreciated.'

'It's the least we can do.'

'Well, business concluded. I must be on my way.'

I hear chairs scrape backwards on the wooden floor. A hip pushes against my table.

'So, sorry.'

I look up at Doctor Ipsen. His face is panicked. 'Oh, it's only you Doctor Gachet,' he says, then quickly calms down again. 'Good morning, nasty day.'

'Unforgiving,' I say.

'Yes, well,' Ipsen says, looking around to see his associate walk out. 'I'll see you at the hospital.' He even lifts his bowler hat to me and that makes the demon rise inside me. The waitress comes and I mumble something about feeling sick and needing to leave. Once on the street the savage wind bites at my skin. I cannot help myself. I run down to the riverbank and kick a sack of apples left on the quayside. The coarse material ruptures and dozens of green orbs tumble out after me, rolling and bruising and falling into the Seine like a fairy-tale of rats. There are barrels of oysters and mussels. I punch one of them several times.

'Hey!' a voice calls out.

I hear footsteps running towards me, mingling with the blood that's pumping in my ears. As the skin on my knuckles rips, I hit the barrel again, almost topple it with naked bone.

A hand grabs my shoulder, turns me round. A stranger's fist hurtles towards me. I grab the man's arm and hit him in the guts with a ragged hand. He falls backwards into the barrels and squirms on the floor. I start walking backwards.

'I'm sorry,' I say. 'Sorry. Sorry.'

Wiping my mouth I turn around to make my way back up the stone stairs. I catch Doctor Ipsen looking down for just one second before he walks away. My assailant grabs me by the shoulder again and this time when he turns me towards him, he pummels my face till I see the moon rise behind my closed lids and feel my spine scrape its way down the rocky wall.

I lie there for some time, my neck propped up on a rock, my clothes dishevelled, watching a gang of dockers pat my assailant on the back.

'Thanks mate, we could have lost the lot.'

'Couldn't let him get away with it,' my attacker replies.

'Do you think he'll be all right?' another asks.

They all turn to look my way. I am *Portrait of the Well-Beaten Man.*

'He'll live,' their hero tells them. He picks up a stray apple and hurls it into the river. 'He's a thug who only got what he deserved.'

I think to move but my limbs fail me; a thwarted effort despite my sense of urgency. Eventually the cold inspires me to try and move again. Getting up is difficult. My body feels arthritic. I come onto all fours and hang my head, giving my neck some relief, but my swollen eyelids are hard to open, and in this position especially, they throb. I look up and almost cry. I crawl to the street where I sit by the kerb and wave down a hansom. Several pass me by. One stops. The coachman jumps down.

'I appreciate this,' I manage to say

'You've been inside my carriage before. Doctor Gachet, isn't it?'

I nod.

'Do you remember me?' he says.

I see a tall, well-built man with curly hair.

'I'm sorry.'

'You're the homeopath. We had a long conversation about my father. You recommended Benzoic acid 30c for his gout. Works like a treat. He gets it about twice a year now instead of all the time. Whenever I give him the remedy it shuts him up fast. So, I owe you a favour. Where to?' he says, hurling me inside.

Sometimes I do believe that there is a God. What were the chances of entering the hospital mid-morning and Catherine being the first and only person I see?

I lean up against the wall and pant.

'Where's Madame Lemont?'

'She's had to go home, her mother is ill. But what happened to you?' There is a slight lilt to her voice, a sense of amusement as if she is talking to an errant schoolboy.

My face took all the blows but my body feels the most bruised and weak. I almost keel over. 'It's a long story. I got into a fight,' I say, as she hauls one of my arms over her shoulder, takes my weight and urges me to walk. If she marries they shouldn't revoke her right, it is innate for her to be a nurse.

In the medicaments room, also thankfully empty of any other staff, she dresses my wounds and administers Arnica 30c from a small vial she extracts from her pocket and gently rubs Calendula cream on my bruises.

'I'm very grateful,' I tell her.

'Well, others might but I couldn't leave you there propped up by the wall.'

'Sit down, Catherine, I have some bad news.'

'You didn't murder the other chap?'

'No.' I laugh and cover my face with my hand to hold it still against the pain. When I've composed myself I look up.

'This afternoon will be the last time I'll have the opportunity to see Bella. They're dismissing her from the hospital. Handing her over … .'

'To that horrible man?'

I place my head in my hands and see the Café Guerbois and Victorine blowing Turkish cigarette smoke up in the air. A man with a botched scar, his arms around a girl in a faded blue dress. Bella. She sways as if drunk.

'Look, as far as the Faculty are concerned, the homeopathy experiment has failed.'

'But I don't understand.'

'Do you know why Doctor Ipsen is so against homeopathy? He takes bribes from a laudanum manufacturer. I overheard the fraudulent dealings this morning whilst having breakfast in a café. You know, I've thought about it, he makes more money if patients don't get well.'

'What can you do?'

'I have no proof, no influence, there's nothing I can do.'

Catherine sits down. 'My mother always said it's a rotten world.'

It's Bella's final consultation. Doctor Ipsen is very much noted for his absence. Catherine sits behind me as usual but this time she doesn't write anything down. She stares trance like as if she doesn't want to be a witness to what is being said. Bella sits on a hard-backed wooden chair before me. I am in my usual position, propping myself up on the side of a bed.

'I had a visitor,' she says, beaming.

'Oh yes?' I answer. 'Who?'

'Victorine. She wants to paint me. She also said that if I ever get out of here, her mother will give me a job as a laundress.'

'And the man you are frightened of?'

'Yes,' she says, looking down. 'There is always him.'

'Bella, I don't know how to tell you this. The hospital has agreed for him to be your guardian. When he comes next time he has the right to take you home with him. I'm so sorry, if it was up to me this circumstance would never have happened.'

Bella looks at me impassively. With her fingers, she plucks out her eyelashes, one by one.

After seeing Bella, I walk out of the hospital, disregard the pebbled path and stain the bottoms of my trousers with mud as I walk across the damp grass.

'Doctor Gachet! Doctor Gachet!' booms a voice. Fast, heavy footsteps squelch in the mulch. Next, heavy breathing in my ear. Charcot.

'Oh my God, what's happened to you,' he says, panting as I, a devilish sight, turn round. 'Never mind, don't answer that, but please, I need to talk to you, come back inside.'

He marches me back through the hospital to his office like a brigadier. He shuts the door firmly and sits behind his desk.

'Genvieve is well,' he says. 'I am so grateful to you and homeopathy for that. You are an honourable man. I've spent many, many hours over the last half a day unable to concentrate on anything else but clarifying my own thoughts about you and your medicine and I've come to the conclusion that I should advise you not only as a colleague but also as a friend.'

'Advise me about what?'

'To be careful. Look, no one has suggested that I dismiss you but I've been advised that you are going away.'

'You obviously know something that I don't.'

'Exactly. Look Paul, you're playing a dangerous game with powerful people.' He rises to lecture and pace. 'I've seen it with my own eyes. Yes, homeopathy works, but would I give up my career for it, my life? Of course not, I have a family to think of, a wife.' Now he is standing behind his desk, holding onto it fast with ghostly hands and leaning forwards towards me like a bird of prey. 'I don't need homeopathy Gachet, I value my career already.' Restless again, 'You make me nervous,' he says, turning towards me, a hand reaching for two glasses from his cabinet. He sits down, splashes brandy into one and pushes the other and the bottle towards me.

It is my turn to stand. 'If it wasn't for homeopathy your daughter could be dead. Don't you think everyone should have access to this wonderfully effective and safe medicine?'

Charcot pulls the bottle back towards him, pours another measure of spirit into his glass, swigs and pours again. 'Have some,' he says. 'It will calm you down.'

My face aches overwhelmingly and I'm tempted by the offer of alcohol to burn its way down my oesophagus on a mission to deaden my pain.

'Come on,' he tempts me.

'Thank you for the talk, I'm going home to pack,' I say, and walk out.

Darkness and Light
November 25th

*'Common sense tells us that the things of the earth exist only a
little, and that true reality is only in dreams.'*

Charles Baudelaire

The same chipped paintwork, bare floorboards and the smell of
mouse droppings; the same posters advertising an exhibition at
the Louvre, five years ago; the same thumbprints on the wall, and
the same squeak on the stairs. But everything feels different. I
pause before reaching the top, follow the turn in the staircase and
darkness is swallowed by light coming through the open door.

'Gachet! You haven't been here for a while,' Père Suisse says,
aiming his sputum into the same aluminium cup he sometimes
used to collect student fees. 'I knew you'd be back; they all come
back.' He wipes his mouth with the back of his hand and stares at
me inquiringly.

'Thank you Suisse, it's good to be missed.'

Despite everything, I'm determined to be positive. I look
around the room. Nothing's changed: chairs set before easels; a
model on a stand sitting on a plush guilt and velveteen chair with
a shawl draped casually over her groin and one breast. She holds
a brass jug and looks towards it. Before her, five or six artists, as
usual, struggle for their own idea of perfection. Same old scene
except there isn't anyone here I recognise.

'Where is everybody?' I ask.

'They'll be back; they always come back.' Suisse replies,
sitting down on a stool, leaning forwards, hands on knees. ' …
Mostly.'

261

'Old man, I hate to disappoint you but I'm not coming in today either.'

Père Suisse nods. His eyes are misty, probably from too much absinthe and wine. I'm not in the mood to sketch with strangers, and although I feel I owe him something more by way of an explanation, I can't think of anything pacifying to say. In the end I just leave, touching the peak of my cap and wishing him a good day. I make my way through the darkness back out into the street where I buy several newspapers. I will read them tonight. I am heading for home to paint and make the most of the good light, so rare in November. On the corner of my road I am accosted.

'Doctor Gachet.'

A woman grabs my arm. She wears a navy cloth coat and scuffed, misshapen shoes that she has matched with a misshapen hat. She holds tightly onto a child's hand, a female aged around six. The child hits her repeatedly with her free hand.

'Get off me, you cow!' the little girl screams. 'Get off me, get off me, get off me!'

'I need help with her,' the mother says. 'I was told to tell you that Florette is walking now. Her parents said that I should wait outside your building and that you do not keep regular hours. They said I should come anytime and wait for your return. Would you be able to see my daughter?'

'What's wrong with her?'

'She has the devil in her. Would you be able to help?'

'I don't know,' and thinking of Bella's deep mental pathology, add, 'Yes, maybe, there is a good chance that I could.'

'You are not my mummy. I hate you. I don't want to see that ugly man.'

The child's mother looks at me. 'She lies all the time and doesn't care what she says. She's brandished a knife at one of my sons.'

'Come on follow me, best for you to tell me all of this in my consulting room.'

'The whole family is frightened to go to sleep at night. I've got six children and she could easily do one of us in – more than one of us.'

We manoeuvre our way through street vendors and mounds of litter.

'Ow! She's bitten me, the witch.'

The mother lets go of her child's arm and stops to suck at the tattoo of teeth marks on her wrist.

'What do I have to do, hang you up by your hair?' she screams at the girl.

'Bet you would if you could catch me,' the girl replies, sticking out her tongue, hands on her hips like a woman of the night.

'I was always such a good girl, I can't believe she's mine,' the woman tells me.

We arrive at seventy-eight.

'Come in,' I say. 'This is not a conversation we should be having on the street.'

I lead the way up to my apartment. The little girl kicks at my heels from behind as we climb.

'Don't do that,' her mother cries.

'I'm not doing anything.'

'Yes, you are, you're kicking the doctor.'

'No, I'm not.'

'Yes, you are.'

My key is in the lock. The door sweeps aside a pile of letters. One of the envelopes bears my father's handwriting. A sudden dark-grey cloud covers the sky and it feels like dusk. I pull down the light and strike a match. The girl kicks the coalscuttle. A puff of soot stains the brickwork of the fireplace.

'I'm so sorry,' says the mother, grabbing hold of her daughter's hand.

'Get off,' the child says, trying to pull away.

'Please take a seat in front of my desk.'

The mother sits down obediently. The girl wanders into my kitchen/dispensary.

'No!' I shout, running behind her, fishing her out.

'What do you like to do ... .'

'Edith,' her mother says.

'What do you like to do Edith?' I ask.

Her answer is an angry face.

'Can you draw me a picture?'

She shakes her head fiercely.

'Of anything you like. It doesn't have to be nice.'

She nods and says, 'No.'

Folding back my rug and carpeting the floor with newspaper, I set up an easel with drawing paper pinned at every corner and reluctantly hand over a piece of charcoal to Edith. Once behind my desk, I ask Edith's mother to tell me her daughter's story.

'She was born in August. The medium said she's a lion, what do I expect? I told her not this, definitely not this. All my children are washed, clothed and fed. I don't push them out into the street. My husband and I don't drink. We pay our bills. We have principles. There are those that judge me by Edith's behaviour. People who steal, people who cheat, selfish parents; they call us filth. Can you help me to understand that?'

I sit back in my seat, look over to the left wall for inspiration. A smaller copy of the original *Dejeuner sur l'Herbe* hangs there unframed. A present from Edouard.

'I don't think I can, but there's some evidence that a homeopathic remedy might encourage Edith to calm down.'

I glimpse at the girl. Her palms are blacker than a chimney sweep's. The paper on the easel is a mess of scribbles and she is tearing through it with a remnant of the charcoal and her nails.

Samuel Hahnemann's idea is that syphilis with its caries and ulcerative symptoms equals destruction in the body. Clemens taught me that a human being is one – the body is a mirror image of the mind. I'd wager there is syphilis in Edith's ancestral history. I'm also longing for this child to be gone before she takes the destructive mind set out on my furniture, especially the embroidered foot stool which Blanche brought over from her home especially for me to rest my feet upon.

'Please, watch over Edith whilst I make up her remedy,' I say to the mother, who up until now has been intent upon watching me.

It is dark in my kitchen/dispensary and I ignite a few candles. In the flicker of light and shadow, I prepare a dose of Mercury 1M, the remedy for destructive processes and syphilis. Once again the silence in the well grabs me, this time making my skin crawl and the hairs on the back of my neck stand like the hackles on a cat. As if I were in some bizarre children's game, I carry the remedy on a spoon to my patient.

'Look up there,' I say to Edith. 'What's that you've got in your mouth?'

In the failing light, she looks at the ceiling, opens her mouth with her fingers pulling at her lower jaw and I shovel the remedy in. She spits it out onto the newspaper covering the floor. It doesn't matter. The remedy coats the pills and it has seeped into her etheric body via her saliva. In my understanding she has taken the remedy.

'She's had the remedy.'

'She spat it out.'

'Trust me, she's had the remedy. You can take her home.'

Shuffling out her daughter, the mother says, 'I'm not paying for this. You've hardly asked me any questions. How do you expect her to get well with one pill that landed on your floor?'

'And bring her back next week,' I call out after them as they descend the stairs.

The room wears Edith's ruinous spirit. As I tidy, Edith melts into a pool of bizarre clinical encounters in my mind. Then I hunt through my store cupboard beside the bedroom for a clean sheet of canvas. It's time to paint *Night*. I set up my easel and line up the pastels on a clean wooden board: midnight blue, royal blue, and bitumen. With big sweeps of my arm I create a background of the compost-scented royal blue. I have no pending clinical situations to think about and there is nowhere else that I am supposed to be. I kick aside a nebulous, uneasy feeling, pick up the midnight blue and mould shapes into the canvas with the side of my hand of buildings vaguely resembling the Louvre and Notre Dame. My mind feels strangely relaxed. Blanche will be pleased. Tonight, I will make *her* dinner for a change.

I'm trampling my newspapers underfoot and I've just realised they are spoiled. I would like to have taken them later to a café to read. Rudely distracted from my creativity, I pick up the shredded papers off the floor, sit on the sofa with my feet on Blanche's footstool, and look over the articles that are not torn or smudged. One in particular, in small print on the penultimate page, catches my attention. At first I notice it because it has a homeopathic remedy stuck to its centre and then because the newsmonger mentions my name:

I was sitting next to a medical man the other day at the bar in my favourite inn. When I told him my name he remembered me as the writer who compared the cholera mortality rates between allopathic and homeopathic medicine in this newspaper some months ago.

He told me his name, which I promised not to mention in print, although I can say that he is a senior member of the Faculty of Medicine just finishing an investigation into homeopathy at the Hopital la Sâlpètriere in Paris. What I can also say is that he is an extremely generous human being when it comes to red wine.

His passion for controlling the quality of medicines came through most ardently in his speech. A point of view that he made great pains to suggest that I write about. In his opinion, medicines should be regulated by the Faculty of Medicine and should only include those that have been manufactured to a high standard and approved by an expert druggist. Remedies such as herbal quackery and homeopathy should be outlawed.

He related a recent incident concerning a Doctor Gachet, who had been granted permission by the Faculty of Medicine to treat a prostitute named Bella Laffaire with homeopathy for a diagnosis of manic insanity. Except when our hero examined the patient himself, he found that it was not insanity that she suffered from but waywardness. He said, 'Doctor Gachet claims great success because this woman can be released from hospital to go back into her old life. Such is the chicanery of homeopaths and homeopathy.'

I did not tell him that my daughter was saved from cholera by homeopathy.

November 26th

It seems as if everyone I have ever met is at Ernest Hoschedé's. Ernest fills parties with frequenters of the bohemian cafés in the same way his father fills up a department store with customers; enthusiastically. So, this get-together proves to be a much less decorous affair than Madame Manet's. There are no waiters here. Nevertheless, effervescent alcohol flows like surf over the necks of bottles held high above people's heads as they wade through crowded rooms. There is a large vat filled with the stuff over by the window in the main room. The air pulsates with human bodies all pushing close to one another. People, continually jolted, look around, find another familiar face, and in this way conversations are cut short and new ones initiated.

Blanche hangs on to my shirtsleeve. I can feel the heat of her through her lace dress. The din of ascending voices makes it hard to focus on the one you are meant to be listening to. Someone behind me says, 'Have you seen Sarah Bernhardt?'

'She's here?' another asks.

'I think she's just left.'

This is one gathering where there will be no guitar, piano or violin playing. Blanche, for once, can be social without being hampered by her instrument. Not that she would see it that way. She tugs at my arm.

'Victorine's over there, can we go and talk to her?' she asks, and I realise that for over ten minutes we have been in the centre of the milieu, silently looking around like foreigners stunned by an alien world.

'Of course, yes, let's go over there.'

She is by the window, behind the table generously bearing a

large, frosty, silver bowl of caviar, toast, and sour cream. A woman absently strokes Victorine's arm whilst she speaks with her lips close to our friend's ear. As we approach, I have second thoughts about disturbing the couple and look over to Blanche who tilts her head towards that side of the room.

'Paul,' Victorine calls, loud enough for a dozen guests to acknowledge with their eyebrows. We continue to shove ourselves through the throng in her direction.

'It's like Saint-Lazare station tonight,' she says, kissing me on the cheek and reaching out to clutch Blanche by the hand. 'This is Lilliene, my new girlfriend,' she giggles and says. 'Lilliene, this is the most wonderful doctor in the world, Paul Gachet. He can cure syphilis painlessly and prevent it. And this is my most favourite violinist of all time, Blanche Castets.'

I follow the direction of Victorine's line of vision as she throws back her head and relieves her face of a few strands of stray hair. Edouard speaks with Ernest, Claude, and two nameless ladies in the corner by the door. He has his back against the wall and his posse in a semi-circle around him.

'The last time I was in a place this crowded, Edouard was being ridiculed over *Dejeuner sur l'Herbe*. Being the model, I didn't feel too good either,' Victorine continues.

'And now?' asks her lady-friend still stroking her arm.

'Lilliene, such a shame you don't paint,' Victorine answers.

Someone pushes at my back. I lose my footing and fall forward into the round of our small group. When I look over my shoulder Charles is mouthing *bonjour*, although I'm not sure it's to me. My back is pushed again from the other side. I twist around to see Doctor Quackenetre standing next to Bella's pimp. Both of them look as if they want to talk to me. Their unspoken camaraderie is unlikely, looks wrong and feels ungainly.

'Excuse me,' I say, preparing to turn back to my female friends.

'Quite a lady's man,' the pimp says. 'I should give you my card.'

'After the last time we met, I have no intention of renewing our acquaintance.'

'Doctor Gachet is a homeopath. One of a growing number who deal in useless medicine and false ethics,' the doctor says to his new friend.

That familiar feeling of dread that seems to come upon me so frequently recently, has struck me dumb.

'Not a man you can do business with either,' the pimp says.

'No, not a businessman at all. There are many people here who like the idea of magic pills. It is a romantic notion that's taking over from religion. I see it as part of my job to integrate and help these people embrace reality. Although, reality can be pleasurable too, as you and I both know.'

'This is a strange conversation to be having in my presence,' I manage to say.

'Not really, you have to get a grasp of how things actually are. 'You see,' the doctor continues, now addressing his ally, 'one has to have a good understanding of the world in order to survive. You have it. My colleagues in the Faculty have it. I like to think I have it. The world has to turn. Decisions have to be made and men have to get on. Doctor Gachet here isn't in touch with the way things work but I think we can talk him into it given enough time. Now excuse me, one must socialise. It's lesson one.'

I catch them before they move off in different directions.

'One minute,' I call, taking a few steps forward to make our liaison more intimate and not to cause a scene. 'You are not worthy to shine Bella's shoes,' I say to the pimp. 'And you sir, are a bigot and an ass and should know better.'

Quackenetre affords me a disfigured smile.

I look over my shoulder. Victorine and Blanche are engrossed in conversation. Lilliene watches. I can hear their conversation. 'Musically you have something unique too. You say I involve my whole being when I play, but you involve the whole of life when you introduce a song and suddenly, the sound from the guitar, your voice, and the story, become one like a series of pictures in sound,' says Blanche.

'Thank you, that means so much, especially from you,' Victorine replies.

When I turn back, Quackenetre and his teammate have gone. I tell Blanche that I'm going to get another drink and ask if anyone would like one, but really it's an excuse to escape the conversation, any conversation. I meander through the crowd into an equally peopled and humid room and out again into the white marbled reception hall and sudden brightness, through the front door into a courtyard, where it's night again and teeth-chatteringly cold.

I break into a run.

When I return, Blanche is looking for me by the front door.

'Where have you been?'

'For a run, I needed to get some air.'

I look down at myself. My shirt is hanging outside my trousers and my tie is askew. I can feel clammy perspiration sticking my hair to my brow.

'You really should find the remedy for "acts strange at parties". I suppose you're going to ask if we can leave now.'

She is right. I was just about to say 'Can we go?' But I change my mind instantly, and spend the rest of the evening trying to catch the attention of Georges as he ever so expertly avoids me.

Later. In bed. Naked. Skin to skin. Floating. Blanche sleeps, back towards me. I move a lock of hair and kiss her shoulder.

'I love you,' I whisper.

She moans. I think over the events of this year: Edouard Manet treating Victorine like his girlfriend and marrying Suzanne; meeting Blanche at the protest; Bella Laffaire; The Salon des Refusés; myriad patients; my political situation; Charcot's voice – *I've been advised you're going away.* I pull my body away from Blanche, slowly, gently, so as not to waken her. She moans again. I put one foot on the floor. She throws her body backwards, towards me, awake.

'Paul,' she says sleepily, watching me. 'Come back to bed.'

I don't blow out the candle. I lie on my back. She's in my arms. Her hair tickles my nose when I breathe. There is tension all over me as she sucks one of my nipples and plays with the other.

I need to get back home. I need to start writing everything that has happened to me concerning the Faculty, the hospital and Bella Laffaire. I need to send this account to the journalist whose daughter was cured of cholera by homeopathy, along with my copy of the clinical report.

'Blanche,' I say to deter her.

'What?'

She lifts her head and looks at me with smoky eyes.

'Nothing,' I say.

She smiles.

I watch her kiss my chest. Feel her mouth on my belly. Feel the tension only where it's meant to be.

As soon as she is asleep, I leave her for the early hours on dark winter streets where Paris is like a magician looking over his shoulder checking-up on who sees how the tricks are performed.

Voilà!

Deep in the night, watching Paris with a sense that Paris also watches me. The heart of darkness, the truth scrabbling out from underground, rats that the journals convince are not real in Napoleon's sparkling world. They exist. I hear them. They squeak, grind and hiss and run over my feet, press their fat bodies under my trouser hem like a quick caress in passing. I smell the sewers in their coats. Their red eyes meet mine. We share the same landscape. We are prey, haunted to seek out the solace of this nowhere time.

The drunk at my feet rolls over into the gutter. An empty beer bottle follows him. His corpse-like pose represents the perfect example of a prize trick gone wrong. The tarts on their way home from hotels and the customers who would not pay for the whole night pass me by as if I am invisible or sidle up to me with their musk overpowered by cheap perfume.

'Come on, try it.' A particularly jaded one nudges me. 'You never know, you might like it,' she says, as if selling ice-cream.

Voilà.

The night itself is stiff in its near-frozen temperature. Hausmann's roofs are like the hats that conjure doves. Paris's body is ribbed with bridges, the Seine an icy vein. One solitary hansom jerks through the streets. A low-flying bat lands on the nose of the horse. If you painted that, they'd call it a fantasy, and yet I witness the phenomenal reality. The carriage passes, its passenger a solitary man dressed as a woman, who pulls his scarf across his face like a veil. His exposed eyes are laughing at me. Cutting winds, like the waves from a swordfight, lower my attention to the ground and blow me home.

Voilà.

The strange stillness I have come to associate with 78, rue du Faubourg St Denis is disturbed. Comforting sounds of mortality seep through its walls once more. I place my key in the lock. A baby cries. A door slams. A voice shouts, 'Can't you fucking shut that baby up?' On entering, 'No, I fucking can't', together with the percussion of continued banging on a wall. A dimmed oil lamp shakes on the ceiling and the crystals chime to the pounding of feet. I drag mine upstairs and mistrust what I see. There is light seeping from my apartment. I rub my eyes. It must be an illusion. The brightness must be coming from somewhere else and yet I can't quite convince myself that there's a moonstruck window in the roof that I have never noticed before. I slow my pace, afraid, stand still for a moment considering whether ghosts have taken over or men in white coats have come to take me away, but no, I push the door open fully.

Et voilà.

Mesmerised
Indeterminate dates

'The attacks of which I have been the object have broken the spring of life in me.'

Edouard Manet

He represents safekeeping in our community and therefore I should, but don't, feel satisfaction at his presence. In fact, I feel quite the opposite and especially so because he is sitting behind my desk. He has even bought himself a cigar to mark the occasion. I am surprised he hasn't planted a flag. I just stand there at the entrance watching him.

'I knew you'd be out when I came,' he says. 'Yes, don't think I don't see you cavorting with women and getting drunk in the cafés. I've been on night duty half my life.' He takes a long draw of tobacco and looks at its source with appreciation. I watch the curls of smoke form a cumulus. He nods. 'I know you Gachet. I know you better than you know yourself. I know the subversive company you keep. I know the strange receptacles I find in your rubbish and I know what you are plotting.'

He leans back in the chair, looks around and points his cigar at the Manet. 'Degenerate art goes well with quack medicine, does it?' he asks.

'Why don't you come to the point?' I answer the question with a question, an *Aurum* characteristic – gold – a remedy for depression and suicidal tendencies. I remind myself that doing a thing once does not in itself infer the need for any medication.

Fornier sits forward. 'The point is that I'm arresting you for the murder of Philip Breton.'

I go and sit on the sofa by the fireplace, stunned. Fornier, whose waist has expanded to fill the whole of my office chair, hauls himself out of the seat. He comes and stands beside me, blowing acrid smoke at me like a form of punishment.

'Aren't you going to say something, a man like you, so devious and clever?'

Elbows on my knees, I clasp my hands. I sense that he wants me to look up at him. I fix firmly on the floor.

'Well, you'd better get up then,' he prods, throwing his cigar into the grate.

I think I should run but as soon as I rise from the chair, Fornier is upon me, turning me to face away from him, pinning me up against the wall, knocking the *Dejeuner* sideways, pulling my upper arms to bring my hands behind my back. My cheek is squashed next to the painting, cold metal twisting the skin at my wrists.

'Start walking,' he commands, extinguishing the light, shutting the door.

By the stairs, I almost trip, unable to steady myself. My heart rate accelerates and I can feel the blood rushing to my face. I manage to gain my composure and remain still for a few seconds in the dark, knowing that if I don't move soon I will probably get pushed.

'Go on, I'm going to enjoy this,' Fornier says, with a shove.

I go slowly, concentrating hard on my feet in relation to the stairs and jamming my body into the banisters for support. I hear the gruff strike of a match behind me. Fornier sweeps down to my side and grabs my elbow. I get into a rhythm with my feet.

The cold air outside is sobering. An infantile moon is shy tonight. The street is ghostly, empty but for the sense of presence that lurks in shadows thrown by streetlamps.

'How long ago? And where did you find Monsieur Breton's body?' I ask. My voice gets entangled with an owl's warning note. Fornier propels me along the road.

'Don't ask questions. We have proof that it's you.'

'This is ludicrous. You can't have proof. There is no proof. I didn't do it.'

'Tell that to your fellow inmates. I have it on good word that you won't be having your say in a court of law.' Fornier chuckles.

Outcasts from society hear this I am sure, from their homes in doorways and alleyways and peeping out of secret passageways that lead to vaults underground. They keep me company, even though they hide.

'The truth will come out,' I say.

'You give me the creeps,' he replies. 'A man like you needs to be put away.'

Being taken in the early hours I am spared a real audience of people standing shoulder-to-shoulder, spitting and gossiping, as they line the road. There are no witnesses to my disappearance, credible or otherwise, which is obviously the reason they have chosen to arrest me at night.

'You might call yourself a policeman, but despite your petty self-righteousness, you stoop low, Fornier, very low.'

He swings me round and hits me in the mouth. I almost topple like a drunk but manage to catch myself as the stars on this clear night jump into my eyes. A corner of my lip widens painfully. I get a sense of the fragility of my gaping flesh and wish to protect it. I taste iron. Blood coats my chin. A swelling grows like an island in a red sea. Inspector Fornier pushes me on.

I'm in a cell, on the floor. My lip has dried to a crust. There is dust in my mouth and a wound that could turn septic. I'm craving water, thirsty for my own saliva. Grit sticks to the walls of my windpipe. I swallow, but the irritant persists. Coughing. Unable to clear the airway. Coughing. My eyes bulge. Coughing. My bruised cheek bangs against a surface that's as rough as a barber's itch. I stop coughing. My arms are tied behind me in a single clipped wing. An aural snap. The crackle of a flare. The glow of a match. Beside me, an old boot with holes nudges my naked wrist. Brown leather, bleached and softened by wear, no laces. A pale ankle caked in grime. The light goes out.

'They put you here when they want to forget you exist,' says a gravelly voice, surprisingly female.

I don't answer; can't answer. The back of my tongue sticks to my palette.

'Are you dumb? Have they pulled out your tongue? Hum, I've seen them do that before.'

I hear the flap-flap as the boot moves away. Quite unbelievably, I fall asleep, wakening to a grey triangle of light on the floor.

'I've been watching you all night. Gave me something to do,' my cellmate says.

The damp is palpable. Black walls glisten with moisture and are decorated with moss. I hear the drip, drip of water into a cask. Ironically, parched is an understatement. I can't even swallow. 'Water,' I try to say but only a low, hoarse moan comes out.

She moves across the cell in her calico skirt that has no petticoat, and is holey like mouse-nibbled cheese. There is something wrong with one of her hips. She stands before the cask and beside her a small pool on the floor generates a stench of ammonia, with fetid water darkening the ground. She takes a ladle full of liquid from the barrel and seesaws over to me.

'Just lick your lips,' she says, pouring the contents over my head. 'You'll die if you gulp it, and vomit violently from a few sips.'

She waits a few moments, standing in the light.

'Let's get you up now,' she says.

Her legs are splayed over me. She has her hands in my armpits. She pulls but I am not moving. She lowers her grasp to my waist and pulls harder. There is a crackle in her heavy breathing. 'Aaargh,' she yells. My back arches towards her. I bend my knees. I am on all fours now and my hands push into the floor so I can lift up my head.

'Well,' she says, pointing. 'You'll be more comfortable over there where there's a load of straw.'

You could say there is loads of straw in haystacks on the fields in Auvers in late summer. But this is hardly more than the amount of straw on the floor in Edouard's studio, a few wisps covered in a slimy, black substance.

'Thank you,' I manage to say, crawling towards it anyway.

'You're welcome, I like to help others,' she says.

Propped up against the wall with wet seeping through my skin, we sit on the straw facing each other. Our breakfast is some thin gruel smelling of old cheese and a strong broth of sour herbs.

'Drink it,' my cellmate advises when I screw up my face. 'Eat and drink, you'll need the strength. What they give you is safe.'

'How do you know?'

'I've been here a while. I've seen quite a lot of them, men like you. They come and go, sometimes overnight.'

'What happens to them?'

'Some die from the contaminated water. Some get out I suppose, else are tortured to death. I don't like to think about it.'

'And you, what about you? Why are you here and how have you survived?'

Shadows from the bars across the windows fall across her face. Heavily lined as if she is very old but her eyes are clear and fiery and her smile belongs to someone much younger.

'You certainly ask a lot of questions.'

'I'm trained to.'

'What are you trained in?'

'Medicine.'

'Well, I haven't survived because of that,' she spits into the middle distance, carefully avoiding our tatters of straw. 'My own mother knew more than the doctors will ever know.'

'Paul Gachet,' I say, offering my hand.

She grabs it. 'Rose Martin. Protesting. I'm here for protesting. They think I don't know what they're up to, what goes on, but I know. I've got eyes. They can't fool me. I've outsmarted them a number of times and they don't like it.' She rubs her thighs with

278

her hands as if polishing her palms. 'I was taught to read and I've read enough to know. I'm a political prisoner, that's what I am. They can't try me because I've done nothing wrong, but it doesn't stop them from using their might. They want to keep me quiet so they lock me inside.'

'I see. Look Rose,' I say, feeling my bladder swell into that bearing down feeling, 'Where can I, you know, urinate?' I'm crossing my legs tightly.

'In the barrel,' Rose says. 'And count yourself lucky that I didn't let you drink from it.'

Once there, I look over my shoulder.

'Are you going to watch me?' I say.

'Yep,' she chuckles. 'It's the only entertainment I get.'

A musty offensive odour is coming from my hair. I've been trying to get away from it all morning.

'You got nits?' Rose asks. 'They make you jumpy.'

'Yes, and they can also make you peevish.' I touch my lip. It's sore and swollen but definitely healing.

'Now that I come to think about it, that's true, Jean had nits and he was always irritable – Jean being the boy next door when we were small. She scrubbed his flesh till it was raw and weeping, that woman who claimed to be his mum. So, I shouted across the road to her, "My mum thinks you're making it worse". She looked at me funny and ran inside like I was going to fly and hit her. I lied. My mum would never have passed judgement. She used to say, "poor woman, God hasn't granted her an awful lot of sense but she's doing the best she can". It was the doctors who advised the baths.'

'Do you get nits living here?'

'Nah, what would they want me for, I'm covered in filth.'

She scratches her head. 'Am I irritable?' she asks.

Rose sharpens a pebble on the floor. She says it will come in useful but doesn't say what for. The grating sound breaks up hours of silence. I sit inside a shadow with my arms around my knees, watching a fly crawl up the wall, wondering if it will fly away before reaching the arched ceiling. I'm practicing the preliminaries to meditation. It's lethal for me to think, and in spite of my earnest efforts, tears roll down my face. I sniff and wipe my cheeks with my dirty hand.

'What keeps you sane in here?' I ask.

'I'm safer here then I've ever been. No one tells me what not to think.'

The fly disappears inside a crack. The grating sound starts to aggravate.

'Can't you stop doing that?' I ask, my voice more aggressive than I mean it to be.

'No, I need to finish. This is going to be an indispensable tool.'

'But can you stop doing it anyway? The noise is playing on my nerves.'

She carries on.

Whereas before all my joints were stiff with aching, I get up from the floor with pliant limbs and march over to Rose. In one sweep I tear the stone away from her hand and aim it across the cell. It bounces off the wall and lands in the barrel with a plop.

'You're angry,' she says.

I have my hands on my hips and pant. 'Yes,' I say. 'I am very angry.'

'I was angry too, but I've been here a long time.'

'You make it sound like an epiphany.'

'A what?'

'An inspiration, an illumination, the god-damn awakening!'

Rose is quiet. She scrabbles on the floor for another stone.

'Well?' I scream at her.

She looks up at me and says, 'In a way it is.'

I don't like to be this person, too many raw moments are pregnant with self-pity. If it would do any good I would attack the door, screaming, 'Fuck you, you bastards, this is not fair.'

'This is not fair,' I say, calmly.

'I know.'

Much later, with the onset of darkness without a moon, I ask, 'How come you had a match when I first arrived?'

'The guard who brings dinner dropped it one time.'

'Oh.'

'Anything else you want to ask?'

'Yes, actually, yes. Why aren't you angry anymore?'

Rose looks at me. 'That's a big question,' she says, looking to the ceiling. A drop from above falls onto her face, like a tear. 'I was so angry I pulled out my hair.' She looks away and says no more as if she has just told me the definitive answer.

'And?' I ask, eventually.

'History, it's all in the history. People take sides, but it's always some powerful bastards manipulating things. Very few of them care about ordinary folk. It made me realise that I was a clodpate to think that I could ever do anything about it.'

'What's the answer then?'

'There is no answer. Agh … ,' she says. 'You're bringing it all back.' She hits her forehead repeatedly with the heel of her palm.

I lie on the light coating of dirty straw with my back towards Rose, the two of us odorous, and even though we don't touch, strangely intimate. I can't sleep. She's right. Throughout history the balance of power shifts, but, fundamentally, human nature remains the same. But she's wrong – in theory at least, there is an answer and I'm wide awake and excited by the possibility. What if the whole picture of disease is not expressed solely by any individual, the individual being merely one part that makes up the whole, like the stomach, the heart, a leg or an arm? And the whole body is a family, a country, society, humanity … .

It is night. I must remember that it is night and such thoughts only seem less fanciful because of the lack of sunrays. But what remedy would heal, say, the staff at La Sâlpètriere?

Characteristics shared generally by the nurses, Doctor Ipsen and Doctor Charcot are: *love of power but respectful to superiors, deceitful, ambitious.* My heart pumps wildly with enlightenment. The remedy is Lycopodium. I imagine creeping through the hospital with a bottle of high-potency Lycopodium dust and sprinkling it into the air for everyone to ingest.

I turn towards Rose. Clouds have shifted and her face is a luminous blue in the moonlight. There's a rattle in her chest that I'm sure has been instigated by the awful and relentless damp. Sometimes it makes me want to hang on to the window bars and haul myself up just to breathe something fresh. Rose's mouth hangs open and a small trickle of saliva rolls down her chin.

Jagged lumps of stone dig into my flesh. I manoeuvre my body then toss myself to face the other way. And Paris? What remedy would I put in the water that supplies Paris? I can't think of an answer but the world suddenly appears very small and all the people in it interconnected in some way. Perhaps we are like ants, each one of us taking part in some vast mission, but only aware of our own individual task? And therefore, maybe, what appears to be might not really be so. It suddenly feels dangerous to presume or even to contemplate mass healing when no one person can be privy to the whole. Therefore, how can anyone judge any outcome? What to do if there's a healing crisis? On second thoughts it is best to stick to the curing of individuals.

I sit up and rub my damp forehead with clammy palms. Of all the things that I don't understand, my most immediate question is, how have I ended up in a sewer like this?

Some afternoon follows some morning. I'm watching the light. It delivers memories. The sun behind a skeletal tree beams onto the door and it reminds me of May in Blanche's downstairs room. I tell myself that no reminiscence is allowed, and instead look towards the dark, wet corner and the gloom, hearing the scratching of rats, the parting of dry bracken and the painful cry of a fox outside. I breathe in Blanche's phantasmal scent, have the

282

taste of her skin on my tongue. Rose watches as I tremble and sweat with longing.

There is a certain time of night when the wall is splashed with moonlight and the world is mysterious, which reminds me of Montmartre. I'm inspired to capture it in pigment upon canvas, but have to make do with going through the motions in my mind.

My stomach nags with hunger. I can feel the jutting bones crunch in my shoulders. It feels as if I haven't eaten for days. A loud clang jolts me. Light from a lantern is a shaft through the peephole that makes me scrunch my eyes. I use my hand for a shield. The door squeals open. Blinding white bursts through the dam.

'I've brought you some food,' our jailer says. 'I hope you're satisfied. I've got out of a nice warm cosy bed with my wife to come and feed you two. Couldn't sleep when I realised that I'd forgotten your rotten needs. Not many men are as generous as me,' he says, his voice trailing towards us.

'What's he here for? It's the middle of the night.' Rose's words are so close to my ear I feel the condensation of her breath against my already moist lobe.

'He's brought us food,' I whisper back.

'About bloody time.'

My sight has adjusted. Our man's eyes are two pieces of shining coal and the ruddiness of his cheeks glows in the light. His large stomach prohibits bending without a clumsy effort. He bangs a tray down before us. Cold broth slaps over the side of a small metal pan. A wedge of bread sits on a bed of its own crumbs, and next to it, a chunk of cheese with a layer of mould that's a more muted emerald shade than the bright moss on the walls. He strokes his unruly beard. Rose and I are wide-eyed before him like children in a fairytale.

'Done my bit,' he says, before walking out.

Rose hits her forehead with her palm several times.

'You really must stop doing that.' I say.

Then, as if someone has given us a shotgun start, we are silhouettes in the dark, tearing and gobbling food like lions at a slaughter. With dry bits lodged in our throats and threatening our breath we pull at the pan from one to the other, losing more liquid over its side. I catch myself out and let go slowly.

'You first,' I say.

Rose looks at me with animal eyes, gulps noisily. By the light of the moon I see the whiteness of her throat and its muscles tighten and relax as she drinks. I pray to whatever deity might listen that she saves me some, and she does, but I'm so thirsty for liquid it is a tease and nowhere near enough. I watch Rose lick the pads of her fingers and use them as magnets for any fragments of food.

'What are you staring at?' she asks.

'Rose?' I say, with my hunger heightened and not sure whether I am any better or worse off now. 'Nothing.'

She sucks at her fingers as if they're lollipops.

'It's just that … .'

She lifts her chin questioningly.

'It's just that I believe the world needs people like us. Ultimately, nothing changes it's true, but if we don't fight for what we believe in then the world has got to be worse off, surely?'

She looks through me.

'Rose?'

'Without us in here, you mean?'

'It's not just us Rose, there are others too.'

'I don't see them,' she says, twisting her head to look over one shoulder and then the next.

'Well, you're in here.'

'And if there were others, they'd be picked up like us and dumped in here too.'

'You don't believe that.'

'Of course I believe it. It doesn't do you any good to be

284

caring. It bothers you and bothers you and bothers you until you have to yell, aim a rifle, or spit in someone's face, but it doesn't do you or anyone else any good, you just end up in here!'

Rose picks her teeth with her fingernail then lies down again. A gust of cold wind whistles and shoots itself through the window at my thinning body until I shiver and wrap myself in my own arms. Rose shivers too.

'In my next life,' she tells me, 'I'm not going to care.'

Days and nights slide, one upon the other, like shuffled cards. How many days? How many nights? Must be quite a few. I walk round and round the circumference of the cell, moving through a forest of shadows and light. Rose lies on the wisps of straw wheezing loudly. Her hair is wet and slimy like seaweed. I have touched her forehead. It radiates a furious heat. Impotence from having no remedies at my disposal has created a knot in my stomach and a lump in my throat. The feeling brings me back to a long ago time when I paced the floor in my apartment with terrible frustration. Ayush has come back to visit me in my mind.

'It's no good Ayush, I can't concentrate on my breath.'

'Yes, you can,' he says. '"Can't" is a restriction you impose upon yourself.'

'But I have thoughts that seduce my mind all the time.'

'Then banish them.'

'How do I do that?'

'Please, sit down, you are becoming worried and that is the opposite of the peace and serenity that this practice is trying to bring you.'

'Peace and serenity, huh.'

'You must sit down. You are feeling too much tightness in your throat.'

'How do you know that?'

I slump on the floor.

'Relax the tightness in your throat. Make your spine straight and your head light as if someone is pulling your hair towards the

285

ceiling. Close your eyes. Feel the breath and see it entering your lungs. See it leaving your nostrils to mingle with the air. You are not forcing your mind. It must be effortless effort. Only have the intention and the rest will come.'

I have the intention. I have asked our jailer to fetch us a remedy and I have recited Georges de Bellio's address to him several times.

'I do enough for you hopeless prisoners,' was his response.

'You could save her life. Could you live with yourself if you don't?' I appeal to his shadowed face.

'What good would it do? What's her life worth living in here, anyway?'

'*Natrum sulph.*' Natrum sulph – the compound mineral with characteristic symptomatology of asthma worse for dampness.

'Excuse me?'

'The remedy you need to bring for Rose is called "*Natrum sulph.*" '

'Is that her name?'

'Yes.'

'I've been bringing her food for two years and I didn't know that.' His eyes glaze over in thought.

'Do you remember the address?'

'Yes,' he comes back to life.

'*Natrum sulph.*' I can't remind him too many times.

Worn out, I am reduced to a shivering wreck. I wonder if it's New Year's Eve. There are voices outside, singing. It sounds like festivity. The temperature has dropped suddenly. A sharp, cold wind blows through the iron bars. I look up at the whiteness of the moon as if it could answer my prayers for warmth, Rose's health, and flesh on my bones.

Can it really be true, what has happened to me? A question I ask myself many times a day. There is no doubt that I have been a trusting fool, a stupid puppy with an ugly master. Looking back, I didn't stand a chance. The Faculty of Medicine must have sent

Ipsen to humour me, never thinking that insanity would benefit from a remedy with the overwhelming ingredient being water. They allowed me the stage upon which to hang myself, slowly. After all, I'd been nipping at their member's heels for years.

How they must have panicked, especially Ipsen when Bella began to improve. And how they must have patted themselves on the back with relief when they realised they could get away with denying that she was ever mad. And Charcot, my friend Charcot, brilliant, yellow, cowardly, but gleaming like the sun.

And what does that make me? An insipid do-gooder? I thought I was more than that. I thought I was passionate. *To restore the sick to health, to cure, as it is termed* – homeopathy for the world and the world returning to Atlantis, when in reality, who would forgive homeopathy if it stripped the world of its palette of colours, its conflict and its stories? Religions have their gods, and the astrologers would have it that the universe dictates. On Earth there is no utopia, and yet, the idealistic desire for it lurks strongly within me. Perhaps I am a dangerous man after all.

1864?

'I remember that, although I was full of fervour, I didn't have the slightest inkling, even at forty, of the deeper side of the movement we were pursuing by instinct.'

Camille Pissarro

Through the hole in the wall that I increasingly refuse to call a window is a pearly white screen. I stare at it for hours with eyes that feel as if they are protruding through their lids. Sometimes I see an iridescence that brings a smile cracking through the frozen bones in my face and warming the numbness in my brain just a bit. Even my lashes are frozen. If I had dexterity in my hands I would pick at the tiny icicles and eat them.

The membranes in my throat are glued together, my lips have split and my mouth is so dry it is raw. My muscles are locked and my skeleton is brittle. I can't move, so I just stay where I am in this catatonic state.

I'm not sure how long I have been here. Maybe I've seen dozens of moons. We don't seem to be visited by the jailer anymore. Just stillness. A, wet, cold stillness and a silence that hums around me whilst my innards have turned to flames. My breath rolls out of my mouth in clouds. I am hungry for air, trying to stay with it, not abandon myself too soon.

And then I hear voices, the human sound of fraternity and communication, a beautiful memory breaking through the barrier that separates me from the world. Faraway voices, soft, quiet tones becoming louder and more distinct, getting closer.

My lips try to widen into a smile. The pain of broken flesh is worth it just to know that there is a pulse in my heart after all.

Laughter. The clack-clack-clack-clack of stepping feet that can still feel their toes. 'I'm here,' I try to say. 'In here.' But my throat is clogged and I can't make a sound.

'It's intolerably cold.'

'That's an understatement.'

'It's starting to look doubtful. Every one of these cells seems empty. No sound from any of them. It's the middle of winter, they've all probably died.'

'Who?'

'The prisoners.'

'Ah, yes, of course. How's your leg?'

'It's all right.'

'Maybe it's healing at last, it's normally worse in the cold.'

Metal upon metal. Clunk, clunk, clunk, squeak and boom, and a gust of wind. They are inside now. The door. My heart lifts but my neck is too stiff and won't obey the desperation to turn my head around.

'Oh, my word.'

Mucus blown into a handkerchief. 'Excuse me.'

'Would you gentlemen care to get this over with quickly? The note said that you are to take him, not hang around to enjoy the view.'

'Is that him?'

'I can't tell; he has his back to us.'

'He's alive.'

'How do you know?'

'He's sitting up.'

'He's slumped, he could be dead.'

'I really think we should prod him and find out.'

'You mean test his breathing.'

'Yes, and with the stench in here, I wouldn't blame him if he's not.'

Fingers dig into the waning muscles of my arms and the ache is so insupportably deep that an animal cries and the beastly noise is coming from me.

No more white light. No more frost in my lungs. Or needle sharp breath. No stinging of flesh. Just warmth. Lovely warmth of soft bedclothes. My resting spine is bruised and aching, but my fingers move. I'm not in a prison cell. I'm not in my prison cell! My heart skips a beat. Maybe it was a nightmare that didn't really happen.

Where am I then? I can't feel my feet. Were they blackened with frostbite? Did I have them removed? The ceiling light is on. Powdery blue velvet drapes are drawn. It must be night. That's a small version of *Olympia* on the opposite wall. I have never seen this room before. Have I seen this room before? Have I lost my memory? I test myself. I am Paul Gachet of Lille, doctor, and there is pain in that thought. Paul van Ryssel, artist. That's good. That's very good. I remember who I am.

'*Bonjour*. You're are awake.' I know the voice.

I just can't seem to find the will to turn my head and look.

'Georges, is that you?' I say.

Daylight pushes through a gap in the curtains and lies on the floor like a sleeping child.

'Georges?'

'Yes.'

'How many days since I came here?'

'I think about ten.'

'Do I have all my limbs?'

'Yes, but you have been very ill.'

'And now?'

'You are recovering.'

'What remedy?'

'*Carbo veg*, at first, then *Agaricus*. Saving life and limb quite literally in your case.'

There's a pink light coming through the curtains, gentle and womanly.

'Georges?'

No answer.

The silence that mocks me is like a woman too, a woman with a tongue in her cheek. An oak cupboard stands sentinel to one side. A china jug in a basin poses on the dresser ready to be painted. *Olympia,* its colours in shadow are hard to make out.

'Anyone?'

A fly or something has landed on my forehead. With one hand I attempt to swipe it away and find delicate fingers grasping mine, firmly and briefly. I try to open my lids but I see only black.

Thirst. Water. Reaching out a little frantically to the bedside table. Knocking the glass that arrives by magic at my lips. Water. Warm and moist on my tongue but my body suddenly shivers uncontrollably with the cellular memory of iced temperatures freezing the marrow of my bones.

I sit propped up on pillows holding a china teacup, creating a stir in a vervain infusion with trembling hands. I have just been told that I have been slipping in and out of consciousness for the last three weeks. Georges and Edouard sit beside my bed with their hands in their laps like an audience that is difficult to entertain.

'You're a bit of a celebrity at the Guerbois these days,' Edouard says.

'Competition,' I smile.

'Yes, the jury's out as to which one of you has created the biggest scandal,' says George.

'I've been in prison?'

'Where do you think you've been, on a yacht in Montpellier?'

I ignore Edouard's remark and ask Georges, 'Have you forgiven me?'

'Have I what?'

'I guess you have then.'

'Ah, that,' he says, remembering.

More silence. The screech of mating birds, the distant sound of a Pianola.

291

'Well, I'd better be going. I was just passing on my way out to lunch.' Edouard stands up and falters like a drunken man. I notice he does not have his cane.

He walks to the door almost perfectly but leans slightly to the right. Standing in the doorway he turns around, 'Who is Rose?' he asks.

I think about the cafés. An endless whirr of multitudinous conversations amidst the chink of glasses and the clattering of plates, the scent of pipe tobacco mixed with alcohol, the tang of boiled seafood, and the implausible truth that Edouard's world hasn't changed a bit. He asked me a question. What was it?

'Pardon?' I ask.

'Blanche asked if I knew her.'

'Rose?' I say.

'Yes.'

'Rose was my cellmate.'

He hesitates. I nod my head slowly.

'Oh, the old lady we found next to you with the cadaverous smell?'

I close my eyes, a little touched.

'Well I'm off then,' he says, eventually.

I always used to think Georges a little spoiled and yet he lives alone, without staff, and has the makings of a very good wife. The chicken broth he serves is excellent and he leaves me alone for hours at a time, always making sure there is fresh water on the table next to me when he goes out. However, my sheets have not been changed for quite a while. The odour of my own perspiration is unhealthy and a little disconcerting as I notice it for the first time. I make a mental note to ask him for a bath and clean sheets when he comes home. I'm still unaware how I came to be here and how Edouard and Georges happened to show up and rescue me like musketeers.

'I'm very grateful,' I tell Georges when he comes in next time.

'For what?'

'For this.'

'You don't think I could leave you to rot in a stinking cellar do you? Saving people is my role in life. I am a homeopath, like you, dear boy.'

'How did you find me?'

'You sent someone asking for some remedy or other. A Monsieur Detramp, which I thought was strange; I've always known you to make your own medicines.

' "You don't think I'm just going to give it to you?" I said to the man, and told him that I'd be glad to help but wanted to deliver the medicine myself.

' "Well, you'll have to speak to Inspector Fornier then, because he's the one that gives the orders concerning this case," he said, in very bad French.'

' "Inspector Fornier?" I asked.

' "Yes," he said, "Your friend is in jail." '

'I was shocked. Shocked.' Georges stands by the window, looking out as if he's expecting someone. 'I couldn't think what stupid thing you might have done, so I told Detramp to take me to this man Fornier straight away. He stood there with his hand out, the fusty sod, rubbing his grubby forefinger and thumb.'

Silence.

'And what happened then?' I asked.

'Where was I? Oh yes, I saw Fornier. He met me in your apartment. It's been ransacked, by the way.'

I can feel myself wince.

'Strangely enough, your kitchen/dispensary is untouched and there's a painting of Camille's, one of Victorine's and a *Dejeuner* still hanging on the walls; I had to put them all straight of course. It seems to be your case-notes that have gone along with every book you've ever owned. Tell you what, you don't need to get a new carpet, your clothes are making a very nice job of it on the floor.'

'Bella's case-notes,' I say, remembering I was going to send the folder to the journalist.

'Who?'

'I've shown homeopathy can work on diseases of the mind. I received permission from the Faculty to treat an advanced case of delusional insanity under the supervision of a Doctor Ipsen, head of pharmacology. He watched my patient's thought processes grow more balanced over a relatively short period of time.'

Georges slowly seats himself in the chair at my bedside.

'Go on,' he says.

'I was invited to lunch at Doctor Charcot's home, my boss. I was told that my patient – Bella Laffaire – had been misdiagnosed. That madness cannot be cured and therefore Miss Laffaire was never really ill.'

I attempt to get out of bed but I am weak and have to be content with sitting on the side, naked, lowering my head in order to muster up some energy. I would make a good portrait of a skinny man.

'And they have the audacity to damn homeopathy when they have nothing curative to offer themselves. Charcot's daughter, who had a sudden dangerously high fever when I was there, was saved by one dose of Aconite, Belladonna and *Chamomilla*, to which Charcot was very grateful, but not grateful enough to stick out his neck for me or homeopathy,' I say, my weak voice in an ascending pitch throughout. My speech seems to have tired me. I have a pain in my chest that I try to locate with my fingers. I hear the distant click of the front door opening and look up.

'Georges I've brought the soup,' a voice calls and the door to the bedroom sweeps open. I start to tremble uncontrollably again. Georges walks out of the room.

'You're safe,' Blanche whispers in my ear as she puts a blanket around my shoulders.

I nod a little too ferociously. She pushes my shoulders back towards the pillows, and kisses my forehead.

'I've been worried about you,' she says and I laugh.

'You disappeared. I didn't know what to think.'

'Rose was my cellmate. She died.' Silent tears are falling.

'You need to sleep,' she says, standing up.

'No!' I call out. 'I've been sleeping and now I'm awake.'

She allows me to hold her and I cry like a baby in her arms.

December 18th

We are having breakfast in George's overlarge kitchen with its black and white tiled floor, cream painted walls and frosted glass windows. It was Blanche who made the broth and now it is I who have introduced Georges to croissants. I decide that those wifely aspirations I perceived in him are not his forte after all.

'You still haven't told me what Fornier said to you.'

'After two minutes in his company I decided to take him to the Bade for dinner. He came as soon as he was off duty and I bought him enough alcohol to loosen his bureaucratic tight-lipped tongue and do you know what he told me?'

I widen my eyes.

'He said that when he received word that he was to arrest you for a murder you never committed, he had been delighted to do it and throw away the key. When I asked him why, he said he has reason to believe you are planning to overthrow Napoleon! Talk about deluded.'

'Unfortunately, I think he really believes that,' I say. 'What about Breton?'

'He's been born again as a man of property in Provence.'

'I'm obviously worth quite a lot locked up, how did you get me out?'

'I took out an envelope stuffed with rather a lot of francs and asked if this would change his mind about your role in organising a coup. He seemed to be very accommodating after that. Oh, I forgot to tell you, I found a note pushed under your door from a lady called Catherine.'

'What did it say?'

'She's lost her job, but she has a friend who works at the

Hospital for Sick Children who has been sending her homeopathy patients because you have obviously gone away. She asked if you'd get in touch upon your return.'

'Do you have the note?'

'No, Fornier grabbed it out of my hand and tore it up. I have no idea of what he thought I might do with it – give it to you I suppose. It had her address on it.'

'It's time I went home.'

'Thank God for that,' he says, slapping me on the back.

December 19ᵗʰ

Having no key, I hire a man to change the lock. He asks me several times whether I am sure this is my apartment. I tell him to go and check with Inspector Fornier who is conveniently pacing the street below. He looks at me oddly, but he changes the lock anyway. When I finally get inside, home acts like a stranger, even after I've cleared up the debris of torn paper and ripped clothes. It is the walls that alienate me in the way of an abandoned pet upon the owner's return.

'Am I different?' I say aloud.

I go to sit on the stool in my kitchen/dispensary.

'This is *my* basket of logs. I just left them down here whilst I carried the other one upstairs,' a sweet woman's voice berates from the well.

'Are you joking? It's mine. I need them. The temperature might have risen slightly but it's going to snow tonight,' a gruff and aggressive male voice replies.

'Precisely, that's why I bought two baskets and carried them all the way from Montmartre! I can't fight you. You're bigger and stronger than me. But, what am I going to do, you bastard, when it's freezing tonight and my baby cries? If she dies her father will kill you.'

'I think not, I don't see him around.'

I can't find the energy to run downstairs. It used to feel as if Paris was my city and I, intrinsically, belonged to it. Lately, as I lay awake for hours staring at the floral cornice of George's guest room ceiling, all I thought about was London as described to me by Henri with its embrace of modern art and its open-mindedness.

Hands in pockets, I stand by the window. Through a small pane of clear glass I see an angular piece of brickwork in shadow against a white marble sky and a bird in flight.

'Are you harassing this woman?' another man's voice.

'I was just asking if she wanted me to help her carry that basket of wood up to her apartment.'

'It sounds like she's declining your generous offer.'

'Good riddance then.'

So, Paris can manage without me.

December 20th

Victorine lets me in. 'She's upstairs. I suppose you want to know why I'm here.' She leads the way and I am jealous of her sense of belonging. 'We've become good friends,' she explains.

Blanche's bedroom greets me like a guest. I stand at the threshold momentarily, case in hand. Blanche lies on the bed fully clothed facing away from me. I am nostalgic for what used to be in this room. I go forward and hold onto the brass bedstead at the foot of the bed. Blanche turns and stares at the case – a still life by the door.

'Hello,' I say.

She doesn't move. I sit next to her and take her hand in mine. We stay like that for quite a while. There are no neighbours squabbling outside the window, you can't even hear a carriage rolling over the pebbles. This is a much quieter part of town. She lifts her head and looks at me.

'You're too thin,' she says.

'I'm not the same.'

'I'm not sure I know how to react to that,' she says, swinging her legs over the side of the bed.

'Yes, and don't go teaching Victorine any of your naughty ways,' I say.

Blanche laughs.

I squeeze her hand.

'Oh Paul, this is so difficult for me.'

'I know, but you have a life here whilst everything about me is lost and uncertain.'

'And you don't want me to come with you.'

'No,' I say. 'Not at this time.'

December 20th
Night

That conversation with Blanche plays on my mind: her lips, soft on my neck, and the definite arousal conceived by her body against mine. I am angry with myself for not saying how difficult this is for me too, that if she came with me she would end up hating me, that I'm troubled and must do this alone. It's six-thirty in the evening. I'm in the back of a hansom riding out of Paris towards Calais where I will board a boat to Dover in the early hours. I look behind me at the road. Snow has just started to fall as predicted. My departure will probably be delayed. Cafés give way to tree lined roads but the moon still follows me. It feels like midnight a long way from home.

Epilogue
1883

The door clicks closed. Paul Gachet looks up from his notes and looks around him. The walls host a whole collection of impressionist paintings, hung, what might first appear randomly but is in fact, with great precision. Works by Camille Pissaro, Edouard Manet, Claude Monet, Armand Guillaumin, August Renoir and others. He takes a satisfied breath and leans back in his chair to admire the artwork. Paintings, like homeopathy, have the power to change one's perception if you let them. Paul chooses to let them have their way with him constantly.

His final patient has just left. He looks at his watch: three o'clock, there's still time to catch the train to Auvers sur Oise. Increasingly, he dislikes staying overnight in Paris these days. The city often feels like the loneliest place in the world and the countryside is a soft balm for his melancholia.

He recalls an afternoon when he'd spent a day painting by the window in his old apartment in rue Montholon and he was struck with a deep and perceptible malaise. He had dabbed the canvas with pale colours that lent nothing to lifeless forms. Ayush was there at the time eating strange food and observing Paul.

'Melancholy is a sickness of the privileged,' Ayush said, 'Satisfaction can only be maintained when there are no expectations.'

Paul is yet to meet the European who is satisfied with what he has. Maybe it would be the wrong decision to go home tonight, he thinks. Perhaps he should attend the dinner arranged by Camille for his painter friends. He could spend some time visiting Le Salon beforehand. It is always interesting to know what the judges at Le Beaux Arts have chosen to exhibit.

He takes down his frock coat and hat from a hook by the door, locks up and begins to make his way downstairs. A liveried coachman ascends at the same time. Paul stands to one side to let the man through.

'Doctor Paul Gachet?' the coachman asks, lifting his hat.

'Yes, why?'

'Monsieur Edouard Manet is desperately ill. I have been asked to come and find you to ask if you would accompany me to his house.'

Eugenie Manet opens the door.

'Doctor Gachet, I really don't think there is anything you can do,' she says.

'Well, perhaps I can still see him, now that I am here,' he says, taking off his hat.

Looking smaller and less imposing in these more modest surroundings, she leads the way through the corridor to Edouard's bedroom, lets Paul in and closes the door behind him.

Edouard lies in a bed opposite. Suzanne and Leon sit by his side.

'Hello, Edouard,' Paul says, clutching his remedy case in front of him.

'I'm dying. Like my friend Baudelaire. How can you bear to come and see me?' Edouard asks. 'The rheumatism has turned to gangrene. They won't tell me – is it syphilis?'

'May I examine you?'

'I should have asked you to do that years ago.'

Edouard has a golden quilt over his body that matches the curtseying swags at the window. The odour in the room is pungent and foetid.

'May I?' Paul asks, grabbing hold of the edges of the bedspread and pulling back the quilt to view a leg like raw meat that has been burnt at the edges.

There is a deposit on the cotton sheet the colour of scarab. He places the pad of a finger upon each of Edouard's lower lids and gently pulls them down. The conjunctivae are yellow and a luminescent green pus has settled in the corners.

'Tongue' Paul commands.

The organ is spongy with a border of bite marks, a Mercury characteristic.

'Other symptoms?'

'I sweat and drink buckets at night.

'What medicine are you taking?'

'Mercury.'

'And Georges has given you?'

'Mercury again. He said there is a difference. I don't understand.'

Paul sits on a gilt chair opposite Edouard's wife and the young man.

'It's not good, Edouard,' he says.

'My lovely people,' Edouard says, turning towards Suzanne and Leon. 'I need to discuss something with my physician.' He pats Leon's knee and his wife's hand.

Reluctantly, the two stand a little awkwardly and file out.

'They adore me,' Edouard says.

'They're your family.'

'Yes, that's right, you remembered, they're family. Leon is my son.'

'Pardon?'

'I love Leon like a son. It's all been such a rush and I don't feel up to it, but I've re-written my will to include him, against Maman's wishes. He's spent the whole of the last few weeks running from physician to physician to try and help me. Now he's found a Doctor Tillaux who said he can save me.'

Paul gets up to stand by the window. Rain pelts the glass like shattering stones till all he can see is blurred light. He puts his fingertip to the glass. A drop of condensation falls away like a tear. Rubbing a wet thumb and forefinger together, he says, 'Yes, you have syphilis and the disease has gone too far. No one can save you, Edouard.'

'They want to operate. Take the leg off.'

'And you want my advice?'

'Yes.'

'If it was me I wouldn't do it.'

'He is the professor of surgery at the School of Medicine.'

'I don't care who he is. The disease is inside you. It's all over your being, in your liver, in your skin, in your tongue, in your eyes. Think about this rationally, an amputation has got to be about the most painful thing that you can do to a man, and it won't take away the disease, just your leg. The shock alone will kill you.'

'So what can *you* do for me?'

'I can administer a remedy but what it will do for you is out of my hands.'

'So, what do you think it will do?'

'What I hope it will do is bring you peace before you die.'

'Jesus, you are candid.'

'I would have thought you would have wanted the truth at this stage.'

There is silence between them.

'And what remedy would you give me then?'

'I'm not sure. I need to ask you some questions.'

'Ask me anything you like.'

'How does it feel to be you right now?'

'Frightened. Sorry for my family. Suzanne will not have an easy time from my mother after I've gone. And Leon – I was the man in his life.'

'Go on.'

'Do you know what Charles said before he died? I am like a match that has gone out. I think that's a very good analogy. I am a match that has gone out too.'

Paul half-smiles, and rubs his chin.

'I have a remedy for you Edouard,' Paul says, fishing in his bag for a bottle of Phosphorus 10M. 'At the very least, it should help you with your fears.'

Sitting alone in the Café de Bade, Paul sips his coffee. He reads in *Le Figaro*:

> *Yesterday at 10 o' clock, Doctors Tillaux, Siredey and Marjolin came to the patient whom they found in excellent spirits. The limb to be amputated was in a deplorable state. Gangrene had set in, resulting in a condition so critical that the nails of the foot came off when touched. The patient was chloroformed and the leg amputated below the knee. Manet felt no pain. The day went as well as could be expected, and yesterday evening when we came for news, his condition did not suggest any serious complications.*

'Suzanne, I've come to see Edouard.' Paul says, standing at the door.

She is still in her nightgown despite the hour being almost lunchtime.

'Please, come in. Do you think there is anything you can do?' she says, leading him hastily through to the bedroom. She opens the door and Edouard is lying in the foetal position shivering violently. He continually repeats the letter 't' with his tongue and his hair is wet with sweat. Paul immediately hopes that Edouard is in some sort of an unconscious state. He walks over to the patient and lays a hand on his brow. Edouard flinches.

'He is in a very dangerous pyrexic state,' he says. 'What are the doctors giving him?'

'Morphine.'

'And yet, he still suffers greatly. I'd like to give him another dose of the homeopathic medicine.'

'I will have to ask Leon.'

'Where is he?'

306

'He was up all night with Edouard and now he's asleep.'

'Suzanne, why are you hesitating?'

'The doctors have said not to give him anything homeopathic. They were very vexed when Leon told them you had been here. They called you a quack.'

'Suzanne, look, look over there, look at what those eminent men have done for your husband so far.'

'Please, Doctor Gachet, leave the medicine with me and I shall discuss the matter with Leon when he awakes.'

Paul hasn't returned home to Auvers but has stayed in Paris for the last ten days. The atmosphere everywhere, on the streets and in the cafés, is morbid, but Paris is somehow the only place he wants to be. He is tempted to join the crowd that has gathered outside Edouard's building. It is hard to work when an old friend is dying.

Paul hears the sound of his own shoes scraping the floorboards. Back and forth. Back and forth in his consulting room. He feels the enormous emptiness of his apartment and he thinks to himself how grief makes you old, that death is part of life, and life must go on because you have no choice. He will visit Le Salon.

He arrives to be told that his entrance is barred. The exhibition hall is holding a private viewing, but someone recognises that he is a painter and ushers him in. Remembering when his own work hung on the walls of the Palais d'l'Industrie, he walks tall through to the exhibition rooms.

He begins to look at the first painting when a silent chill descends upon the room. An official from the Beaux Arts enters and stands in the centre.

'Edouard Manet has just died,' he booms.

Silence.

Paul Gachet looks to the floor. When he raises his head all hats in the room have been removed.

Asnières, July 31, 1883

Madame,
I beg you to excuse me if in what follows I revive your grief over the extraordinary and greatly mourned Monsieur Manet.

You know without doubt that I posed for a great many of his paintings, notably for Olympia, his masterpiece. M Manet took a lot of interest in me and often said that if he sold his paintings he would reserve some reward for me. I was so young then and careless ... I left for America.

When I returned, M Manet, having sold a great number of his works to M Faure, told me that he was going to give me something. I refused, enthusiastically thanking him, adding that when I could no longer pose I would remind him of his promise.

That time has come sooner than I thought; the last time that I saw M Manet he promised to help me get a job in a theatre as an usher, adding that he would give me money to secure it ... You know the rest, and what a rapid sickness ravished your loved one.

Certainly I had decided never to bother you and remind you of that promise, but misfortune has befallen me: I can no longer model, I have to all alone take care of my old mother, who is now utterly incapable of work, and on top of all this I had an accident and injured my right hand (a broken finger) and will not be able to do work of any kind for several months.

It is this desperate situation, Madame, which prompts me to remind you of M Manet's kind promise. M Leenhoff and M Gustave Manet can tell you that M Manet certainly intended to come to my aid. If in my misfortune, and in remembrance of him, you will be so kind as to interest yourself in my destiny and can do something for me, please accept, Madame, my deepest gratitude.

I am respectfully yours, Victorine Meurent,

7, Boulevard de la Seine,
Asnières
Seine.